UNLEASHING MAYHEM

DEMON BOUND
BOOK 4

GRAE BRYAN

Content warnings: Moderate violence (including discussion of torture), child abuse (past, off-page), child abandonment (past, off-page), MC with unaddressed PTSD, explicit sexual content, somnophilia

PROLOGUE

Matty's mother was here. He wasn't sure why—he hadn't seen that woman in over a decade.

What was weirder than her unexpected presence was that he could only see the back of her, a mass of long dark hair flowing down over her too-thin frame. And that no matter how much he shouted, she never turned around. She and her hair stayed exactly as they were, silhouetted in a doorway at the end of a long, narrow hallway.

And the longer Matty walked toward her, the longer the hallway grew.

He didn't even know why he was walking toward her in the first place. He didn't want to see her, not after what she'd done—what she'd *failed* to do. But he couldn't stop his feet from moving in her direction.

And now there were doors lining the hallway, misshapen wooden things, all of them shaking and pounding, like whoever or *what*ever was behind them wanted out.

Matty didn't want them to come out. He knew what he'd find if one of those doors opened.

Icy fingers wrapped around his heart, and suddenly Matty was dizzy with fear. It wasn't a new feeling—not at all. Fear was like an old friend to Matty, if a friend was someone people hated and resented every single day of their life. But the *intensity* of the fear was off.

Matty had been feeling okay earlier, hadn't he? He remembered feeling almost...safe.

Why had he felt safe?

The answer came to him in an instant, burning brightly through his mental fog. He'd felt safe because of Kai and Sascha and Seacliff. Their cozy home in Maine.

How had Matty gotten from there to here?

I'm dreaming, Matty realized in an instant. Immediately, his panic spiked sharply. *Oh fuck, I'm dreaming.*

It was the worst place to find himself: in a dream where he couldn't direct the outcome. Because *he* was bound to appear. He always did.

Always.

Wake up, Matty told himself. *Wake up right* now.

He didn't. Of course he didn't. He wasn't in control here. He was never in control. And any minute, one of those creepy doors was going to open.

Right on time—summoned by Matty's thoughts, no doubt—a familiar voice called out, "Matteeeeeooooo." The voice was singsong, falsely juvenile. Taunting. "Come out, come out, wherever you aaaare."

Matty started running. Or at least, he tried to. But his dream legs were leaden, sinking deep into the ground no matter how hard he pushed himself to sprint.

The hallway grew longer and longer and longer, the doors all around him pounding and shaking.

Matty kept trying anyway. Running was the only solution. He needed to keep running and running. And if this stupid goddamn hallway ever stopped growing and he came to a real exit, then he needed to hide. Hiding was good, even if he was always found eventually. At least it delayed the inevitable.

At least it gave him a few moments without pain.

"Matteo!" The voice was growing louder. Bolder. Meaner. Sharp as the knife its owner always carried. "Get the fuck back here, you little bastard!"

Matty couldn't help looking over his shoulder. There was nothing but dark hallway behind him—too dark to see anything clearly. But was that a shadow there, coming slowly closer?

Matty whimpered, his heart racing so fast now that he thought it might explode.

But suddenly there was no more hallway in front of him. Matty hit something horribly solid and slammed backward, landing on his ass.

He stared up at the obstruction. A person. Sort of. From Matty's sprawled position, he was mostly staring at long, unnaturally thin legs. Spindly like a spider, dark gray and blending into the shadows around them.

Familiar.

Matty looked up. Up and up and up. He saw white hair sprouting from a strangely elongated human skull, one with sharp, flesh-shredding teeth and glowing white eyes. Large, branched black antlers topping it all.

Relief flooded through Matty, so powerful he instantly started crying.

He blinked up at the apparition, trying to calm his hiccuping sobs. He swallowed hard. And then he smiled, shaky as the gesture might have been.

"Oh," Matty said, his voice thick with tears as he stared at the monster looming over him, that fanged maw opening wide. "It's you."

———

NIGHTMARE OPENED HIS EYES, staring out at his dim, dusty cave. He licked his lips, savoring the traces that were left there, his shadows dancing around him in delight.

Sweet and tart. Sugared lemon.

Nightmare smiled into the dark, a flash of sharp teeth with no one there to see them. He wished he could return, but the dream had already faded. He would have to wait another night.

It was a dull proposition. The Void had long grown tedious, even before Nightmare had lost his companions. He still hadn't decided if the trio he'd been stuck with had made it more or less so in the first place, but the answer was of no consequence.

Nightmare would be leaving soon.

It was a matter of *when* and not *if* now. Nightmare could sense the soul magic in his summoning mark, all the way across the ether in the human realm. He could feel how it had dislodged itself from the Book, seeking the right soul to aid their escape.

Nightmare knew which human his magic sought, but he was less certain if fate would be so considerate as to allow it.

It mattered little either way. Nightmare would make his own fate.

He may not have anticipated the Book getting lost in the human realm for centuries—an oversight if there ever was one—but Nightmare hadn't wasted his time here. He'd worked slowly and patiently, feeding as best he could on the tattered dreams he was able to access through the veil of the Void. Leeching off human fear, bitter and potent even from a great distance. Consolidating his power and building his reserves.

Nightmare stretched his long limbs, cracking his neck to the left. To the right. He closed his eyes once more, slipping back into the dream realm in the quiet of the empty Void.

For now, he would find a lesser dream to ease his boredom. He could be patient a little while longer, here in the prison of his own making.

After all, there was something sweet waiting for him on the other side.

1

_____

Matty

S creaming. Blood everywhere. A knife hacking away at an unsuspecting victim.

Matty tucked himself deeper into his multilayered blanket burrito, popping more sour candy into his mouth as the movie played. When his phone rang a moment later, he already knew whose name he'd see on the screen, requesting a video call.

Only one person ever called Matty. And that person was usually living in the same house with him, so there wasn't much occasion for it.

But now Matty's housemate Sascha and his demon husband, Kai, were off on vacation, and Matty was alone, so Sascha was calling him daily to check in.

Alone in the house. No one to protect you. Don't think about it, don't think about it, don't think about it.

Maybe Matty should have felt more pathetic about Sascha feeling the need to check on him so regularly, but he could only feel grateful.

He swallowed his candy and lowered the volume on the TV, picking up on the second ring. "Hey, Sascha."

"Matty!" Sascha cried. He looked beautiful as always, with his light hair and pale-blue eyes and delicate features, and his smile was loose enough that it was clear he was tipsy. "I was worried you might be asleep already."

"Not yet."

It was well past midnight, but Matty had no intention of going to sleep, not until he absolutely had to. He could already tell it would be a nightmare sort of night, and he was choosing avoidance over bravery. As per usual.

He planned to keep watching his horror movie marathon through increasingly dry and itchy eyes, relying on a mix of sugar and stubbornness to stay awake. He'd stocked up on sweets before Sascha and Kai had left, so wouldn't run out of candy, at least. With any luck, he could stay up all night, not passing out until it was light outside and the horror of waking from another dread-filled dreamscape would be less potent.

Not that Matty was going to tell Sascha any of that.

Sascha already worried too much about Matty. They weren't even related or, like, normal friends, so it wasn't fair to him. Matty was just a stray Sascha and Kai had picked up and were reluctant to kick out.

A fact for which Matty would be eternally grateful for the rest of his life.

He owed them both so, so much.

"I got your texts," Sascha told Matty, his brow furrowing. "But I have to ask: Are you extra, super, one hundred percent sure you don't want them to come stay with you this weekend?"

"Am I extra, super, one hundred percent sure I don't want your scary older brother and his sex demon to reluctantly babysit me? Yes. 'Fraid so."

Sascha laughed, his face lighting up again, and Matty felt a quick flash of pride. Even that much sass had been beyond him six months ago. It still was, more or less, with anyone other than Sascha or Kai.

There was a reason Sascha's family called Matteo his resident mouse.

"You know Ivan would never actually hurt you, right?"

Matty *did* know that, actually, but before he could say so, a loud scream erupted on the TV. Apparently loud enough to be heard on the phone even with the lowered volume, because Sascha groaned. "Oh my God, I can't believe you're watching one of those movies alone at night. I don't know how the hell you do that."

Because I've met real monsters, and these Hollywood make-believe creations have nothing on them.

Matty didn't say that out loud. Instead, he said what he'd already told Sascha a million times, "I just like them."

Sascha grimaced. "To each their own." Then, in a falsely casual voice he was definitely too tipsy to pull off, he asked, "So, um, have you left the house since our departure?"

Matty had practiced for this. "Yep," he said easily.

"He lies," Kai's deep voice accused on Sascha's end of the phone. Matty saw the edge of sleek black hair and a blue cheek before the demon ducked back out of view.

Well, damn. If Matty didn't think Kai was one of the best nonpeople around—Matty's literal savior from another realm— he'd be really annoyed with him right now.

"Kai," Sascha scolded, glaring off to the side. Then, in a much softer tone, he addressed Matty again. "But, see, Seth already told us you haven't been to the bakery at all. He made extra lemon bars for you and everything."

What. The hell. Seth was going around *tattling* on Matty? Traitors. Traitors all around.

Although, a lemon bar did sound good right about now.

Sascha had started looking plaintive, and Matty let out a breath. "I'll go tomorrow, I promise. But I *have* been out on the porch," he added, maybe a little sulkily. "So I wasn't actually lying."

"Of course you weren't," Sascha soothed. "Kai's just drunk."

"Kai doesn't drink human alcohol," Matty pointed out.

"Well, then *I'm* drunk."

"He tried to keep up with the vampires," Kai butted in again, apparently jonesing to call everyone out mercilessly tonight. "He did not succeed."

Sascha shushed him noisily before turning back to Matty. "But, Matty, are you...You're okay?"

That was a question Matty didn't have an answer for. He cleared his throat. "How's Colorado?"

Because he was good and sweet no matter how much he denied it, Sascha let Matty change the subject. "Oh my God, we're having so much fun!" he cried, color high in his cheeks. "Alexei's vampire den is a total trip. Like, I could definitely get a reality show going with this cast of characters, I swear..."

Matty listened to Sascha gush about his brother's new home as the slasher on-screen kept gutting unsuspecting teens. With his movie, his blankets, and his housemate's voice, Matty could almost convince himself he was safe. Almost.

His eyelids started drooping as he made little sounds of disbelief and encouragement back to Sascha, who was raving about someone named Soren's fabulous fashion sense.

Matty was half-dozing when Sascha abruptly cut off. "Oops, we have to go! We're late for our car. We're going out dancing in the next town over."

It was like a cold bucket of water on Matty's head, and he was instantly alert. "O-Of course," he said, straightening in his blankets. How had he let himself get so close to falling asleep? "I'll talk to you tomorrow. Not that you have to—or that *we* have to—"

"Tomorrow, Matty," Sascha said with a smile, breaking through Matty's stammering. "I promise I'll call."

Matty hung up before he could do something stupid like burst into tears.

Sascha and Kai would be gone on their vacation for three whole weeks, visiting Sascha's brother Alexei and then taking their trip international. It was the first time they'd left for so long since adopting Matty into their home. Originally, they'd talked about Sascha's brother Ivan and his demon mate staying with Matty while they were gone, but Matty had chickened out at the last minute.

It was one thing relying on Sascha and Kai, but Matty was an adult—he should be able to last three weeks on his own. It was pathetic that everyone thought he needed a babysitter.

Even if he kind of maybe did.

There's another option, a tempting voice whispered in his head, and Matty's gaze darted over to the bookshelf, where Kai had once told him a demon's summoning mark was hiding, just waiting to be called.

But Matty couldn't. No way. Demon protectors were for people with real issues. People like Sascha, when he'd been targeted by Matty's now deceased (*may he rot in hell*) mobster stepfather.

Matty didn't have real problems, not anymore. Because Sascha and Kai had saved him, and now no one knew where he was. It was even possible that no one cared. Even...even *him*.

What Matty had were ghosts. Neuroses. Nightmares.

And that would be truly pathetic, wouldn't it, to trade a piece of his soul to keep bad dreams at bay?

Matty could do this. He could get through this night, and the next, and the next after that.

And he'd even do what he promised and go out and be seen by Seth tomorrow so Sascha wouldn't worry. Because Sascha deserved to have a fun vacation without stressing over Matty.

Something creaked in the house, and Matty jumped, his heart racing.

He waited to hear another noise, but it had just been the old house adjusting to the weather. The bones settling, as Sascha called it.

Matty turned up the volume on his movie again. *All the doors and windows are locked*, he reminded himself. And while he'd turned off the lights in the rest of the house, every lamp in the living room was blazing bright. He was safe as he could be.

He tried to get lost in his movie again, to find solace in the over-the-top violence of it.

Sascha might have thought it was weird, a scaredy-cat like Matty watching so much horror, but for Matty it was comforting. Every ridiculously mauled dead body was just a reminder that at least some monsters weren't real.

If only Matty could say the same for the ones that haunted him.

———

AGAINST ALL ODDS, Matty survived the night.

Well, it probably wasn't actually against *any* odds, but it made him feel better to think that it was.

He'd passed out around dawn, into a (thankfully) dreamless sleep, and he'd caught a whole four hours. He was feeling almost good now. Refreshed.

Hungry as all hell.

It was possible he'd forgotten to stock up on actual groceries when he'd stocked up on sweets. Matty had gotten away with a lot of delivered meals so far—thank God for the "leave on porch" option there—and then eating leftovers for lunch. But now he didn't have anything in the house for breakfast, unless he counted his remaining candy.

So Matty was going to do what he'd promised to do and go to the Bakeshop, to be seen by Seth and get delicious pastries for breakfast at the same time.

Lemon bars were a suitable breakfast food, right? They had fruit in them and everything.

Matty showered, changed into a clean oversize hoodie and more size-appropriate sweatpants, and headed out.

The morning was still nice and cool, and Matty breathed it in greedily. He hated to admit it, but the fresh air was beyond decent, even with his hood pulled over his head. He could already feel it cleansing the dust from his lungs.

On the other hand, people were already out and about, and that was...less decent.

Seacliff, Maine, was a small town when it came to population, but it was adorable and coastal enough that it had an influx of tourists every summer. A selfish part of Matty wished Sascha and Kai had left on their getaway in the winter, when the town was dead and he had the residents' faces mostly memorized. Plus, if they'd left in the winter, Matty would have been able to stay inside the whole time and just blame the snow and the cold.

But alas, Matty was venturing out mid-tourist-season, and it was a beautiful, sunny morning. The horror.

Luckily, the Bakeshop was never super crowded. Locals loved it, especially since it stayed open all winter, but visitors usually preferred the town's other diners, where they could get lobster eggs Benedict and crab cake sandwiches or whatever.

Matty loitered on a bench outside until the place was fully empty of customers, then headed in, lowering his hood. It was the kind of bakery that was almost offensively cute, with little ceramic cats and doilies on the counter, supposedly put there by the ever-absent owner, Marjorie.

Matty was greeted by the familiar sight of Seth, the bakery's head baker, all round cheeks and big smile and floral cloth head-band holding back his dark curls.

"Matty!" Seth cried, like he was genuinely happy to see him. "So glad you're here. Did Sascha tell you about the lemon bars?"

Matty nodded, a shy smile of his own on his lips. "He did."

"Excellent. Should I pack one up for you? Or two?" Seth gave him a devilish look, lowering his voice. "Or perhaps even three?"

"Two, please. And, um, maybe a muffin I can heat up tomorrow?"

If Seth was annoyed by Matty asking it as a question instead of ordering it outright, he didn't show it. "Sure thing! Blueberry crumble? Banana nut? Lemon poppy seed?"

"The lemon one, please."

"Sticking with the citrus theme," Seth said, nodding as he began placing Matty's items carefully in a white paper bag. "Respect."

Matty smiled a little wider but didn't say anything back. Seth never seemed to mind that Matty was shy or awkward though. He treated him with the same warmth he gave Sascha and Kai. Like Matty was fine just the way he was. Like he belonged.

Seth rang him up, and Matty took the bag gratefully, peering inside. "Hey," he said after a moment. "You think— It's okay to have a lemon bar for breakfast, right?"

"Psh, of course," Seth said, waving a hand. "There's fruit in them. Just think of it as a sugar-dusted square Danish."

Matty gave him a happy grin and pulled his hood back up, ducking out of the bakery with his prize.

Maybe there was something to this whole leaving-the-house thing after all. It had been nice to see a friendly face. Nice enough that Matty was thinking he could head down the coastal path to the little sandy cove his housemates liked so much. It probably wouldn't be too crowded yet. Or, if it was, Matty could find a corner in the rocks to tuck himself away into. He was pretty small; he wouldn't take up too much room.

He walked off in that direction, grabbing one of the lemon bars out of the bag. Seth made the best ones Matty had ever had, tart but also overwhelmingly sweet, enough to kind of hurt the roof of his mouth. *And* Seth didn't skimp on the powdered sugar—an oft-overlooked metric.

Matty would eat one on his walk and then the other at the beach, and that would be two servings of fruit right there.

He'd been pretty scrawny when Kai and Sascha had found him —living in abject misery hadn't done great things for Matty's appetite—but thanks to Kai's insistence on learning human cooking and Seth's delicious baked goods, Matty had filled out reasonably. He would always be short, but he at least looked like his actual twenty-one years now and no longer like a malnourished teenager. Growing out the buzz cut his stepfather had insisted on helped too; his big brown eyes no longer looked too large for his head.

Sometimes it didn't feel real, that Matty's stepfather was really dead. That he and his main men had been taken out by Sascha and Kai, and that Matty didn't have to cater to that cruel man's every whim anymore. Didn't have to be hurt without remorse when he inevitably failed to please.

Didn't have to worry about being given over to *him*.

For a second, Matty thought he'd imagined it. That the mental image of a familiar face was brought on by thinking of the past.

But Matty looked again, and in the brief moment before the man was swallowed up by a family taking over the sidewalk, Matty could *swear* he'd seen him. One of his stepfather's men. Here. In Seacliff.

It couldn't be real. As far as Matty knew, they all thought he'd died with the rest of the henchmen there that night, another of Kai's deserving victims. And even if they knew he was alive, why would anyone think he was holed up with Sascha Kozlov, the little brother of a rival Mafia leader?

It didn't make sense, but it didn't stop the fear from taking over.

The lemon bar slipped from Matty's shaking grip, landing on the sidewalk, and for a moment he was stuck there staring at it, smashed and broken on the ground.

Then he turned and bolted.

Matty ducked his head and did his best to dodge tourists on the sidewalk before giving up and running in the street. Sprinting back to the house, back to safety. He looked over his shoulder only once, to make sure no one was running behind him.

When Matty got to the house, he slammed the door behind him, checking and double-checking and triple-checking the lock before he went to the back door and did the same.

Then he went to all the windows to check their latches, even the ones on the second floor. Even the tiny circular one in the attic, which turned out to be too high to reach, so Matty just stood there for a long moment, staring at it as he tried to stop hyperventilating.

Eventually he crawled back onto the familiar living room couch, piling blankets up around himself and jumping at every little sound from the outside world. He could have hidden in his room, but if someone made it into the house, Matty didn't want to be stuck on the second floor with an intruder between him and the stairs.

Matty had watched too many horror movies to make that mistake.

He realized he was still somehow clutching the white paper bag from the bakery in his hand. Matty grabbed the remaining lemon bar and took the largest bite he could fit in his mouth, ignoring the powdered sugar that showered over his blanket nest.

Tart lemon. Melty-soft sweetness.

Matty let out a sigh, blowing more powdered sugar everywhere, and tried not to notice that he was still shaking.

He'd imagined the whole thing; he was sure of it. He wasn't Luca Caruso's stepson anymore. That was the past, and Matty was here now. In the present.

I'm okay, he told himself. *I'm safe.*

But Matty's gaze darted again and again to the bookshelf, and he couldn't help asking the same question he'd asked himself over and over, ever since the day he'd arrived here:

Safe for how long?

2

Matty

Matty lasted until nightfall.

He'd done okay for the rest of the day, if he didn't count the frantic trembling and equally frantic rechecking of all the doors and windows. He'd even talked to Sascha briefly and put on a brave face for his friend, though he wasn't sure how convinced Sascha had been.

But then the sun had finally set, the automatic porch light turning on as the outside world plunged to darkness, and that was it.

Matty hadn't been able to stop thinking about that face he couldn't have seen, of phone calls being made, of a group of terrifying men bursting in with guns and knives and—and *him* at the forefront.

There you are, Matteo. Disobedient as always. Now what will I do with you?

Matty could picture it too perfectly: his worst nightmare come to life. And he just...couldn't do it anymore. He was tired, and he was scared, and he'd been both of those things for so long now, and he didn't want to be. Not anymore. Not for another second.

And maybe now was supposed to be the moment in his life where Matty turned inward and looked to his pool of inner strength to become something better than a scared mouse. Something braver. Something bolder.

But whatever inner strength Matty might have held had been broken a long time ago by cruel hands and terrifying threats, and Matty didn't think there was any better or braver or bolder version of himself waiting in the wings.

Matty needed someone. Someone who was *his*. Someone he didn't have to feel guilty about clinging to by his pathetic fingernails.

Sascha and Kai were wonderful, but they had lives of their own, as this vacation of theirs proved. And really, they'd given Matty too much already. Sascha had even gifted Matty with access to one of his generous bank accounts, since Matty had been too terrified of anyone tracking his funds to use the one meager account Luca had allowed him.

Matty was penniless, jobless, and cowardly beyond measure. A failure of an adult human.

But that was all going to be fine because the someone Matty needed wasn't human at all.

Matty had been doing his best to hide from the monsters of his past, but he was done with all that.

It was time to catch a monster of his own.

Matty shook off the blankets shrouding him, rose from the couch, and shuffled over to the bookshelf. He began painstakingly checking between each book, hoping what he was looking for wasn't hiding between any of their pages. He was pretty sure they'd all been left by the previous owner of the house—there was no way Sascha had ever bought a book called *Lighthouses of the*

World: A Beginner's Guide on purpose—and there were a lot of them packed together on the bookcase.

But Matty didn't have to go through each individual book. He found it on the middle shelf: a loose page of strangely thick paper, with words in a language Matty didn't recognize on one side and a foreign symbol on the other. The symbol was painted with thick black lines, smudged and twisted at various points. Some people would probably think it was creepy-looking, but Matty couldn't help smiling as his eyes followed its path.

He thought of Kai in his demon form, huge and blue and horned, able to cut through nine armed human men without breaking a sweat. He thought of Nix, beautiful and sly and willing to stand up to Ivan at his scariest. He thought of the chaos demon, small and kind of cute, but with a predator's edge and talons that Matty had been told shredded through flesh like butter.

Matty traced his finger along the stark black symbol; it was oddly warm against his fingertip.

He hoped it summoned the scariest monster there ever was. He hoped the demon waiting within its magic was vicious and bloodthirsty and willing to do its worst.

Maybe then Matty would finally feel safe in a way that lasted.

He continued to trace the symbol as he tried to remember the instructions Kai had given him when he'd suggested Matty summon a protector.

Copy the symbol. Recite the words. Spill his blood.

Kai had taken his suggestion back that very night and told Matty in no uncertain terms that the demon this page would summon was *not* someone Matty would want around, even in the short term.

But Kai wasn't here right now, was he? He and Sascha had left, and now Matty had to do what he had to do, didn't he?

He just hoped they'd forgive him later, after the fact.

Matty looked around the room for something to copy the

symbol with. He was pretty sure Sascha had summoned Kai with a bottle of nail polish, but that had been a whole accidental thing. *This* was on purpose, and Matty felt like he should make it nice. So his scary monster demon would feel welcome.

Oh! He had something!

Matty ran up the stairs. Sascha and Kai had gotten him art supplies, back when they'd had hopes for him adopting a hobby that didn't involve watching bloody movies and hiding in his room. Matty found the box in his closet and gathered everything he could carry before rushing it all back down to the living room.

He spread the mess out on the floor, seeing what he had to work with. There was some thick, artsy paper—the kind people drew beautiful portraits on—and Matty carefully laid a piece of it on the living room rug, separate from the rest.

He sorted through the remainder of the supplies and finally settled on a plain piece of charcoal. There were other, brighter paints and markers, but the charcoal felt right.

Matty set the demon's symbol next to his blank page. Should he just...go for it? Was a piece of paper and a stick of charcoal really enough to summon a monster?

He hopped up, remembering that Sascha had gotten flowers for the house before he and Kai had left. They were still in a vase on the kitchen table, and Matty selected a mostly wilted and forlorn-looking purple flower and brought it back to the living room, setting it above the blank page where he was going to copy the symbol.

There. That was kind of...appropriately gothic? Maybe?

Although, the more Matty stared at it, the more it looked like nothing at all.

Voices rang through the air outside, and Matty jumped in place before turning to stare through the living room doorway. The voices sounded deep. A group of men? Were they on the street or had they made it to the porch already? Were they coming for him finally? Had he been too slow in realizing he needed protection?

But then there was bright laughter and then the lighter, higher-pitched voices of small children, yelling something about a beach. A tourist family on the way back to their rental, most likely.

Matty sat there clutching his chest, his heart racing much too fast.

He couldn't do this anymore. Couldn't jump at shadows and panic over nothing over and over again.

Appropriately gothic presentation or not, it was time.

Matty waited until his hands were as steady as they were going to be, and then he carefully copied the symbol onto his paper, the charcoal blackening his fingertips. When he was done, he cocked his head and narrowed his eyes, studying the final result.

It looked...close enough.

Matty turned the symbol over and painstakingly sounded out the strange words on the other side.

Now he just needed blood.

Matty refused to touch a knife—not to harm another human, not even himself—so Matty bit down as hard as he could on his lower lip, wincing at the sharp sting. He swiped at it with a charcoal-dusted finger, then smeared the blood on the symbol he'd traced. It messed up the lines a little, but hopefully that wouldn't matter.

Matty repeated the words on the page one more time for good measure, even though he was pretty sure he only needed to say them once.

There. It was done.

Wasn't it?

An icy wind blew across his back, and Matty hunched over his paper to keep it from blowing away. Had the front door opened somehow? It was locked. Matty *knew* it was locked. But...were the wrong monsters already here? The human kind? Ready to steal him away and make him hurt? Make him pay?

But then a dark fog poured in from nowhere, filling the room and bringing with it the scent of smoke and hidden shadows. It wasn't long before the living room floor was hidden from view, the smoke still rising steadily, Matty's hold on his paper the only reassurance that it hadn't disappeared.

Matty grinned around chattering teeth, the pain in his lip sharp and satisfying as the wound stretched.

He'd done it. Matty had actually done it.

His monster was coming for him.

3

Nightmare

Nightmare's smoke and shadow filled the room, obscuring the vision of the human before him but not his own.

Nightmare took advantage of the momentary imbalance between them to feel out the space as best he could from within the confines of the summoning circle.

He'd been summoned into an unfamiliar dwelling, although there were threads of recognition Nightmare could follow. Dream-altered corridors and shadowy corners that had been recreated inside a fearful mind.

Nightmare had walked these halls before, hadn't he, inside his summoner's psyche.

They were in a living room, a large space dominated by a long couch and two overstuffed armchairs, pillows and blankets abounding on all of them, with a gigantic, modern television fixed to the wall.

A familiar demonic signature filled the space, though it had gone stale in its owner's absence.

Nightmare bared his teeth, sending his shadows out into the rest of the house. They returned within mere moments. There were no other humans lurking in the vicinity, according to his companions. Nor demons, for that matter. No threats of any kind.

Satisfied for the moment, Nightmare focused on the human standing before him, the young man craning his neck in an attempt to see Nightmare's face through the smoke. He was short and slight, with a few inches of unkempt dark-brown hair and enormous brown eyes. Olive-skinned and dressed in a garment many sizes too big for him.

Overall, a pleasing flesh covering for the soul emanating within. A soul that might have been almost cloyingly sweet if not for the sour and bitter fissures running along it. Nightmare inhaled slowly, breathing in its essence.

Tart, sugared lemon filled his lungs.

And what a coincidence, that Nightmare had recently developed such a sweet tooth.

Nightmare let the smoke and shadows fall away, revealing the summoning circle fully to the human's gaze. The human blinked, those doe eyes of his widening even further as he stared up at Nightmare.

By all rights the little creature should have been shrieking or trembling at the monstrous sight before him. But the human remained silent, and though his hands were clasped tightly in front of him, they were held surprisingly steady.

Nightmare noted the reddened swelling on the human's lush lower lip, the bit of dried blood there. Nightmare glanced down at the page with his mark, the careful copy next to it, the wilted rose perched above them both.

The human had summoned Nightmare deliberately. That simplified things immensely.

Nightmare allowed his lips to curl at the corners, gracing the human with a rare smile, one that kept his sharp teeth hidden. The human's face drained of color anyway. He still did not speak.

That was fine. Nightmare would wait.

He lowered himself to sit cross-legged within his summoning circle. The removal of the height disadvantage seemed to give his sweet summoner a bit of bravery. The human stepped closer to the circle's edge. "H-Hello," he greeted in a soft, shy voice. "Are you a demon?"

A silly question. Nightmare remained silent.

The color rushed back to his summoner's cheeks, turning them a dusky pink. "Of course you are. I can see..." He gestured to the top of Nightmare's head, to the antlered black horns that branched above him. And then he seemed again at a loss for words.

He was struggling. Nightmare would help him.

"I know you," he told his summoner, watching as the little human flinched minutely at Nightmare's low, husky rasp.

"Y-You do?" The human unclasped his hands, tucking them into his oversize sleeves and folding the fabric over his fingers. "How?"

Nightmare cocked his head and answered a question with a question. "Do you know what kind of demon I am?"

"No." His summoner shook his head and then said, as if fearing offense, "I'm sorry."

"They call us nightmare demons," Nightmare explained. "We feed off the human psyche, namely fear. We feed most often on bad dreams."

"You eat nightmares," his summoner said with wonder. He gave Nightmare a tender, hopeful smile. "I have a lot of those."

Nightmare wanted to trace the soft curl of those lips with his fingertips, feel the shape of them for himself, but the circle wouldn't allow it.

The same restrictions did not apply to his shadows.

Nightmare gathered them from the corners of the room and—after a moment of considering the benefits of restraint—harnessed them to sweep lightly over his summoner's clothed shoulders, down to his covered hands. Nightmare kept the touch light, so as not to startle the shy human. His summoner looked down at his arms, watching the darkness play over him. His brow furrowed as he tried to understand where his sense of recognition came from.

So Nightmare helped him.

The next time his summoner glanced up, Nightmare summoned his skull visage from the ether, switching it on and off again, quick as a blink.

He was rewarded by his sweet summoner stepping forward with a gasp. "I've seen you. I-I *know* you."

As he should. Nightmare had saved Matteo Caruso from the monsters in his dreams often enough. He'd sipped the young man's fear like the finest ambrosia, one made of burned lemon twists and candied citrus peels left to rot.

The recognition seemed to embolden Matteo. He squared his slim shoulders, although he made no attempt to shake off Nightmare's shadows. "I want to make a deal with you." His fists clenched around their folded sleeves. "Will you— Do you want to make a deal with me too?"

There it was. A juicy summer lemon, ripe for the plucking. Nightmare kept his smile contained, nodding once. "Tell me your terms, summoner."

"I need someone to keep me company," Matteo said in a rush, the words almost blending together in his eagerness to get them out.

"Contracts need an end point," Nightmare told him gently.

"Until I feel safe."

It wasn't a lie exactly, but it *was* an untruth. A false covering over the real heart of the matter. But the falsehood didn't raise

Nightmare's ire; his summoner wasn't required to bare his soul at their very first meeting. Not when Nightmare would soon have a piece of that soul for himself.

But the terms were still unsatisfactory.

If Nightmare had his way, young Matteo Caruso would be feeling as safe as could be sooner than he might think possible.

"Why do you feel unsafe?" Nightmare asked. "What do you fear?"

"Everything," Matteo answered immediately. "Noise. Shadows. The dark. My own mind."

"My power would be wasted on imaginary things that go bump in the night." Nightmare paused, then added, "I'm overqualified."

A little joke, but Matteo didn't laugh. He seemed instead suddenly terrified that Nightmare would refuse his offer outright. "I need a protector," he said desperately, and never before had Nightmare seen a human look both so fearful and so brave as this young man standing in front of a monster, begging it to stay by his side.

"From what?" Nightmare prompted.

"From the people who would hurt me."

They were getting somewhere now. Nightmare leaned forward until his antlers were brushing against the edges of his circle. "Names, sweet. Give me names."

Matteo only stared, reluctance painting his features.

Nightmare tutted. "I'm losing patience."

"Dominico Caruso," Matteo blurted, quick as could be.

Nightmare's shadows savored the taste of the soon-to-be dead man on Matteo's tongue. Now he did smile fully, a flash of sharp teeth. "And what would make you feel safe from this Dominico Caruso?"

Matteo raised his clenched fists, clutching them against his stomach. "I want him dead," he said fiercely. When Nightmare only waited for more, Matteo continued, "I want him—I want him ripped apart. Him and anyone who follows him. Anyone who hurts people on his orders. And I want you to do it for me." He was panting by the end of his short speech, the color high in his cheeks, as if it had taken immense effort to get the words out.

Nightmare stood slowly. He gave weight to his shadows, using them to push Matteo closer to his circle.

"I accept your terms. I, Sarkaron of the demon realm, will rip apart Matteo Caruso's enemies, until there is no one left for him to fear." Nightmare tapped a talon against his confinement. "Put your hand in the circle."

"I didn't tell you my name?" Matteo blurted, half statement and half question.

Nightmare inclined his head in acknowledgment. "You didn't need to. We were already acquainted. Your hand, sweet."

Matteo hesitated for only one more moment, then pushed his arm into the circle, fabric still clenched between his fingers.

Nightmare took hold of that small, slight hand, dislodging the fabric from its tense grip. He folded the sleeve over once, then over again, revealing bare, unblemished skin to his gaze. He ran his talons over his summoner's fingers, delicate things with knobby knuckles.

Matteo shivered, little goose pimples rising on his wrist.

Nightmare chose the fleshy pad at the base of Matteo's thumb for his purpose. He raised Matteo's hand to his mouth and bit, letting warm drops of blood fill his mouth.

For all his fear of shadows and noises, Matteo didn't flinch at the bite, nor did a whimper pass his lips. He met Nightmare's gaze squarely, those big dark eyes deep and fathomless. And when Nightmare released him, the summoning circle dissolving around him, Matteo drew his arm back slowly and let the softest, sweetest, "Thank you," fall from his lips.

And then he dropped to the floor.

4

Matty

Matty had a demon in his living room, and he wasn't quite sure what to do with him.

He'd woken up from what he assumed was a dead faint all tucked into his blankets on the couch. And for one horrifying moment, Matty had thought maybe the entire summoning had been a dream.

Except Matty didn't have good dreams anymore, and finally gathering the courage to summon a demon protector definitely would have counted as a good dream.

What he'd *had* in recent months was a dream protector. One who had never once spoken to Matty. He would just appear in all his terrifying glory—the strange white skull and elongated limbs —and keep the other monsters at bay until Matty awoke.

Matty had thought it was something his mind had invented to protect itself. He'd been kind of proud of his brain for its efforts.

But the reality was so. Much. Better.

Because after the shock of waking up on the couch and

worrying he'd imagined it all, Matty had finally seen him. The demon Sarkaron, standing stock-still among the shadows in the far corner. Watching Matty.

Had the nightmare demon carried Matty to the couch? Tucked him in with his slender, taloned fingers?

How strange it was that they already knew each other, in a vague, surreal sort of way.

What a cool coincidence.

And now they were kind of just staring at each other, each of them taking the other in.

Matty supposed Sarkaron might be considered kind of scary-looking, even without the skull. He was almost as tall as Kai in his demon form, some few inches short of seven feet, maybe. And that wasn't including the branching black antlers he was rocking. But unlike Kai's muscled physique, Sarkaron was slender, with dark-gray skin that blended in with the dark shadows that seemed to twist and wind around him whenever they were given the chance.

His face was severe, with sharp cheekbones and all-white eyes that shifted between flat and glowing. He had long silver-white hair and thin lips covering sharp, jagged teeth.

Matty thought he was beautiful.

A demon. A real demon. And he was Matty's. At least for now. At least until...

But no, Matty didn't want to think about the terms of his bargain. What Sarkaron had pushed him into saying out loud. Matty couldn't believe he'd allowed himself to be so vicious, even verbally. That wasn't him, that kind of violence. Or he didn't think it was.

Maybe it was what they'd made him into.

Anyway, they were still having an epic face-off, Matty on the couch and Sarkaron lurking in the corner. The demon seemed to be the naturally quiet type; he hadn't spoken a word since Matty had woken up. Which was fine because it meant Matty got to look his fill and feel weirdly unembarrassed by it.

Sarkaron's clothing was black and layered and hard to distinguish as any specific style. Maybe some kind of linen? And he had really long, thin fingers, blackened at the tips and ending in sharp talons. As Matty stared at them, they clenched into fists.

Did that hurt, with the talons?

Oh. Maybe Matty *was* being rude. Maybe he was making his demon feel unwelcome, studying him like this. He should make conversation like a normal person, instead of creeping like a...creep.

Matty cleared his throat. "Do you—do you have a human form?" he asked.

The other demons he'd met had all had them, but Sarkaron was a different type of demon, he'd said. It wouldn't do to assume. Maybe that skull face he could summon was his only other form.

"You find this form displeasing?" Sarkaron asked in his low, gravelly rasp.

Matty was distracted for a second, hearing that voice again. He liked it, liked the way it sent a shiver down his spine. It was the voice of a creature lurking in the dark, whispering before it grabbed hold of an ankle and *tugged*.

Then Matty registered what Sarkaron had asked. His cheeks went hot. Had he really offended the demon after all?

"No." Matty shook his head frantically. "I find it very, um, pleasing. It might be hard to take you into town though." He waved a hand, encompassing Sarkaron's impressive antlers, which would definitely set off some local alarms if seen. "Unless you can turn invisible?"

Sarkaron cocked his head. "Not true invisibility, not as such. But I can blend with the shadows."

And then he did it.

It was strange to watch. Matty knew the demon was there, and he could just barely make him out, the faint outline of him. But if he *hadn't* known...

It was like one of those horror movie things, where someone sees a figure out of the corner of their eye, but when they turn, it's nothing but the play of light and shadows. A flash of eyes glowing in the dark, maybe real or maybe not.

"That's very impressive," Matty told him.

Sarkaron emerged from hiding again, although wisps of his shadows continued to dance around him, obscuring and then revealing his features. "Fearful of so many things, Matteo. But not of me?"

Matty covered his hands with his sleeves, tucking them under the blankets. "I have other things to fear."

Was the demon going to push Matty again, make him name names and spill truths?

But Sarkaron didn't ask him any more questions. "You've seen my nightmare visage," he said instead. "The sight has sent some men to madness."

Ohh yes, the old skull face. That *was* pretty creepy. Especially in Matty's dreams, where Sarkaron's limbs extended into those unnaturally long, thin appendages to go with it.

But Matty had always been glad to see him, grotesque as he might have been.

He was better than the alternative.

Was Sarkaron offended Matty wasn't more scared of him? If he was a nightmare demon, maybe he prided himself on his ability to terrify.

"I watch a lot of horror movies," Matty reassured him, tilted his head to the TV.

Those white eyes went from flat to gleaming. "You like monsters, sweet?"

Matty shook his head. "I've met real monsters. Zombies and slashers and killer aliens, those are just pretend."

Sarkaron stepped out of the shadows. Or more like, he stepped out of the corner, and the shadows came with him.

"But *I'm* not pretend, sweet. I'm very real."

He approached the couch, not seeming to walk so much as glide. Matty was frozen in place, mesmerized by the way the towering demon moved.

Maybe this was how Sarkaron got his victims. He paralyzed them with the beauty of his unnatural grace.

When he was directly in front of Matty, Sarkaron dropped into a crouch, one arm outstretched. Slowly—so slowly—he splayed those long fingers over Matty's chest.

Matty jerked at the touch. Not because he was frightened but because while Sarkaron looked like he should be ice-cold, in reality he was warm. So *warm*.

It had been the same when Sarkaron had bitten Matty, his mouth hot against Matty's skin, but Matty had thought maybe that was the magic of the summoning circle.

The warmth was nice, as was Sarkaron's scent. Like smoke-laced fog. Was that a thing? Matty hoped it was.

Sarkaron stared into Matty's eyes. Waiting for something.

"You're real," Matty conceded, his chest rising and falling steadily under Sarkaron's hand. "And you're here to keep me safe."

Sarkaron's lips tilted up at the corners, and after a moment he treated Matty to a full smile, all sharp teeth. "Yes, sweet. That's exactly why I'm here."

It was like the warmth on the surface of Matty's chest went inward, filling his chest and stomach and sweeping down to his toes. He had no idea why Kai had warned him that this wasn't a demon Matty would want to keep around after the contract.

Matty thought this demon was *lovely*.

"I'm not really sure what to do now," he admitted. It felt safe to do so. Sarkaron wouldn't scold him for it; Matty was sure of it.

And he didn't. The demon shook his head slowly, his hand still on Matty's chest. "There's nothing for you to do, little human. You're still weak from the contract taking hold. The body and spirit must adjust to losing a piece of your soul, however small."

Right. Because Sarkaron had a piece of Matty's soul now. One he was going to keep.

"Sarkaron." Matty bit at his lower lip, then winced at the sting. "Does my soul— Is it all right? It's not... It hasn't gone bad?"

Matty wasn't sure why he was asking. He already knew it had. When he pictured his soul, he always imagined it rotten on the inside, pockmarked and riddled with some secret disease.

Sarkaron cocked his head, dark-gray lids lowering over glowing white eyes. "Your soul is as sweet as your scent, Matteo. I would take the whole of it, if I could."

Oh. Should that be frightening? It sounded...nice.

Matty grinned at his new friend, yet another weight lifting off his shoulders.

He should have summoned a demon ages ago.

He patted the spot on the couch next to him. "Would you like to sit with me? Have you ever watched a scary movie?"

Sarkaron didn't move. "I've seen the shape of them in human dreams."

"So it would be boring for you?"

Sarkaron stared at Matty for a moment, like he was studying him. His expression was unreadable, particularly with those strange eyes, but Matty didn't mind. What right did he have to try to guess a demon's motivations anyway? Sarkaron could be as mysterious as he liked.

"Not boring, no." Sarkaron rose from his crouch and took the seat next to Matty.

"Okay."

Matty was still grinning. He couldn't seem to stop. He couldn't remember the last time he'd smiled so much. It hurt his cheeks, like his facial muscles weren't used to it.

While Sarkaron sat still as death, Matty worked on getting settled for the movie. He'd tucked some sour Skittles into the couch cushions earlier, and he dug those out as well as the remote. He tucked more blankets around himself and then— after a moment of hesitation—draped a blanket over Sarkaron's lap.

Sarkaron didn't tuck himself in under it, but he didn't object or fling it off either, so Matty left it there.

"Are you ready, Sarkaron?" he asked.

"Sarkaron is my true name," the demon told him instead of answering. "But most call me Nightmare. You may use either, as you like."

"Nightmare," Matty repeated. He bit back a giggle. "So literal. I could just call you Mr. Scary Monster Man."

He flinched as soon as the words left his mouth. He'd meant it as a little joke, but was that, like, mean to say?

But Nightmare only inclined his head. "As you like."

He was so nice. The nicest demon Matty could have summoned.

Matty grinned at him again, holding up the remote. "Human slashers or creature feature? Just..." Matty bit at his lip, then winced again when he hit the little sore spot from his summoning. He needed to stop doing that. "No, um, torture. I won't watch torture porn."

He only had to look into his own memories to see that, and he had no interest.

Nightmare seemed to deliberate for a moment before answering, "Creature feature."

Matty selected the movie, then held out his Skittles. "Would you like some?"

He was rewarded with a small twist of Nightmare's lips. "No, sweet. Keep your candies."

Matty burrowed back into the couch cushions as the movie

began, wriggling around. He couldn't seem to get comfortable, and it took him a moment to realize what the problem was.

He peeked at Nightmare from the corner of his eye and then shifted—slowly, subtly—until he was closer to the demon. Close enough to feel Nightmare's heat against his arm.

Then Matty was able to settle back into the cushions with a contented sigh.

There. That was better.

————

THEY WERE on their second movie of the night, and Matty's eyes were going kind of blurry.

Nightmare—literal as the name was, it was fitting enough that Matty couldn't get it out of his head now that he knew—was watching with the same quiet interest he'd shown the first movie.

Or maybe it was quiet *non*interest? What did Matty know, really?

Even though Nightmare had said he wouldn't be bored, Matty was probably being a terrible host right now. He just couldn't muster up the energy to do anything more. Nightmare had been truthful before: the contract had taken it out of Matty. Passing out didn't seem to have helped at all, maybe because Matty hadn't been unconscious for long.

Now his eyelids were getting heavy and he was out of sour Skittles. He needed something else to munch on. Sour was good; sour helped keep him alert. Did he have Sour Straws stashed anywhere? Had he finished those already?

Before Matty could search for them, Nightmare's low rasp cut through the falsetto scream on the TV. "You need rest, little human."

Matty blinked at him. Nightmare was still watching the movie, his sharp side profile on display. "This *is* restful."

"Allow me to clarify: You need sleep."

"Oh no." Matty let out a humorless laugh. "I don't sleep."

Nightmare slowly turned his head to face Matty. "That is a lie, little human. I have been in your dreams."

Matty fidgeted with the edge of his blankets, folding them over one way and then back again. "Well, sometimes I drift off *accidentally*. And then I have the—the nightmares. And then I wake up again." He tried for a smile, falling a bit short. "It's a whole cycle."

"Lack of sleep can drive a human into psychosis. I know. I have done it."

Oh. That was interesting. Nightmare didn't just scare people in their dreams; he also drove them mad. Did he kill them too? Was he like some sort of dream assassin?

Matty decided immediately that the answer wouldn't change how he felt about his demon. Kai had killed tons of people, and he was *wonderful*.

"You will sleep," Nightmare ordered.

"No." The word fell from Matty's lips before he could stop himself.

"No?"

"No." Oops. There it was again.

The air in the room went still, and suddenly it was a little hard for Matty to get oxygen into his lungs. He'd gotten used to Nightmare's silent presence beside him on the couch, but now he realized just how giant the demon next to him was, especially with those antlers.

Matty still wasn't afraid of him, exactly. Nightmare was here to keep Matty safe, and Matty believed that deep down in his bones.

But he was definitely getting the impression that Nightmare wasn't a demon many people said no to.

Maybe Matty *should* be afraid. Maybe Nightmare was going to lash out with those talons as a punishment for talking back, slice through Matty's blankets and deep into his flesh.

Matty could suddenly hear his stepfather's voice, clear as day. *Take your punishment, Matteo. We need to make you stronger. That is, if Dominico doesn't kill you first.*

But Nightmare didn't lunge or growl or even frown. He just looked at Matty with blank white eyes. "I will stay with you while you sleep."

"In—in my room?" Matty asked.

Nightmare inclined his head regally. So that was a yes to a slumber party.

Tempting...

"In my bed?" Matty asked hopefully. He'd probably be able to sleep at least a little bit, if he had Nightmare's inhuman warmth within reach.

"In your *room*," Nightmare repeated.

Matty had the strange, foreign urge to pout.

As if Nightmare sensed it in him, his lips tilted up at the corners in an almost smile. "I siphon fear, Matteo. I walk in dreams. You won't have nightmares with me here, either in your bed or outside of it."

It was almost too much to bear, that spark of hope Nightmare's words ignited. A physical protector, sure, that was what Matty had been looking for when he summoned a demon. But the bad dreams had been plaguing Matty nightly since he'd escaped his old life, stealing his sleep and bits of his sanity. They had been making it impossible to get his feet underneath him, no matter that he had Sascha and Kai helping him at every turn.

And here was Nightmare—the living embodiment of exactly what Matty had been struggling with—telling him he didn't have to worry anymore.

It was official: Matty had summoned the best demon there was. The *perfect* demon.

"Can you stay forever?"

He'd meant it as a joke, but the words came out much too sincere. Pleading.

Luckily, Nightmare didn't seem to mind. He bared his jagged teeth at Matty again. "Show me to your room, sweet."

Matty scrambled out of his blankets, standing and holding out his hand. Nightmare cocked his head, and Matty held his breath. After a long moment, Nightmare took his hand.

Matty turned before Nightmare could see his grin, gently tugging his demon out of the living room, up the stairs, and to the door of the room Sascha and Kai had given Matty, at the very end of the upstairs hallway.

Matty pointed at the door across from it. "The bathroom is right here across the hall. I'm going to brush my teeth. I'm trying not to get any more cavities."

Nightmare nodded, releasing Matty's hand and ducking his head to enter Matty's room. Matty rushed into the bathroom, getting through his nightly routine as quickly as possible.

He entered his room to find his bedside lamp already on, and Nightmare sitting in the creaky wooden chair in the corner, bathed once again in shadow, his white eyes shining in the darkness.

Matty slipped out of his sweatshirt, which left him in an equally oversize T-shirt and his sweatpants. He climbed into bed, shuffled under the covers, and turned on his side to face the demon in the corner.

"I usually keep my light on," he admitted after a moment.

"You may still, if you like," Nightmare told him. "Or you may turn it off. I'll be here either way."

Matty shut off the light, giving it a try. The room was darker, but he still had the little night-light in the shape of a lighthouse plugged in—a gift from Sascha—along with Nightmare's glowing eyes.

This would work.

Matty lay there, willing himself to sleep. But though his eyes were heavy and dry, he kept staring into the corner, where his demon stared back at him.

"Close your eyes, Matteo."

There was a pattern there, Matty was pretty sure. "Sweet" when Nightmare was coaxing, "Matteo" when he was ordering. Matty took note. He didn't usually like hearing his first name in full like that, but it wasn't so bad in Nightmare's hoarse rasp.

Instead of closing his eyes, Matty scooted back in bed until there was a space next to him on the outside edge. "Just until I fall asleep," he pleaded. "Please."

He waited for the weary sigh or sarcastic snort, the telltale nonverbal cues that Matty and his weakness were a burden. But he didn't get any. Instead, Nightmare slipped silently from his shadows, gliding closer to the bed like a wraith in the dark.

A weight on the bed. Smoke and fog. Heat.

Nightmare had gotten rid of his antlers somehow, though he was still almost too tall for Matty's bed. He sat half-upright against the headboard, hands clasped together on his chest.

Matty reached out, his fingertips just shy of touching Night-mare's side. He sighed happily, letting his eyes fall closed. "Thank you, Scary," he whispered.

A huff of near-silent laughter was the last thing Matty heard before drifting into sleep.

5

Matty

Waking up well rested wasn't something Matty was used to. It had definitely never happened when he'd been living in Luca Caruso's house. Not since Matty had been freed from that place either.

But this morning, Matty felt...nice.

Not exactly like all the damage from countless sleepless nights had been miraculously undone, but less like Matty was clawing himself out of a shallow grave just trying to get out of bed in the morning.

And it was all thanks to his demon.

Matty wasn't even surprised to find himself cuddled up to a long, lean male body this morning. Nightmare was warm, and he smelled nice, and he'd protected Matty all night long. It was only natural that Matty had migrated Nightmare's way at some point.

Matty *was* a little surprised at the...situation the top of his thigh—which he'd at some point hitched up over Nightmare's lap —was brushing up against.

Matty cleared the sleep out of his throat. He already knew Nightmare was awake. He could feel him watching. "I didn't know demons got morning wood."

Well, that was eloquent.

There was a long, slow sigh from above Matty. "You slept well, little human?"

Matty tilted his head to blink up at the demon. With the angle of Matty's bedroom window and the way the curtains were drawn, Nightmare's head was still bathed in shadow. Or maybe those were *his* shadows, the ones who'd tickled Matty's arms the night before.

Matty directed a smile somewhere in the vicinity of where Nightmare's face should be. "I can't remember the last time I didn't dream."

A satisfied rumble left Nightmare's chest. At some point Matty had thrown his arm over Nightmare's stomach too, but Nightmare didn't seem to be trying to get rid of him, so Matty let himself cuddle a little closer. The movement had his thigh brushing up against that same...predicament again.

Matty left his thigh where it was.

"You were alone in the Void a long time, right?" he asked. "With just a few other demons?"

That was what Kai had told Matty. That the Book the demons were all summoned with had been lost, and it had just been the four of them—Kai, Nix, Chaos, and Nightmare—in the Void for centuries, unable to return to the demon realm on their own. Just...stuck.

"Yes," Nightmare confirmed.

"And you didn't have sex with any of them?" Matty guessed. He thought Kai might have mentioned if any of the demons had been dating, but maybe that hadn't been the warrior demon's priority at the time.

There was a longer pause before his answer this time, but eventually Nightmare told him, "No."

Matty hummed in thought. "Then it's been a long time for you."

There was that soft sigh again. Or maybe it was a huff of laughter, Matty couldn't tell.

"Yes."

Matty was being pretty damn nosy right now. He wasn't even sure why, exactly, except that he felt so cozy and protected, and Nightmare was so...odd. Larger than life and powerful enough that it felt like he was outside the normal fear-based restrictions Matty lived by.

What could Matty really do to offend a being like that? Nightmare wouldn't answer any questions he didn't want to.

Still...

Matty rested his chin on Nightmare's chest, peering up into those shadows again. "If I annoy you, just tell me, and I'll stop."

There was no pause at all before Nightmare's answer this time. "You don't annoy me, little human."

Matty couldn't resist snuggling even closer, every inch of his body pressed against the demon in his bed. He'd never cuddled someone like this. He understood why people liked it.

Matty let his thigh brush against Nightmare's hardness again. "I could help, if you want."

The body in Matty's arms tensed, every muscle held still. "Explain."

"Well, you took care of me all night, so I could—could take care of you. That way. If you wanted. I don't really know what I'm doing, but I could figure out a hand job, I'm pretty sure."

Matty might have been inexperienced, but he came from a crude world. He had an idea of what men liked. And Nightmare might not have been a human man, but he seemed to have some corresponding parts Matty was familiar with. By the...shape of it, at least.

What were those pants made of, anyway? Demonic linen? They didn't hide much, whatever they were.

And Matty knew from overhearing Sascha and Kai these past months that some demons *did* enjoy sex with humans. Quite a bit, judging from the sound of it. Like, *a lot.*

"An exchange," Nightmare said, after a moment.

"Yeah." Matty nodded, his chin rubbing against Nightmare's chest. Definitely some sort of demonic linen on the shirt end of things. It was slightly rough against his skin but not uncomfortable.

"There's no need," Nightmare told him.

"Oh."

Matty was weirdly disappointed by that, which was kind of a surprise.

For numerous, life-saving reasons, Matty had pushed down the sexual side of himself for years. No ogling, no flirting, no daydreaming of any kind. Unless it was in the very darkest dark of night, under the covers, when he had occasionally furtively and franticly brought himself to completion.

But cuddling with Nightmare was nice, and it could have been even nicer to really...touch him. Bare skin to bare skin. He was so big and strange and powerful, it made something clench in Matty's lower belly just to be near him. Was that a thing? Were people turned on by big monsters, or was that just Matty being abnormal again?

But the thought of Nightmare calling Matty "sweet" in that low rasp while Matty made him feel good...

Matty shivered. He liked that Nightmare called him that. Matty didn't feel sweet most of the time. He felt...broken, and kind of jagged, but also weak and useless. Basically the worst combination a person could be.

Maybe all humans were sweet to Nightmare though. Maybe

their lack of skull faces and antlers and shadow fingers made them all soft and squishy in his eyes.

"What now?" Matty asked, holding back a sigh. He didn't want to make Nightmare feel bad for refusing him. He probably just wasn't attracted to little underfed weaklings who let bad dreams scare them out of sleeping.

"I have fed," Nightmare told him, and he must have been talking about munching on Matty's fear all night long. "So should you."

Finding something to eat. That was reassuringly practical. "I haven't gotten groceries in a long time," Matty warned him.

"We'll go to the market, then."

"You want to go grocery shopping with me?"

Nightmare made a vague sound of affirmation. "And then you will tell me how to find the men who scare you."

"Oh, I don't know how," Matty told him. Nightmare angled his head down, and now Matty could see his striking face, although his expression was still unreadable. Matty tried for a smile. No change. "I've been hiding from them," Matty explained.

And even with Nightmare here, protecting him, the thought of *not* hiding—of poking his head out of the sand in a way that meant anyone could find him—was too much to bear.

Matty untangled himself and hopped off the bed, stumbling a bit when the sudden movement made him lightheaded.

He looked down at himself. Oh. That was where all the blood had gone. "Oh, look," he said senselessly, pointing to his crotch. "I have it too." He looked back up to Nightmare dazedly. "Maybe I'll shower before we go, if that's okay."

Nightmare inclined his head, his white eyes sort of glowing. He looked...very large, lounging there on Matty's bed. Even without the antlers.

Oh God, did I really offer to jerk him off?

Belated embarrassment caught up to him, and Matty choked on a cough, turning on his heel. "Okay, bye, then!"

He ran into the bathroom, not sure if he imagined the low, raspy chuckle that followed him.

———

MATTY HAD THOUGHT he was prepared for Nightmare's human form.

He'd seen Kai go back and forth plenty of times between demon and human. As a human, Kai became a little shorter (relatively speaking) and a little less blue, and he lost the horns and the sharp teeth. He looked different but not shocking.

Nightmare's human form was...kind of shocking.

It was almost like the negative of a photograph, a darkroom opposite to his demon appearance. Nightmare's dark-gray skin became strikingly pale, and his white hair turned jet black, his irises dark enough to match. Without the shadows, his cheekbones were...startling. And maybe he was shorter, but it was hard to tell—he was still absurdly tall and slender.

In short, he looked like some kind of fae prince, even if his ears were no longer pointed.

A fae prince with intricate black tattoos running along both forearms, stark against his pale skin, presumably continuing under his clothes.

They were standing at the front door, and Nightmare's head was cocked as he studied Matty in turn, although the only thing Matty had changed was his clothes. "You're displeased?" Nightmare asked softly.

Matty's face must have been doing something weird.

"People are going to be all over you," Matty told him, maybe nonsensically. He couldn't stop looking at all the changes. Had

Nightmare's clothes gotten tighter too? They looked more...
modern somehow.

"They won't," Nightmare said. "My very essence is repellant to
humans."

Matty frowned. "I don't find you repellent."

Nightmare gave Matty a look that would have been almost
gentle, if sharp, otherworldly beauty could look gentle. "You've
lived with fear and pain a long time, Matteo."

Ah. So Matty *was* broken, and he'd just had it confirmed. *That*
was why he kind of wanted to climb his nightmare demon like a
tree.

It seemed okay, though, if it meant Matty could appreciate
Nightmare without running in the other direction.

It also seemed right to grab Nightmare's hand as they headed
out the door. Matty belatedly tugged his hood up, then led Nightmare into town at a brisk pace. It was true that—while people
definitely stared—no one approached them. No one tried to get
Nightmare's number or offered him a modeling contract or
anything like that. Everyone kept their distance, like there was an
invisible force field around Matty and Nightmare. That part was
pretty nice.

Still...

Dummies. Dummies, the lot of them.

Matty smiled up at Nightmare when they reached their
destination.

"This is not a market," Nightmare noted mildly.

"No. It's a bakery." Matty pointed at the Bakeshop window,
which had a view of the pastry case. "But the pastries have fruit.
I've even seen a vegetable or two in the savory croissants."

Not that Matty ever *bought* a savory croissant, but still. He'd
seen them.

He opened the door, leading Nightmare inside.

"Helloo— Oh, holy fuck."

"Hi, Seth. This is Night—" Matty broke off. It wasn't exactly normal for people to go by names like *Nightmare*, was it? "This is Night. Sarkaron Night, but he, um, goes by Night. Right?"

Matty looked up to Nightmare for approval, and Nightmare inclined his head slowly, although his eyes were on Seth.

Matty followed his gaze to where Seth was still staring wide-eyed at them. What was Nightmare looking for? Did he think Seth was pretty? Matty did. Seth had soft round cheeks and equally soft curls, and he usually had a bit of something sparkly on his face. Matty had always liked that about Seth, but now suddenly he wasn't so sure.

Matty tugged Nightmare's hand, grabbing his demon's attention. "Do you like coffee? Kai likes coffee."

Nightmare shook his head. "No, sweet."

"Okay. I'll just, um, make my...selections."

Matty didn't really want to let go of Nightmare's hand, but Nightmare didn't seem interested in coming forward to the pastry case, so Matty let it drop. He stepped up and focused on his task.

No lemon bars today.

Seth leaned over the counter, whispering kind of loudly, "*Where* are you all finding these men?"

"Who's 'we all'?" Were there more nightmare demons in town Matty should know about? They probably weren't as good as *his* nightmare demon though.

He already knew he'd gotten the best one.

Seth ticked off on his fingers. "Sascha. Benny. Now you."

"Benny has a dem—a...person?"

Seth rolled his eyes. "He waltzed into town—after disappearing for weeks, mind you—with the prettiest, grumpiest man glued to his side. It was...very odd. Like you, who barely speaks a word to anyone besides Sascha, Kai, and myself, coming in now with this new friend of yours."

"Oh." Matty worried at his sweatshirt sleeves, studying the

pastries to avoid Seth's gaze. "Night and I have known each other a long time though."

It wasn't a lie, not really. Nightmare had been stalking Matty in his dreams for months before they'd formed their contract. It was kind of comforting to think about, actually. Maybe Matty snuggling Nightmare and holding his hand and offering sexual favors out of the blue really wasn't that weird, considering their history.

"Mm-hmm," Seth hummed skeptically. But he didn't look put out or unkind, even if he thought Matty was lying. He never did look either of those things, no matter how shy or weird or awkward Matty was. That was why Matty liked the Bakeshop. That and the actual baking.

"I have key lime Danishes today," Seth finally told him, apparently done with the interrogation. He pointed to some pale-green pastries Matty had feared might be apple-flavored.

"Yes, please," Matty said immediately. "Two?"

"Sure thing. If nothing else, we know you'll never get scurvy." Seth put two in a bag, then added a third thing. "And a blueberry scone. If your...friend wants a taste of the local flavor."

Matty narrowed his eyes as Seth held the bag out cheerfully. Was that a come-on? Seth didn't sound lascivious, but Matty grabbed Nightmare's hand again anyway, not sure why he suddenly wanted to snap and growl at a man who'd only ever been incredibly kind to him.

Matty pulled Nightmare out of the Bakeshop after one last suspicious look at Seth, then guided his silent demon down the town's coastal path, stopping at a bench that looked out at the cliffs. Matty tugged Nightmare down to sit, then slid sideways until their thighs were touching.

"This is the ocean," Matty said, pointing out to the sea beyond the cliffs. "Do you like it?"

Kai had said they didn't have oceans in the demon realm.

"I do." Nightmare nodded regally, pale skin glowing in the

morning sun. It was strange for him not to be wrapped in shadows. Matty had the odd urge to throw a blanket over his face. "Many humans fear it. They dream of drowning, or of creatures in the depths. I enjoy their terror."

"Oh." Matty nodded politely. "That's nice." He took a bite of his Danish. The sharp citrus was tangy enough to hurt his mouth.

Seth really was a genius.

"Were your parents nightmare demons too?"

"Possibly. Unlikely."

Right. Nightmare probably didn't know, because demon parents didn't stick around to raise their young.

"My mom left me behind too," Matty told him, setting his half-eaten Danish on his lap. "Luca didn't have any heirs of his own, so when she left, he...stole me? Or maybe bought me. I like to think he bought me, because she never came back. Never—never tried to get me. If it was a desperate money thing, I would kind of understand, I think."

"He wanted a son, this Luca?"

Matty shrugged. "He needed a successor, and he thought he saw something in me. And when he realized he was wrong...I guess he figured it was just as good having a pet. One he could hurt without anyone caring."

"And Dominico Caruso?" Nightmare asked, his voice deadly soft.

Matty couldn't suppress his shiver, and *not* the good kind. He hated hearing that name spoken out loud. The sun was out, it was a pretty day, and Nightmare was warm at Matty's side, even if he looked strange and human; there was no need to bring *his* name into it.

So Matty changed the subject. "Why didn't you want me to touch you, earlier? Are you not attracted to me? It's okay if you aren't."

Matty knew he wasn't pretty like Seth, but he'd thought he was maybe cute.

There was a long silence. Nightmare really did like to consider his words carefully sometimes. "It's the reverse that interests me."

"Oh. Am *I* attracted to *you*?"

Nightmare nodded, and Matty thought it over. He wanted to give Nightmare the same courtesy Nightmare gave him—a thoughtful answer to a question.

Was he attracted to Nightmare?

Matty was still getting used to this absurdly beautiful human form of Nightmare's, so that side of it was maybe a trickier question. But Nightmare's demon form? Wrapped in shadows, all sharp teeth and talons, more monster than man?

"Yes," Matty decided. "I think so."

"You offered it as an exchange."

Matty tilted his head up to look at Nightmare. "You didn't like that? Lots of men seem to. 'I'll give you this if you do that.' 'Let me do this, and I'll maybe do that.'"

There had been men in Luca's employ who'd been either brave or stupid enough to try for something with Matty, despite what Luca would have done to them if they'd found out. They'd always seemed to approach the prospect as a barter of some kind.

Nightmare straightened, all impressive height and predatory stillness. "And do you accept these offers of exchange, Matteo?"

"No." Matty frowned out at the ocean. "They always scared me."

And while Matty could be stupid, he certainly wasn't brave.

"And I don't scare you."

It was half statement, half question. In answer, Matty leaned his head against Nightmare's arm and held up his pastry. "You want a bite of this?"

"Yes, sweet." Matty could hear the smile in Nightmare's raspy voice again. "Give us a taste."

Matty lifted the pastry to Nightmare's lips, and his demon took a careful bite, his teeth scraping lightly against Matty's fingers.

A shiver went down Matty's spine, the good kind this time. Nightmare's lips were soft, and his breath was hot, and as he leaned back to swallow his bite, Matty missed the feel of them both. He wanted those teeth to scrape against more of his skin— his throat and his belly and the shell of his ear, maybe.

Matty swallowed hard, staring at his pastry again. He looked at that perfect bite mark Nightmare had made, and he brought it to his own lips, pressing his teeth where Nightmare's had just been.

Yes, there was definitely attraction there.

6

Nightmare

Nightmare let his shadows dance and play over his talons as he watched his summoner sleep.

Matteo was active in rest, both in body and mind. It was a constant snag on Nightmare's attention, to keep his little human's dreams from trailing into the darker reaches of his psyche. It was as if Matteo's mind yearned to slip back into terror, to visualize the horrors that chased him. As if it kept running straight toward his fear, the exact opposite of what Matteo did during the day.

During the day, Matteo hid.

Nightmare had tried several more times to name the man who haunted Matteo. The man Nightmare intended to rip apart from sternum to pelvis. The man whose organs he would give to his dear shadows as playthings as soon as they found him.

But each time Nightmare had attempted it, Matteo had shied away, changing the subject without an ounce of shame. Bold even in his timidity.

It was making Nightmare restless, this blind spot Matteo insisted on. He itched to work around the impediment, to catch a glimpse of the face Matteo so feared. But that would require allowing Matteo to slip into a nightmare—allowing him to *suffer*—and that Nightmare would not do.

Now Matteo's brow furrowed as he mumbled something about "sugar toads" and rolled onto his stomach, his arms and legs sprawled out to the four corners of his bed.

Yes, very active in his rest.

He'd been much more docile when Nightmare had been lying beside him, the little human's limbs reaching only to wrap around Nightmare before settling contentedly for the night. But repeating that closeness did not seem wise at this juncture.

Of course, Nightmare had given in to Matteo's subtle pout at the beginning of the night, sitting with his back to Matteo's headboard until his summoner fell into slumber. But then Nightmare had returned to his corner, choosing the embrace of his shadows over the sweet torture of Matteo's clinging form.

Things were progressing much more quickly than Nightmare had anticipated.

He'd been prepared to go years—perhaps forever—without a physical side to their relationship. He was aware he was not the type of demon humans were drawn to, especially tender young men afraid of the dark. Nightmare had been prepared to possess but not to claim. To covet but not to grasp.

But his sweet was full of surprises.

Even now, Matteo's arm shifted again, reaching across the bed as if searching for Nightmare in his sleep.

Nightmare could wake him with soft touches this very moment, could slip Matteo onto his back without a word, could hold back his sharp teeth and taste his summoner's sleep-soaked skin. Nightmare could go further, even. He could slide into him with fingers or tongue or cock, take what he wanted while his little human's body was still lax and unassuming from his recent slumber.

Matteo would let him; Nightmare was sure of it.

But Nightmare could do more damage than good, pressing too soon. Matteo seemed unsure of his own attraction. He'd likely been suppressing that side of himself his entire life, judging from the innocence that glowed from his soul piece like moonstone.

So Nightmare would be patient. He would help Matteo coax it out, this sensuality brimming inside him, just waiting for an outlet.

Nightmare would even enjoy himself in the process.

He thought of the little breathless gasp Matteo had made that morning, when he'd realized Nightmare was aroused. When he'd thought it was a mindless physical response and not a direct consequence of Matteo's small, soft body rubbing against Nightmare in his sleep.

Nightmare's lips curled into a smile, and his shadows trailed out from him, reaching back to Matteo in turn.

Yes, Nightmare would enjoy himself.

He was no mindless brute. He could be kind and soft and sweet with his summoner, for as long as he needed to be. For all of eternity, if that was what was required.

Gentle touches in exchange for pretty, wide-eyed looks. Soft kisses given for breathless, tender smiles.

And when Matteo finally blossomed into who he should have been all along—who he might have been if cruel men hadn't taken him in hand...

A sweet, tender being with teeth as sharp as jagged knives.

Then Nightmare would devour him whole.

———

NIGHTMARE WAS STILL STARING at his summoner—on his back now, one slender arm thrown over his face—when he heard the noise.

Something on the house's porch. Something trying its best to be quiet in the dark. It could have been a prey animal, perhaps, trying to escape a mortal predator.

But there was a scent in the air: the acrid taste of ill intent.

Nightmare sent his shadows out to investigate, and they returned quickly with their findings: an image of a human man, of average height and muscular build, dressed in dark clothing. He was attempting to open a downstairs window; he had a tool to aid him and a human weapon tucked into the back of his jeans.

How interesting.

Nightmare approached Matteo's bed. He lifted Matteo's arm away from his face and stroked his summoner's cheek with his talons. "Wake, my sweet."

Matteo blinked awake slowly. And though Nightmare was in demon form, looming over him like a ghoul, he woke with a smile. "Is it morning?" His brow furrowed immediately, and he shook his head. "No, it's still dark. Was I—was I snoring?"

Nightmare's lips twitched at the corners. "No, little human. But there's a man breaking into the house."

Matteo immediately tried to jolt up and out of bed with a strangled cry, and Nightmare pressed a hand to his chest, holding him down. "Hush, sweet. It's all right. No one will harm you." He took a seat on the bed, brushing Matteo's hair from his face. Nightmare's shadows were keeping an eye on the would-be intruder; they were in no hurry. "Tell me why you summoned me now, Matteo. At this time. What prompted it?"

Matteo's large eyes were still wide with shock, but he lay there docilely enough, with Nightmare's hand on his chest. "I thought—thought I saw someone." He swallowed, loudly enough to be heard in the quiet of the night. "In town. One of his men, maybe. But I was just imagining it, I think. I—I thought."

"Mm." Nightmare considered, then stood. "Stay in bed. I'll call you when he's subdued, and you may come see if it's the man you thought you saw."

Matteo's hand shot out to grab Nightmare's wrist, his grip desperately tight. "No! *No*. Don't leave me alone. Please."

"You want to come with me, sweet?"

Matteo nodded frantically. "Yes."

"I'm going to hurt him," Nightmare warned.

"Good. If—if it's him. Then *good*."

Nightmare leaned down to press a kiss to Matteo's hair, a small reward for them both for this little glimpse of viciousness. Matteo gave him a shy smile—its own reward, that—and Nightmare held out his hand. "Come."

Matteo jumped up, clinging onto Nightmare's hand like a lifeline as Nightmare led him down the stairs in the dark. They made their way to the foyer, where they could hear the gentle scratching sound of a man still trying to open the window.

Nightmare let him through.

He did not open the window first.

Glass sprayed, and wood splintered, and Nightmare sheltered Matteo with his shadows, his little darlings whisking away anything sharp that dared head in their direction.

The stranger ended up on the hardwood floor, bloody and groaning. "What the f-fuck?"

He gathered his senses fairly quickly—Nightmare had to give him credit for that—and his eyes gleamed as he caught sight of Matteo, Nightmare too shrouded in shadow to be visible to the human eye.

"It's you." The intruder started laughing, blood gleaming on his teeth. "I knew it. Everyone thought there was no way you were hiding out with Dimitri Kozlov's boy, but Dominico knew." His laugh turned into a sneer. "He *knows* you, Matteo. He's coming for you. What happened to Luca, huh? Dominico's going to take it out on your skin, pretty b—"

That was enough of that. This was obviously the man Matteo had thought he'd seen, and Matteo was shaking with fear now.

Nightmare released his shadows, wrapping them over Matteo's form to warm him. He hadn't given Matteo enough time to slip on his hoodie over his thin shirt, an error he would not be making again. Matteo's human body was fragile and in need of more particular care than Nightmare was used to, but he would adapt.

Nightmare stepped into the moonlit patch of floor in front of the stranger, and the man's eyes widened as he tried to scramble back, his retreat halted by the wall behind him. "What the— What *are*—?"

Nightmare grabbed his skull mask from the ether, pulling it into place with his shadows. He let his limbs thin and stretch.

The man's face contorted into pure, unadulterated terror. "What the *fuck*?" he whimpered.

Nightmare crouched, his limbs bending and twisting to accommodate. The man stared, almost seeming to hold his breath, perhaps waiting for Nightmare to say something. He smelled suddenly of urine.

But Nightmare had no speech for him, no message for this unwanted intruder to send back to his master. This man had signed his life away the moment he'd approached this house, disturbing Matteo's precious slumber.

Nightmare struck, clawing his talons into the man's chest, letting his venom seep out as the man screamed. He watched the paralysis take over, stilling the human's clawing hands and freezing his vocal cords, silencing him forever.

Nightmare's magic allowed only the smallest hint of movement, the barest inflation of the human's lungs. Just enough to keep the man sufficiently alive to feel the agony of his own slow suffocation.

Nightmare let his shadows enter the man's mind next. They wriggled into his darkest corners and found every fear, every inner horror, every twisted thought. They brought them out into the light, amplifying and contorting and displaying them back to him.

The man couldn't scream as he lost his senses, not with the paralysis working through him. The best he managed was a strangled garbling.

But it was a delicious meal all the same, his terror. Full-bodied. He'd seen much to corrupt him, and Nightmare's shadows had their fill to work with.

Sometime later—when he'd plundered everything there was to take—Nightmare slipped his talons back into the man's chest and pulled out his heart before dropping the bloody mass onto the floor.

Nightmare stood and turned as his skull mask dropped back into the ether and his demonic visage slipped back into place, his limbs shrinking back to their usual size.

Matteo was there, still draped in Nightmare's spare shadows, no longer shaking now. He was standing straight-backed and motionless, his eyes locked onto the dead man slumped onto the floor.

"Do you wish me to erase this from your mind, sweet?" Nightmare asked. "You need not live with it."

Nightmare would never have let Matteo see such horrors if he didn't have a way to clear them from his memory.

"You tortured him," Matteo said softly, his eyes still on the corpse in front of him. "Inside his head."

"Yes."

"And killed him."

"Yes."

Matteo took a deep breath, then clutched the edges of Nightmare's shadows to his chest like the clasp of a cloak. He slowly walked over, looking much too soft to survive in this world, with his short, mussed hair and his giant, tired eyes.

Matteo tugged gently at Nightmare's shirt. "Bend down for me, please."

Nightmare lowered his head, and his sweet, tender summoner pressed a soft, chaste kiss to his lips. "Thank you," Matteo murmured.

"Again and again and again," Nightmare promised. "As many times as needs to be done."

Matteo kept hold of Nightmare's shirt as he said, slowly and clearly, "When it's Dominico's turn, I want it to last longer. I want it to *hurt*."

Bright, acidic lemon filled the air. Tart and perfect.

"Yes, sweet," Nightmare vowed. "I swear."

And then Matteo was throwing himself into Nightmare's arms, clutching at his waist with surprising strength. "Thank you." He peered up at him, blinking up at him through thick, sooty lashes. "Can we watch a movie now? I'm not tired anymore."

7

Matty

Matty watched the end credits of the movie blankly, making no move to grab the remote just yet. He might have liked to put on another, but Nightmare had let him watch this one curled up in his lap, warm and safe and cozy. Matty was worried that if he moved, Nightmare would come to his senses and shove him off.

Okay, he probably wouldn't *shove*. But maybe he'd slip out like one of his shadows. And then Matty would be cold and alone and sad, with no one's strong arms surrounding him.

And maybe Nightmare hadn't *let* him so much as Matty had just crawled up onto the demon's thighs and settled in, wrapping blankets around them both before anyone could protest.

So. No moving.

But it didn't matter, because Nightmare was already slipping out from under Matty, just like Matty had thought he would.

Although, less expected was how Nightmare knelt in front of the couch, his hands on either side of Matty's folded legs. The position put them at eye level with each other, and Nightmare's pair were a flat white at the moment, narrowed slightly as he stared at Matty.

"Hello," Matty said.

Nightmare stayed silent. Watching. Waiting.

Ugh. It was time for Matty to start talking, wasn't it? The thought made him weirdly petulant. "There's still a body in the foyer," he pointed out. "A dead one."

Nightmare didn't even twitch. "My shadows will take care of it."

"And the glass?" Matty frowned at him. "Sascha's been really nice to me. I don't want him to come home and find everything all messed up."

"My shadows will repair the damage."

Matty picked some fuzz off his blanket with a scowl. "They can do just about anything, huh?"

If Nightmare thought Matty was being a brat, he didn't say so. He only nodded regally. "They can do many things, yes."

His antlers were so close. And because Nightmare had yet to refuse him any sort of touch (except that one time Matty had tried to jerk him off, and Matty wasn't letting himself think about that time because it was too embarrassing to mention), Matty reached up, stroking one of the branches. It was velvety soft. He pressed his thumb against it to test its strength. Solid. Sturdy.

"Matteo."

Matty sighed, stroking the velvet...fur? Skin? He wasn't sure. He stroked the velvet *whatever* of Nightmare's antler. "What do you want to know?"

"Who is Dominico Caruso and why does he haunt you?"

Straight to the point. How mean of him. Matty stalled for time by studying his demon, his monster of the dark, not just in form but in spirit.

Because Matty had seen Nightmare's face when he'd been

torturing Dominico's goon. Nightmare had enjoyed it. A lot. His white eyes had been glowing and his skull face's teeth had been bared in a jagged grin.

And Matty didn't care.

He *should* care, shouldn't he?

Matty let out another sigh, dropping his hand from Nightmare's antler and twisting his fingers in his lap.

"He was my stepfather Luca's cousin. Or maybe half brother? They were never straightforward about it. Either way, he was a psychopathic dog, and Luca held his leash. He was—*is*..." Matty tried to find words for it that didn't make him want to dry heave. "He took a liking to me early on. When I was still a boy. Luca put him in charge of—of my punishments. He enjoyed them." Matty let his eyes drop to Nightmare's crotch pointedly. "*Really* enjoyed them."

Nightmare let out a low growl, and the dangerous sound bolstered Matty the slightest bit. He kept going, pushing the truth out before he could think too hard about it. "He wanted to do more than punish me. He wanted to keep me as one of his pets. Sometimes— Sometimes I'd wake up in the middle of the night to find him in my room, sitting on my bed. He'd tell me everything he had planned for me."

Dominico had made a habit of it, especially at the end. Whenever he was due to report in to Luca, he'd skulk into Matty's room in the dead of night and whisper horrors to him in the dark. Luca had allowed it, as long as Dominico didn't touch Matty without his permission.

Matty had been terrified of falling asleep. Terrified of finding Dominico waiting in the shadows when he woke. The monster he couldn't seem to shake.

Matty blinked back stubborn tears. He was safe here. Safe to talk about it. Safe to remember. "So Luca held it over both of us—giving me to Dominico. A threat to keep me from running or talking, and a promise to keep Dominico obeying his orders without question.

"I—I saw some of the boys he kept." Matty swallowed through a thick throat. "Their bodies afterward. He's—he's *evil*." He made himself meet Nightmare's eyes, made himself admit the truth. "But so am I."

When Nightmare only cocked his head, silently demanding Matty keep going, Matty told him, "I stood by while they did awful things, Sarkaron. The pair of them, and the men who followed them. I let fear make me complacent. I should have killed them both, or gone to the FBI, or—or *something*. But I was too afraid Luca would catch me. Afraid he'd give me over to Dominico when he did. And over time..."

Matty twisted his fingers together so hard it hurt. "Luca wanted to break me. To make me into the kind of man he could use. The kind who would hurt innocent people and not care. A real successor and not just a scared little boy at his side."

Matty leaned forward, dropping his forehead onto Nightmare's shoulder, unable to bear letting Nightmare see his face as he let the truth spill out. "Maybe you can taste it in my soul, Scary. That they succeeded. Because I *liked* watching you hurt that man. I'm glad he's dead. I wish he'd suffered more. I didn't used to be that way. I—I used to be good, I think. But they broke me like they wanted, and now I want to cut them all with my jagged pieces. Cut them into *ribbons*."

Matty waited for Nightmare to shove him off. To hold Matty accountable for all the rot inside him. Any minute now Nightmare would tell Matty that he was too wicked to deserve anyone's help, even a demon's.

But there were only gentle fingers in Matty's hair, stroking softly as Nightmare asked, "Why didn't you trust Sascha and Kai to keep you safe, Matteo?"

"They're trying to get out of Mafia business," Matty explained.

Sascha had told him all about it once. How much he hated the world he'd grown up in. How much he wanted to keep himself and Kai away from it all. "They want to stick to the light. To keep it to legal businesses and no violence. And Dominico... He works in the shadows."

Nightmare let out a quiet, raspy laugh. "Sweet summoner, I *own* the shadows."

Matty heard that simple statement for what it was: a promise. Nightmare was going to protect him, even though Matty was rotten and weak. Maybe that was because of the contract—maybe Nightmare didn't actually have a choice—but still...

No one had ever protected Matty. Not his mother, not his step-father, and certainly not his stepfather's men. But this demon would. This monstrous creature would stand by Matty's side, keeping him from harm.

Nightmare tugged Matty's head gently off his shoulder and cupped Matty's face with his large, warm hands, stroking those slender fingers against Matty's cheeks. "I will be your jagged pieces, Matteo. I will cut them into ribbons for you."

Matty's eyes were wet. He was pretty sure he was getting salty tears all over Nightmare's fingers. "Why are you so nice to me?"

"Selfish pursuits," Nightmare whispered, his white eyes beginning to glow.

"You want something from me?"

A nod.

"Something bad?"

No answer.

Matty sniffed back more tears. "Whatever it is, you can have it."

Nightmare made a quiet tutting sound, like Matty was being unreasonable. "And if it's your very soul, whole and complete and mine to devour?"

"You can have it," Matty told him instantly. "It's yours."

"Foolish little human," Nightmare whispered, soft and dark as one of his shadows.

And then he pressed his lips against Matty's.

Other than the thank-you kiss Matty had given Nightmare in the foyer, Matty had been kissed only once before. It had been stolen by a vile man in the organization who'd reeked of stale beer and was found dead in a river the next day. He'd shoved his meaty tongue into Matty's mouth and made him gag.

Nightmare's kiss was nothing like that. His lips were thin but so warm, and his soft tongue swept gently against Matty's mouth, coaxing it to open.

Matty let the demon in, his skin suddenly too tight and too hot. Nightmare smelled like smoke-laced fog, and secrets in the dark, and his touch never hurt, and Matty wanted more of it.

Matty leaned so far forward he fell off the edge of the couch, but Nightmare caught him, tugging Matty into his lap, never breaking the kiss.

It was a good position, because it meant Matty could wrap around him like a limpet, craning his neck up so Nightmare could keep kissing him. Nightmare was so much bigger than him—so much stronger—and it did something weird to Matty, made his belly swoop and all his blood rush south.

Safe in Nightmare's lap, Matty let go of all his terrible thoughts and fears, let himself be reduced to nothing more than a warm and willing body grinding against Nightmare, mindlessly trying to get more pressure against his swelling dick.

Nightmare broke the kiss, still stroking Matty's cheeks. Matty wasn't crying anymore, so that was good. But he was...aching in a way he never had before. He was aching and hard and wanting.

"What do you desire, sweet?"

Matty knew the answer. "I want to feel good. Please. For once in my life, I want to feel only *good*."

And Nightmare really was the best demon Matty could have

ever hoped for, because taloned fingers left Matty's cheek and trailed down to his sweats, working nimbly to slide them down and untangle them from Matty's legs until he was nude from the waist down, still in Nightmare's lap, his hard cock red and weepy with precum.

Oh God. Nightmare was going to touch him. Stroke him. Make him come.

Matty could barely breathe, overwhelmed by this ferocious need for all of it.

He looked down, watching those slender fingers wrap around his cock. Matty was large for his stature, but Nightmare's fingers dwarfed him easily.

"Pretty," Nightmare crooned, his thumb sliding over Matty's cockhead, spreading his precum around, making Matty gasp. "So pretty, sweet. Every bit of you."

He stroked down, precum easing the glide, and then he squeezed as he lifted back upward and— Oh. *Oh.* That was—that was *so much better* than when Matty touched himself.

"Oh my God." Matty dropped his forehead into Nightmare's chest, rolling it back and forth as he looked down, unable to stop watching Nightmare touch him.

Before he'd summoned Nightmare to his side, Matty had almost only ever been touched in cruelty, and this was—

Matty would give his soul over without question, if he could have more of this.

As if reading his mind, soft warmth creeped under Matty's shirt, sliding along his ribs, teasing at his nipples, petting along his neck. Nightmare's shadows. The ones Matty had seen rip into Dominico's goon's mind and drive him mad. The ones he'd seen tear a man through a closed window.

They were teasing Matty, and they felt *wonderful.*

Matty moaned. He didn't think it had been very long at all, but he could feel something building at the base of his spine, swirling deep in his belly, and his need was too strong for him to hold any of it in. He couldn't stop squirming and writhing, and it was only Nightmare's strong arm around his back that kept him from sliding off his demon's lap onto the floor.

"I-I'm going to come," Matty said, the words coming out in a desperate whine as he rocked his hips. "You're making me come."

"Yes, sweet," Nightmare hissed, still gliding his hand around Matty's cock in a steady, perfect rhythm. "Give it to us."

Matty cried out, a high-pitched screech that maybe he'd be embarrassed about later. But his orgasm was a hundred times stronger than anything he'd ever done for himself, and it choked the air out of his lungs as he came.

A deep, satisfied rumble left Nightmare's chest, and he continued stroking Matty through his release until Matty was trembling like a leaf.

Matty panted, blinking down as Nightmare finally released his hold. White cum on gray skin. Nightmare's shadows congregated on the demon's hand, and then the cum was gone.

Did they...eat it?

Matty's brain was too fuzzy to figure it out, and also he was kind of distracted because he was sitting on something hard.

Matty scooted back, stroking a hand over Nightmare's clothed lap, gasping at what he found. Another erection, this one *definitely* because of Matty.

"I'd like to see," he said.

Nightmare said nothing, but nimble fingers danced down to unlace something or other, and then there was his cock.

Oh wow.

It was just like the rest of Nightmare, scary large and scary-looking. It had twisted black veins branching along it, and the head...

It was bulbous, thicker than the rest of him, and the foreskin was...strange. Like the bud of a closed flower, petals covering the tip, leaving a little open star at the very center.

Before he could stop himself, Matty stroked a finger along one of those petals. It lifted, a stream of smoky gray *something* pouring out.

Was that...demon precum?

Matty cocked his head, fighting the strange urge to lean down and *lick*. "Do I turn you on, Scary?" he asked, and he barely recognized the low croon of his own voice.

Another rumbling growl left Nightmare's chest. This one was in affirmation; Matty was sure of it.

"You want to—to put that inside me?" Matty stroked another petal, watching it lift. The cockhead hiding under those petals was dusky black and so very wet. If Matty stroked them all, would they peel back and reveal it fully? Would it taste as dark and dangerous as it looked?

Would it fit inside him?

Nightmare laid a gentle, restraining hand on Matty's wrist. "Another time, little cocktease."

"Is that what I'm doing?" Matty asked dazedly. He didn't seem to have many brain cells left after his first partner-induced orgasm. He could only think, *Nightmare cock, Nightmare cum, Nightmare fuck.*

Or something like that.

But Matty supposed he was—very literally—teasing Nightmare's demon cock with his touches.

But shouldn't Nightmare want Matty to tease him *more*?

"Won't you be uncomfortable if you don't...finish?" he asked, lifting a finger to brush another petal.

Nightmare grasped Matty's hand with his own, effectively removing it from his cock, and tucked his erection away.

Matty made a grumbled sound of protest. He'd been enjoying himself. He liked looking at Nightmare's cock, and he liked touching it. He thought he might like putting it in his mouth even more.

Soft, careful fingers gripped Matty's chin, lifting it until he was meeting Nightmare's glowing white eyes. "I'm a patient demon, Matteo," Nightmare said quietly. "I know how to wait for what I want."

Matty swallowed. Was he talking about Matty's body or his soul?

Matty wasn't sure he cared either way.

Nightmare's lips twitched into a small smile, like he knew what Matty was thinking. "You need more sleep, sweet. Let me take you to bed."

"And you'll hold me again?"

It was kind of a trick question. Nightmare hadn't held Matty the night before. He'd lain *next* to Matty, and Matty had snuggle-strangled him in the night.

And maybe it was mean to even ask, when Matty had just come and Nightmare was left all hard and wanting. But Matty was feeling...demanding in his soft, postcoital state.

And Nightmare would give it to him, wouldn't he? He'd give Matty anything, it seemed like, and all he was asking for was everything in return.

"And I'll hold you," Nightmare confirmed.

Matty could barely contain his smug, tired grin as Nightmare lifted him into his arms and carried him up the stairs.

He really had summoned the most perfect demon.

8

Matty

Matty stopped short at the bottom of the stairs.

Sascha's entryway was pristine.

No dead body, no broken glass, not a sliver of splintered wood to be found. The floor even looked cleaner than before, the hardwood almost sparkling in the early morning light.

Matty felt more than heard Nightmare come up behind him.

"You doubted me, little human?"

Matty shivered as that low rasp caressed the back of his neck. He hadn't doubted his demon at all, but seeing the reality of it was different. It also begged the question—had Nightmare's shadows *eaten* the dead man?

It probably didn't matter. Either way, Matty didn't want to know. The body was gone, and that was enough.

"Your shadows did a very good job," Matty admitted grudgingly.

Nightmare let out a low chuckle behind him, and a weight

settled on Matty's shoulder, followed by a tickling touch on his cheek.

Had one of Nightmare's shadows just *kissed* him?

Matty sighed, reaching sightlessly behind him to grab Nightmare's hand and tug the demon into the kitchen. It was too hard to hold on to a bad mood when adorable, murderous shadow monsters were distributing cheek kisses.

It was a shame though. Matty had really intended to grump around for a bit, at least until his better sense got the best of him.

He'd woken up disturbingly well rested. He'd been wrapped around Nightmare again, both of them clearly aroused, and Nightmare had just...let Matty get up and get started on his day. He hadn't asked for a hand, or offered Matty one, or alluded to the night before at all. And Matty had been too nervous to do it himself.

But he'd wanted to. He'd really, really wanted to. Nightmare had been so big and warm against him, and Matty had wanted to... slide around on him. Under him? On top of him? Or something. He wasn't sure, exactly, but it probably would have involved rubbing *on* or rubbing *off* the demon. Rubbing of some kind, definitely.

But no rubbing had been offered, and thus had come the grumping.

Matty sat Nightmare down at the kitchen table, placing him in the oversized chair Kai usually chose. Then he set to work toasting his day-old blueberry muffin, since Nightmare didn't seem to have any interest in "sampling the local flavor."

He could feel Nightmare's eyes on him, watching Matty in that unblinking way he had. The way that made Matty feel like nothing could ever escape Nightmare's notice.

"What distresses you, sweet?"

There it was.

"Nothing," Matty lied, peeking out of the corner of his eye to see how well that untruth landed.

Nightmare cocked his head. He'd disappeared his antlers again during the night, but they were back now. That was good—Matty had missed them. "I left not a trace of blood."

"Clearly."

Matty's snark was met with silence, and Matty didn't attempt to fill it. He was all weird and itchy and uncomfortable in his own skin. He wasn't used to playing the brat. He wouldn't have survived it in his old life and he was too scared of losing everything to try it in his new one. But he was...irritated. And he didn't even know why. And that was *doubly* irritating.

"I do desire your touch, sweet."

Matty froze at the counter, a tub of butter in hand. "You do?" he asked, not daring to turn around just yet.

"Did I not tell you I came to this realm with selfish pursuits in mind?"

Matty frowned down at the counter. "Some would say actions speak louder than words."

"And what about my actions do you find displeasing?"

"I'm not sure," Matty hedged.

He really wasn't. He knew enough to know he was being unreasonable. He wasn't owed Nightmare jumping his bones at every opportunity. No one was ever owed the touch of another being.

But Matty wasn't used to *wanting* things. His life before had been about survival. Avoidance. And now he'd summoned this demon to his side and the demon was bigger and scarier than anything Matty had ever seen and Matty wanted him to *stay*. And he wanted him closer. And he maybe wanted to crawl under Nightmare's skin and fuse them together so Nightmare couldn't ever leave.

It was terrible, this wanting.

And possibly not very normal.

But Matty would worry about that part later.

Matty finally summoned the courage to turn around, only to find Nightmare leaning forward in his seat, his taloned hands clasped on the kitchen table. He looked so strange and out of place in this quaint New England kitchen. Tall and gaunt and gray, his antlers wreathed in shadow.

"We have a task to complete, Matteo," Nightmare told him, his raspy voice as gentle as it was capable of. "I need you to aid me in finding Dominico Caruso."

Matty bit his lower lip, only distantly aware that at some point his wounded skin seemed to have healed. "So you can leave?"

"So I can keep you."

The hope those words induced was sharp and painful, so Matty ignored it, choosing instead to butter his muffin in silence and bring it to the table.

Nightmare grasped Matty's wrist when he was within reach. "How do I find Dominico?"

After a moment of deliberation, Matty motioned for Nightmare to scoot back from the table, then took a seat on his lap. If they were going to be talking about terrifying things, Matty wanted to be as close as possible to his terrifying demon. "I don't know."

"Who does?"

Matty thought it over. "Ivan, maybe. Sascha's brother. He'd be keeping track of Luca's key players."

"Ivan Kozlov. The incubus's mate."

Matty twisted to look back at Nightmare. "How do you know that?"

"Call him," Nightmare ordered brusquely, completely ignoring Matty's question.

Matty looked down to his muffin. If he ate slowly enough, he could delay things by...twenty minutes? He'd need to chew really thoroughly though. Crumb by crumb.

"*Now*, Matteo."

Matty sighed, reaching across the table to where he'd set his phone earlier. He pressed Ivan's contact, mildly shocked when Ivan picked up promptly.

"Matteo Caruso," Ivan greeted in his cold, monotone voice. "Did you change your mind about the babysitter?"

A lot of people found Ivan pretty scary. His name was whispered with fear in plenty of circles; Matty knew that much. And Matty even got it—he really did. Ivan was a cold and intimidating mob boss, and Matty had only ever seen him smile for his gorgeous incubus mate.

But also, a couple months ago, during one of his visits, Ivan had walked up to Matty—nestled in blankets on the couch, fighting back tears as he selected another horror movie to keep himself awake—and apropos of nothing, had told him, "The kind of men who raised us, they should never have been in charge of children. *Fuck* them."

And then he'd walked away without another word.

So overall, Matty thought Ivan was pretty okay.

"No, um...I haven't changed my mind about the babysitter. I have a request."

"Sascha isn't giving you enough funds?"

Before Matty could reassure Ivan that Sascha was more than generous with funds, he heard Nix's voice in the background. "Ohh, is that Matty? Put him on video call! I want to see the little chickadee."

Ivan let out a loud, put-upon sigh, but he also immediately did as his incubus asked, so the sigh seemed more like a performance than anything else.

Matty accepted the video call, smiling shyly when the screen revealed Nix's beautiful face in front of Ivan's, sly grin included.

The grin fell in an instant.

"By the Book," Nix whispered, his pretty purple eyes wide and focused on the demon behind Matty. And then, much louder, "Holy fucking dick and balls!"

"What is it?" Ivan tilted the phone toward himself, presumably so he could see what had Nix so surprised. His lips thinned. "Who is that?"

Nix snatched the phone back, his brow furrowed in an uncharacteristically serious expression. He cocked his head, his long red ponytail swishing behind him. "Matty, little darling, are you doing okay?"

"I'm fine."

"And can you perchance see the infernal creature lurking behind you?"

Matty turned around with a start, but there was only Nightmare, still seemingly content to be used as Matty's chair, staring at Matty's phone without any particular expression.

Matty turned back to Nix. "Of course I can see him. I summoned him."

His words didn't seem to reassure Nix at all, and now Ivan was looking decidedly cranky. "As I currently have the Book in my possession, *how* did you summon him, Matteo?"

"Dominico Caruso," Nightmare interjected, and though his voice was quiet, it halted any other discussion immediately. "Where is he?"

Nix murmured something that sounded like, "Best to answer him, darling," and Ivan's jaw clenched.

"I don't know."

When Nightmare said nothing more to him, Nix started making crazy motions with his eyebrows, and Ivan added, "Cooper has gathered some surveillance data. Nothing he nor I would be comfortable sending over digitally."

"I can't come to New York," Matty told him immediately.

"Can't or won't?" Ivan asked icily.

"Won't."

Even with Nightmare at his side, Matty wouldn't do it. And he knew it made him cowardly and stupid, and he didn't care. New York was Dominico's territory. Matty would be staying far, far away.

Ivan gave him a single sharp nod. "Give me a moment, then." He stepped away, and Matty could see him in the background, picking up his office phone.

Nix gave Matty a strange sort of smile. "It's always lovely to see you, Matty, but let me talk to Nightmare for a minute, hm?"

Without you present were the unspoken words.

Matty slipped off Nightmare's lap and took a seat at the other side of the table. He could only hear vague murmuring on Nix's side of things—apparently the brash incubus could be quiet when he wanted to be—but Nightmare said nothing.

When Matty's demon finally *did* speak, his raspy voice was colder and crueler than Matty had ever heard it. "I don't answer to you, incubus. Interfere at your own risk."

And that seemed to be that, because Nightmare put the phone down on the table, and Matty had to slide back over onto his lap to reach it.

He found Ivan back on the other end, Nix nowhere to be found. "Cooper and his demon can meet you in Portland," Ivan told Matty without preamble.

Matty winced. "Or we can just wait for the next time you vis—"

"We will meet them," Nightmare said.

"I'll let them know." Ivan was shamelessly studying Nightmare now, his expression blank. He looked so similar to Sascha—who was always vibrant and occasionally mercurial—that it was always strange to see that same face so unanimated. "Is this a permanent sort of—?"

"Yes," Nightmare answered, and then he put the phone face down on the table again.

Apparently he was done with talking. Although, he didn't actually press any button to end the call, so hopefully Ivan would take care of that on their end.

Maybe Matty wasn't the only one in a grumpy mood this morning.

Nightmare shifted Matty further back onto his lap, wrapping an arm around his middle. His shadows pulled Matty's plate closer. "Eat your muffin, sweet."

So apparently they were going to Portland. To get information they needed to find the person Matty most dreaded ever having to see again. So Nightmare could complete the contract they'd made.

Matty bit into his muffin with a scowl.

Yeah, this morning was the actual worst.

9

Nightmare

There was something going on with Nightmare's little human.

There had been since the previous morning, when Matteo had crawled out from Nightmare's arms and rolled from the bed with a strange pulse of disappointment-tinged anger emanating from his soul piece.

Now they were several hours into their second bus ride of the day—Matteo couldn't drive a vehicle, so they were taking public transportation—and Matteo was a jumble of emotions so conflicted that Nightmare was having trouble parsing through them.

It was...frustrating.

Part of that may have been due to lack of experience, Nightmare had to admit. Terror, shock, awe, defeat—those were Nightmare's expertise. Hope and resentment and lust and shame—all of them blanketed under a fear that had been growing heavier the further they strayed from Seacliff—those were more challenging.

It was a pity because, if not for his concern, Nightmare might have enjoyed modern human travel. Every now and then, one of their fellow travelers would fall into a fitful sleep and provide Nightmare with a little snack. He didn't usually prefer to feed in his human form, but after so long in the Void with no variety at all, the novelty of the experience made it well worth it.

Matteo, of course, did not doze off. He was too wary by half, even with Nightmare on the outside seat of their bus aisle. In addition, Matteo seemed to find it his duty to lean over Nightmare and glare out of his hoodie at anyone who dared stare at Nightmare too long. It was perplexing and amusing, the strange sort of protectiveness that lit up Matteo's soul piece when he did so.

Humans were...odd.

Case in point: Why didn't Matteo want Nightmare to find Dominico?

Matteo's current state was evidence enough that it was necessary. He was jumping and twitching over every shadow not belonging to Nightmare, his hands clenched into fists inside his sleeves.

Living under that kind of fear for so long twisted a soul into knots. It was unacceptable that Nightmare allow it to fester inside Matteo any longer.

What Matteo needed was to watch Dominico get torn from this mortal plane by way of a million bloody pieces. Matteo needed to see it with his own eyes and understand his past would never come back to haunt him again. He needed to understand that Nightmare would rip the hearts out of anyone who dared try.

What other use was Nightmare for, if not to rend his future mate's enemies into scattered bits of flesh?

The bus stopped with a loud lurch and a plume of smoke.

"We're here," Matteo said with a sigh. He pushed gently at Nightmare until Nightmare was standing in the aisle, and then he walked them off the bus.

There was a man in a suit and a cap holding a sign that said "Mr. Kozlov." Matteo stopped far back from the man's line of sight, cocking his head. "I think that might be us?" He pulled out his phone, reading something on the screen and nodding. "Ivan set it up. Same with the hotel."

He approached what Nightmare could only assume was a hired human driver, giving the man a small, uncertain smile. "Hi. We're your passengers?"

The man smiled back at Matteo, and there was something lustful in his gaze as he took stock of Nightmare's human. Nightmare made a note of the man's psychic signature; he'd find his way into the driver's dreams sooner rather than later.

Matteo was not this man's pet to ogle.

The suited driver took them to a hotel, and after a short registration process—wherein Matteo acted as if every question the concierge asked had to be answered under penalty of gruesome death—they ended up in a luxe room with two beds, neither quite as large as Matteo's at home.

Matteo still whistled in approval as they entered. He seemed impressed enough with the costly fabrics and spacious bedroom. Even more so with the large bathroom and its demon-sized shower and standing bathtub.

Nightmare cared little for the room, but he was pleased to finally shed his human form again. He stretched his neck in relief, relishing the solid weight of his antlers.

"Ivan really set us up," Matteo finally said, carefully placing his backpack on one of the beds and taking a seat next to it.

He'd dropped Nightmare's hand when they'd entered the room, and he hadn't picked it back up again. The distance was...displeasing.

"He's fond of you, this Ivan?"

Matteo shook his head. "Ivan's only fond of Nix and Sascha.

Everyone else he tolerates. But we've got certain similarities in our upbringing. I guess he sort of...gets it."

"Raised by cruel men," Nightmare surmised.

"Yeah. But Ivan took that past and became a scary badass mob boss that nobody dares to fuck with, and I became"—Matteo waved a hand, gesturing in a way that encompassed all of him —"this."

Nightmare stepped up to the bed, tugging Matteo's hood down slowly, his shadows dancing over Matteo's short, mussed hair. "And what's wrong with *this*?"

"Are you serious? I'm weak." Matteo frowned down sullenly at his hands. "A coward."

"You fear someone who would do you great harm. I see only logic in that."

"You don't know much about toxic masculinity, huh?"

Nightmare tried to parse through that riddle. "Fearing for your life makes you less masculine?"

Matteo sighed. "When someone threatened Ivan and his family, he gathered a group of demons and vampires and loyal men and executed all the traitors in his midst. He didn't get himself adopted like a kitten and use it as an excuse to hide out for the rest of his life."

"Do you not wish to do the same?" Nightmare asked. "To execute your pursuers? Is that not why you called me?"

Matteo didn't seem to find Nightmare's words comforting. His frown deepened, the space between his brows furrowing. That strange resentment festered in his soul piece again. "No. I don't know." He bit at his lower lip. "I want them gone."

"That's what we work toward." Nightmare traced a finger down Matteo's cheek. "You need not be the cruel executioner, Matteo. You have me."

Matteo batted Nightmare's hand away, glaring up at him. "You're just saying all that so you can leave!"

Ah. Yes. Humans were indeed strange and confusing.

Hadn't Nightmare told Matteo he was staying? Told him he intended to keep Matteo for his own?

Why was Nightmare's word not enough?

Nightmare's shadows whirled around his chest, pinching and poking at him. *The truth,* they seemed to say. *The whole of it.*

Nightmare glared down at them. Matteo wasn't ready. But Nightmare couldn't allow him to stay in this stew of agitation either.

And what did it matter if Matteo was ready? Nightmare wasn't letting him get away, no matter the outcome.

Nightmare cocked his head, staring down at his summoner. Matteo was looking down at his feet and nibbling at his lower lip again, as if ashamed of his outburst.

"Take a shower, sweet summoner. Wash off the scent of foreign souls."

Matteo nodded, the very picture of dejection.

Nightmare placed a finger under Matteo's chin, lifting his head. "When you're done, I'll tell you a story. Would you like that, sweet?"

Matty blinked large, sad eyes at him. "A true one?"

Nightmare nodded.

"One that will make me feel better?"

Nightmare couldn't promise that. "One that will assure you I am here to stay," he said instead.

———

SOME TIME later Matteo emerged from the steam-filled bathroom. He wore black sweatpants that hung low on his slender hips and a damp towel pressed to his chest, covering most of his skin.

"I left my shirt in my bag," he told Nightmare, doing a strange sort of side step to his bag, one that kept him facing toward the room.

But when he bent to grab his shirt, the towel shifted, revealing...

"*Stop*," Nightmare ordered.

His shadows were out before he could halt them, blanketing Matteo's torso like a protective covering. Nightmare peeled them away with great effort.

He needed to see.

Nightmare stalked toward his summoner. "Dominico?" he asked, voice deadly soft.

Matteo nodded slowly, letting his towel fall now that he was caught out. "The punishments," he explained dully. "He always preferred knives."

That fact was clear enough. Matteo's chest and back were a network of crisscrossed scars, raised white lines shocking in their number. They stopped at his neckline and arms, a deliberate choice. There was nothing anyone would see when Matteo was clothed.

And so far, Matteo had always been clothed with Nightmare. His top half, at least.

Something cold and dark and vicious snaked through Nightmare's veins as Matteo turned to show Nightmare his back, seeming to sense Nightmare needed to see all of it.

Nightmare stepped closer, his shadows swirling in agitation.

One death hadn't been enough for Luca Caruso. One death wouldn't be enough for Dominico either. The man deserved an eternity of punishment. An eon of pain.

Nightmare found himself tracing his talon along the white lines. Matty stood still, allowing Nightmare to look and feel his fill.

"Kind of ugly, huh?" Perhaps Matteo was trying to be flippant, but there was a vulnerable edge to his soft question.

Nightmare scoffed as he followed another line. "I already told you: Every bit of you is pretty, Matteo. Even these."

He was so beautiful, Nightmare's summoner. Slight of build and tender of heart, with eyes a demon could get lost in. The scars only added texture, rough patches over distressingly soft skin. Nightmare could choose to despise them, evidence as they were of the pain Matteo had suffered. But they were a part of Nightmare's summoner, and as such they weren't something Nightmare could ever hate.

Nightmare placed careful hands on Matteo's shoulders and turned him around.

"I'm not ashamed of them," Matteo told him, though his large eyes were shining with unshed tears. "It's just—people always have questions."

Nightmare laid a hand on Matteo's cheek, coveting the way his human leaned into the touch. "So beautiful, sweet."

A bright bit of lemon blossomed in Matteo's soul piece, and he rose onto his tiptoes, tilting his head in clear invitation.

Nightmare had been holding himself back, demonstrating immeasurable restraint when it came to his sweet summoner. He'd been concerned that if he broke that last barrier between them completely, he'd lose sight of much-needed vengeance.

But a kiss, sweetly asked for—Nightmare couldn't deny Matteo that.

Nightmare lifted Matteo from the floor, taking his mouth. He kept his sharp teeth to himself, but soon Matteo's tongue was at his lips, begging for entry. Nightmare blunted his fangs and let him in. He was rewarded with a soft sigh, Matteo's legs wrapping around his middle, immediately rocking against him.

There was such hunger there, in the way Matteo ground against him. Nightmare knew the feel of such want. It matched his own, an insatiable craving that only grew and grew.

When Matteo's became more urgent—his hard cock pressing

again and again against Nightmare's belly— Nightmare hissed, halting Matteo's movements with a hand to his hip. "Patience, sweet."

Matteo leaned back, glaring at Nightmare with the same fierceness he'd shown their fellow bus passengers. "I'm twenty-one years old, and I've never once been touched in the ways I want. And now you're here, and you think I'm beautiful, and I want *you* to do the touching. Why am I being patient again?"

It was a reasonable question. Nightmare wished he had a reasonable answer. Instead, he had dark urges and fierce needs and his murderous shadows whispering to him about truths that should be revealed.

Nightmare pressed a kiss to Matteo's temple. "I have a story to tell you, sweet. Remember?"

"Is it a sexy story?" Matteo asked, his lower lip pushing out into an unconscious pout.

Nightmare had the foreign urge to clear his throat. "Some parts could be considered—"

"That's a no," Matteo said with a sigh, cutting Nightmare off.

Nightmare lowered him gently to the floor. "Sit, little human."

They ended up cross-legged on the floor. Nightmare had delved into the room's mini refrigerator and set up a selection of beverages for his human. Matteo chose a small can of alcoholic cider. He was still shirtless, and his bare skin with all its history seemed like a gift. One Nightmare hoped wouldn't be rescinded.

"My kind—"

"No," Matteo interrupted. "You said a *story*."

Nightmare's lips curled into a smile. So demanding when he allowed himself to be, his summoner. "A story, then." He settled his hands on his bent knees. "Once there was a type of demon, rare and solitary. No friends, no mates, no companions of any kind."

Matteo settled into a slouched sort of posture over his crossed legs, listening raptly over his cider.

"One day, one of these demons agreed to be spelled into a Book. Contained there in exchange for access to the human realm. For, you see, demon dreams are dull and monotonous. It's *humans* who hold the variety, in their varied fears and terrors and twisted thoughts."

"And the demon got stuck?" Matteo guessed.

Nightmare nodded. "And the demon got stuck. But it was no matter because he was strong and he was singular, and he could still access the human realm in dreamspace. He was well fed, despite his captivity. He was powerful. And he was bored."

It had been a surprise, the boredom. Nightmare had thought feeding from human terror would awaken something in him—align him to his terrible purpose. But the novelty had worn off after barely a century, and Nightmare had realized there was no purpose in it at all. Only survival.

And there was nothing beautiful or interesting about merely surviving, was there?

"And then one day the demon tasted something new. A thread of something...special. He followed that thread to a nightmare. And within that nightmare, he saw a face. Large brown eyes wet with tears, and a sad little mouth begging for mercy."

It seemed at some point Matteo had stopped breathing. He was holding himself unnaturally still, his beverage forgotten as he listened to Nightmare's tale.

"The demon gave it to the human—as a lark more than anything—and the human smiled at him, though the demon's form was terrible."

Whatever happened, Nightmare would remember that smile for the rest of eternity. The slight tremble in it, the wet tracks of tears still running down Matteo's face. A cousin to the smile Matteo was giving him now, amazed and a little bemused.

"And with that gesture, the demon could taste it, out from under that bitter coating of fear—a sweet, tart bit of soul. Lemon cake with bitter peel. And the demon began to covet. To desire to keep it for his own."

Matteo licked at his lips, seeming to come out of his trance. "He—he liked the human because the human was so scared?"

"He liked the human for what lay *underneath* the fear."

Matteo's brow furrowed. "But didn't the demon like fear the most out of anything? Didn't he need it to survive? To feed off of?"

Nightmare sighed. "And I have been doing so for a long, long time, Matteo. Fear sustains me, yes. But it is...a vegetable. I need it, but I can tire of it. You, my little human, are dessert. Sweet and delectable. Driving me to gluttony. Do you know what I'm telling you?"

Matteo shook his head, his eyes wide.

"I connected with your psyche despite the multitude of barriers between us, and I tasted your soul long before our contract. So no, Matteo, you won't be rid of me. I could be sent back to the demon realm this very instant, and it would not matter. I would find my way back." Nightmare leaned forward. "You let a monster in that night, Matteo. And I am never, ever leaving."

Nightmare's proclamation was met with silence, those big brown eyes still leveled at him. He cocked his head. "Are you frightened of me now, Matteo Caruso?"

But it wasn't fear emanating from Matteo's soul piece, Nightmare realized after a moment. It was awe.

Finally, Matteo rose onto his hands and knees across from Nightmare on the floor. He either didn't notice or didn't care that Nightmare's shadows had come out to wind around his wrists and forearms. "Can I tell you a secret, Scary?"

Nightmare nodded. He would take every truth Matteo wanted to give him.

"I'm not supposed to be alive right now," Matteo whispered.

"Dominico was growing restless with all of Luca's false promises about me, and Luca had given up on me ever taking over. After they got rid of the Kozlovs, Luca was going to either kill me or finally give me to Dominico to do the job for him. Sascha and Kai freed me, but I knew I was living on borrowed time. I knew that Dominico would find me eventually."

Matteo crawled forward, placing his hands over Nightmare's on Nightmare's knees and using them as leverage. "So I'm not even a real person, Scary," he continued in that quiet whisper. "I'm the ghost of a lost boy who was given away, forced to use a name that was never even his." He tugged on Nightmare's shirt, coaxing Nightmare to bend his head. He cupped Nightmare's cheeks. "But you're here now. And you being here makes me feel *real*. You covet me? You can have me. I'm happy to be yours. I would have been dust otherwise."

Was this what it always felt like when a demon found its mate? It couldn't be. No other creature could have felt a triumph this sweet, this perfect.

Nightmare grinned, all sharp teeth and shadow.

He'd known it from the moment he'd caught the scent of Matteo's soul, back in that wretched Void. He'd known Matteo was destined to be his.

Nightmare had found his terrible purpose, and it was more beautiful than anything else in all the realms.

10

Matty

Matty stared at Nightmare's sharp-toothed grin, momentarily frozen in place by pure, unadulterated joy.

Nightmare wanted Matty. *Coveted* him, he'd said. He planned to keep him.

He'd planned to keep Matty all along.

Something heavy and warm and wonderful settled in Matty's chest as Nightmare stared at him with naked hunger in his strange white gaze. Matty had been claimed by this creature of the dark without even knowing it, and it was a better fate than he ever could have hoped for.

And maybe Matty should have longed for freedom after a lifetime under Luca Caruso's cruel thumb. Maybe he should have wanted independence, a chance to find his inner bravery. But Matty had tried life on his own here in Seacliff, and while it was better than what he'd left, he'd still hated it.

He didn't *want* to be alone. He wanted what Sascha had with

Kai. He wanted to *belong* to someone. Someone so strong and fearless that nothing could stand in their way.

And maybe that made Matty weak, this need to be protected. But he'd already known that about himself, hadn't he?

It was silly to expect him to resist, anyway. Nightmare was perfect. He was exactly what Matty needed. What he *wanted*. Darkly compelling but also tender. Ripping a man apart in one moment and talking sweetly to Matty in the next. He fit around all Matty's broken pieces, his shadows filling all the painful gaps.

Matty didn't even care if Nightmare was acting that way just to seduce him into a bond. Let the seduction continue forever, then. Matty was game for it.

There was a gentle tug on Matty's wrists. Nightmare's shadows, urging him even closer. Matty went willingly—easily—crawling fully into Nightmare's lap.

"Kiss me now," Matty ordered, tilting his chin up in invitation. "Please."

Nightmare did, wrapping strong, slender arms around Matty's back. Matty stretched up as much as he was able, slinging his own arms around Nightmare's neck, tugging him down so he could kiss his demon back with all the yearning in his veins. The kiss was sloppy, messy, and hungry. Nightmare didn't seem to mind. He let out a rumbling growl as he ravaged Matty's mouth, encouraging Matty to rock against him, Matty trying desperately to get friction against his aching cock as all his blood rushed south.

This was good. Very good. Talking and confessions of eternal devotion were fine and all, but really, there should have been more kissing all along.

Eventually Nightmare allowed Matty to breathe—*overrated*—and Matty instantly started tugging at the ties on Nightmare's pants. "Take it out. I want to see it again."

Nightmare huffed a laugh, but he unlaced the ties, lowering

his waistband to release his cock. Matty scooted back on Nightmare's thighs, making room for the monstrosity.

Why did the sight of that strange cock make Matty so *hungry*? There was something about it—large and dark and unlike anything he'd seen before—that made him ache inside. He wanted to rub his face against it. And his...chest? And his dick. Definitely his dick.

For the moment, Matty settled for rubbing his thumb against the head of it, enjoying the way it made Nightmare's rumble deepen. "Do the petals stay like that?" Matty asked.

"Petals?"

"These." Matty brushed one deliberately, watching it lift, smoky gray precum leaking out.

Nightmare gently knocked Matty's hand away and wrapped his own slender fingers around his cockhead. He slid his hand down, and the petals bunched down around the head, revealing the bulbous black tip to the air, shimmering with precum.

Matty's own cock jerked at the sight, and he squirmed on Nightmare's lap. "I want to touch it," he breathed. "And—and suck it. And I think you should fuck me with it."

"Is that what you think, sweet?" Nightmare asked, his voice deadly soft.

Matty reached out a hand, wanting to touch it again, but Nightmare's shadows held him back. Matty settled for palming his own clothed cock, hoping some sort of pressure would make him less desperate.

It didn't work.

Matty licked his lips, staring at the branching black veins. "Will it really fit inside me? The whole thing?"

It seemed unlikely. The head was so fat, the petals bunched under it so strange.

"Yes, sweet. It will fit."

"And it'll feel good?"

"We'll make sure of it."

"You should—you should give it to me. Right now." Matty squirmed harder now, fighting against the shadows holding him. It was like all the lust and want and naughty thoughts he'd been ignoring for a lifetime were pouring out from inside him. He felt ravenous and needy and a little crazed.

Nightmare rose from the floor, lifting Matty with him effortlessly. Matty tried to wrap his legs around Nightmare's waist, but he was held back by something. The next thing he knew, he was being tossed on the hotel bed, and then he was sprawled on his back, spread-eagle, his demon's shadows holding down each limb. Nightmare stood over him, his cock rising rigid from his open pants.

"Stay," the demon ordered darkly. He was huge and scary and perfect.

Matty melted into the mattress. "Okay. I'll stay."

The shadows around Matty started peeling off his pants and underwear. All the while Nightmare stood there, looming over him.

Maybe Matty should have felt exposed or embarrassed, being stripped like this, all his scars on display. But he only felt beautiful. Not cute or adorable or anything like that. *Beautiful.*

Eventually Matty was naked, his hard cock jutting out from the dark thatch of curls at his groin. His erection wasn't as strange or impressive as Nightmare's, but Nightmare seemed to like it. His gaze was locked on it, and he'd wrapped a hand around his own cock again, gripping tightly.

"Am I still pretty?" Matty asked.

"Yes, sweet. Every inch."

Matty's breath caught as Nightmare lifted a knee onto the mattress. The demon leaned down close, running his nose along Matty's neck, his long silvery-white hair brushing Matty's skin.

Matty could feel the heat emanating from him, an inferno waiting to envelop him.

"So sweet," Nightmare murmured. And then he moved down, running his nose along Matty's collarbone, his chest. He followed a path all the way down to the creases along Matty's groin, ignoring the way Matty jerked as his hair tickled Matty's cock.

It didn't matter if Matty jolted though. Nightmare's shadows were still holding him securely.

Nightmare didn't stop at Matty's groin. He traveled down Matty's legs next, upper thigh to ankle. Sometimes Matty thought he felt Nightmare's lips brushing him, but mostly it was skin against skin. Scenting him or marking him or sizing him up to eat him, who knew?

Matty had thought he'd experienced all types of torture, but this one was new. He'd never been turned on like this, aching for any tiny bit of touch. He'd never been so completely desperate, with absolutely no idea how to relieve any of it.

Well, he had *ideas* of how to relieve it. But he wasn't being allowed to act on them.

It was overwhelming. Scary. Perfect.

But not enough.

"I hurt," Matty whispered as Nightmare moved on to examine each of his individual ten toes.

"Where do you hurt, sweet?" Nightmare asked, one of his shadows shifting to caress Matty's cheek.

"Everywhere."

Matty meant his aching arousal, but he also maybe meant a lifetime of broken hopes and horrible pain finally catching up to him. He thought Nightmare got it though. He thought maybe Nightmare was the only creature who could.

Nightmare rose over him again, his palms settling on either side of Matty's head. He smelled of smoke and secrets, and his white eyes were glowing. "And how can I make it better, little human?"

"Touch me all over," Matty whispered, tears leaking from his eyes for some reason. "Make me come. Make me—make me yours."

And then Nightmare was finally kissing him again. Matty sobbed into it, desperate and aching. And Nightmare must have made his teeth blunt again because Matty didn't cut his tongue, no matter how aggressively he fucked it into Nightmare's mouth.

He was grateful for the shadows holding him back now. Otherwise, Matty might have tried to climb into Nightmare somehow. Burrow under his skin. He thought that might be the only way to assuage this hunger.

But at least now Nightmare was doing what he'd asked and touching Matty all over. Matty couldn't tell what were Nightmare's fingers and what were his shadows, but there was warmth and pressure everywhere, petting his skin and rubbing his tender places.

And then Matty knew exactly where Nightmare's fingers were because they were brushing against his crease. Matty whimpered into Nightmare's mouth. Permission. A plea.

Nightmare pulled away, his breathing harsh and jagged. "Has anyone ever touched you here, sweet?"

"No." Matty pouted. "No one's touched me anywhere."

"No wonder you hurt, my sweet summoner."

Exactly. *Exactly.* Something warm and slippery rubbed against Matty's hole—lube or precum or who the hell knew what—and Nightmare's shadows or maybe his fingers wrapped around Matty's cock at the same time.

Matty whimpered at the touch.

"Relax, sweet," Nightmare soothed. "Let me in."

It was hard to do. Matty was too impatient, too desperate. Nightmare nipped at his chin, then at his neck. He laved Matty's nipples with his hot tongue, his teeth just barely scraping the tender buds, one hand tugging Matty's leg up and around his hip. "I have you, Matteo. Let go."

Matty let out a long breath, and Nightmare's finger slid inside him. It was a strange pressure but also...good. Good because it was his demon, and Matty wanted his demon everywhere. And then good because there was another finger, and a specific spot and— *Oh.*

Matty arched up, and Nightmare's hand started pumping his cock with more of that warm, slippery stuff. "There you are, sweet," he crooned. "Find your pleasure."

It wasn't hard to do anymore. Not with Nightmare's fingers inside him and around him, his shadows kissing Matty's skin.

But Matty needed him *everywhere*, so he lunged up, taking Nightmare's mouth again. And then Nightmare's tongue was in his mouth, every bit of Matty consumed, and it was finally perfect.

Matty rocked his hips into Nightmare's touch and whined and whimpered into his kiss, and then everything broke and spun and shattered, and he was curling up and coming into his demon's hand, and he was also maybe crying, and it was wonderful and perfect but also too much and scary and—

"Sh, sh, shh," Nightmare soothed. He'd broken the kiss at some point, and he was pressing his mouth to Matty's cheek. "I have you."

He flattened Matty back onto the bed, and Matty could breathe again. He was spent and limp as a noodle, his belly sticky with traces of cum.

Matty nodded to Nightmare's cock. It looked even bigger than before, and the black veins on it were bulging. "Now you." When Nightmare only looked at him, Matty begged, "Please."

"You will stay still," Nightmare commanded.

"I will," Matty agreed. Nightmare's shadows were still at his wrists and ankles anyway, though their touch was more comforting than constricting. "So still."

Nightmare straightened, standing over Matty again at the foot of the bed. Looming. He started stroking that big cock, and the petals bunched and shifted with each swipe of his hand. More of that gray substance poured out, coating his cock and hand both. Matty was pretty sure that was what Nightmare had used to ease the glide of his fingers inside Matty.

Matty had been boneless and sated just a moment ago, but warmth stirred in his belly again, watching Nightmare. Seeing the way his gaze traveled over every inch of Matty as he stroked himself. Getting himself off to the sight of Matty, naked and vulnerable with his own cum on his belly.

Matty could relate. He liked watching Nightmare just as much. Nightmare was so beautiful. So eerie.

"One day I want to get naked and rub all over you," Matty told him. "Hump you until I come."

Nightmare's hand lost its rhythm for only a moment before starting up again. "You may do with me whatever you wish."

"Except move right now?"

"Except move right now."

"You act nice, but really you're kind of bossy."

"I'm aware."

"Are you going to fuck me one day?" Matty asked. He kind of wished he could stroke his cock too, but it might hurt this soon after coming.

"Yes."

"When?"

"When we bond." It was subtle, the way Nightmare's breath quickened. The way his hand moved just a bit faster. But Matty was watching closely, so he saw it all.

His demon was close.

"When will that be?" Matty asked. He was ready now, if Nightmare wanted. Especially if it meant getting fucked in the next five minutes.

"Very soon."

"And then I'm yours forever?" Matty asked.

"*Yes*," Nightmare hissed. "Mine forever."

And then the dark, fat head of his cock pulsed, and gray cum spurted all over Matty's groin and stomach and chest.

There was a lot of it. Matty was covered, sticky with it, and somehow it *still* wasn't enough. He wanted it inside him, filling him up.

He was maybe not a very patient person, Matty was learning. Maybe he was even greedy.

How strange to only be learning that about himself now.

Matty made do with watching the rise and fall of Nightmare's chest. Watching as he tucked himself deftly back into his pants.

"You like that idea a lot," Matty said, voicing his realization out loud. He'd said the words right before Nightmare had come, hadn't he? "Me being yours forever."

Nightmare's lips twitched into a small smile, and his shadows finally released their hold completely, trailing all together to drape over Matty's neck instead of holding his limbs down. It was nice. Like a weird, smoky scarf.

The bed dipped as Nightmare climbed next to him, lying on his back with his hands folded over his belly. Matty turned on his side, cuddling into his demon with a happy sigh.

Matty had been so tense on the bus. Jumping at every vaguely familiar-looking face, only to find that they were a stranger after all. Maybe Nightmare was right, and Dominico really did have to be dealt with before they could live their lives. But for now, Matty's tension eased with the comfort of Nightmare's body next to his, his shadows tucked around Matty's neck.

Everything in Matty's life had been temporary so far: his days as his mother's son, his time with Sascha and Kai, his very life. But Nightmare claiming him—that would be permanent.

Matty could relax, maybe for the first time ever.

"You're going to keep being nice to me, right?" Matty asked, his eyelids drooping closed against his will. "This isn't some elaborate trick?"

"No tricks, sweet. If I ever harm you, you may banish me from your side."

"And you'll go?" Matty frowned into Nightmare's chest. That didn't sound permanent at all.

"No. I'll watch from the shadows, wanting you always. Waiting to return to your good graces."

"Ohh, that's nice."

Matty drifted off to the soothing rumble of Nightmare's laugh.

11

Matty

Matty was warm and safe and well rested. How funny. So maybe he was dreaming?

But he didn't usually have dreams like that—the good kind—at least not before a certain skull-faced monster showed up and saved him.

Matty burrowed deeper into the smoky warmth surrounding him. A pair of strong arms tightened around his middle, and some sort of sentient, scarf-like thing started stroking Matty's cheek.

Matty sighed happily. "Good morning, Scary. Good morning, shadows."

"Good morning, sweet."

"You kept the bad dreams away."

"Of course."

Matty wriggled a bit in place. His erection brushed against the top of Nightmare's clothed thigh with the movement.

Matty's *bare* erection.

"I'm naked." He didn't know why he was surprised. He'd fallen asleep nude, hadn't he?

"I tried to clothe you. You kicked off your sweats in your sleep."

"I did?"

"Quite forcefully."

Damn. Even Matty's deeply unconscious mind had become a horny, horny place, hadn't it?

But rubbing his bare dick against Nightmare's pants felt pretty good, so Matty did it again. He craned his neck to peer up at Nightmare, who was already looking down at him. It was hard to tell sometimes with that all-white gaze, but the demon looked...concerned?

"Why do you seem worried?" Matty asked.

Nightmare narrowed his eyes. "Yesterday morning, this is how you were: soft and eager and writhing against me. And then suddenly you were quite upset."

"Oh. I wanted you to touch me."

It had been so strangely hard to admit before, but it was easy to be honest now. What with Nightmare swearing he was going to keep Matty no matter what and all.

"Why didn't you ask?"

"I didn't know I could," Matty told him. "And I'm not really used to asking for the things I want."

"Ah. And *this* morning?"

Matty grabbed one of Nightmare's hands, tugging it away from his waist and placing it down over his ass. And since Nightmare was wonderful and perfect, he immediately used his grip to encourage Matty to rock against him.

Matty moaned, rubbing his forehead back and forth against Nightmare's chest as he moved. "Mm. 'S nice." He grinned up at his demon.

Nightmare's white eyes began to gleam.

Matty kept humping him gracelessly, Nightmare's grip firm on his ass now. Matty did it because it felt good and it seemed to turn Nightmare on and Matty had already admitted he wanted to.

He eyed the bulge in Nightmare's pants hungrily. "Why do you want to wait until we're bonded to fuck me?"

"Because I might frighten you."

Oh. Matty paused his rocking, ignoring the ache in his dick as he considered that. "And you want us to already be stuck together? So I can't leave?"

"Yes."

"Wow." Matty giggled as he slid his cock up and down Nightmare's leg again. The movement was a little uncomfortable with the rough cloth rubbing against his tender skin, but the pressure felt good.

He was vaguely aware he was letting his brokenness show again. He should probably be outraged by Nightmare's admission —the inherent manipulation in it—and not flattered. But Matty *was* flattered.

Flattered and horny.

"But I don't mind if you scare me a little," he admitted. "It's— it's okay if it's you."

"Me and your horror films."

Matty giggled again, maybe a little lust-drunk at this point, like all the blood was in his dick and there was none left for his brain. He let his hand wander down to Nightmare's clothed hardness. "Why didn't you take care of this while I was sleeping?" he asked, palming that intimidating erection.

"You wished to be held."

"You could do both." Matty found the bulbous end of Nightmare's cock, fondling it. "I wouldn't mind."

Nightmare's grip tightened around Matty's ass, his taloned fingers digging in almost painfully.

"You like that idea?" Matty guessed. "Touching yourself or—or touching *me*? In my sleep?"

Before now, Matty had been starting to think that maybe Nightmare just didn't have that high of a sex drive. Which would have been fine, of course. Matty would have simply become more acquainted with his right hand to make up the difference. But now he was thinking that maybe Nightmare was just very...self-contained.

He had more self-control than Matty; that was clear. Although, that wasn't a very difficult record to beat at the moment. Right now a honey badger in heat probably had more self-control than Matty.

"Is this okay?" he asked, moving faster against Nightmare's leg.

"It is more than okay."

Matty sighed in overwhelming relief. Maybe the wanting wasn't so bad, now that he knew it was reciprocated.

He squirmed and writhed frantically, heat building steadily in his belly. He burrowed his head in Nightmare's chest, a whine leaving his throat.

Nightmare's big hand massaged and caressed his ass. "What do you need, sweet?"

"I don't know!" Matty cried plaintively. He was close to something big—something like the orgasm from the night before. But the pressure or the pace or *something* wasn't right, and his release kept escaping him.

"Come here."

And Matty was suddenly being lifted by those massive hands on his ass—as easily as if he weighed nothing at all—and then he was straddling Nightmare's chest.

Matty stared down in a daze. Positioned like this, his bare, weeping cock was mere centimeters from Nightmare's lips. "Um. Hello," he said stupidly.

"Like this," Nightmare rasped. He bared his teeth, revealing blunt tips.

"You want me to..." Matty rocked toward him, barely holding himself back. "In your mouth?"

"Yes, sweet."

Matty's lower belly clenched, and another low whine left his lips. ""What if I—I've never...I could hurt you."

"You couldn't."

"I could *choke* you."

"I can go without breath for a very long time."

Nightmare's hands pushed Matty forward. Matty's cockhead was right there, at Nightmare's lips, the demon's hot breath ghosting over him, and then— *Oh.*

So wet. So hot. So *good.*

"Oh my *God.*"

Matty's hips jerked forward, and Nightmare let out a low rumble of satisfaction. Except his mouth was around Matty's cock, so the rumble sort of...vibrated. And Matty almost came right there.

He had to forcibly hold himself very, very still and look anywhere but at Nightmare's glowing white eyes.

This was— How was Matty supposed to survive this? Was this what fucking someone felt like? How did people go about their lives, knowing this was an option?

Although, no one else had a Nightmare of their own, so maybe the masses had no idea how good they could feel.

When Matty had the barest thread of control back, he started a mindless, rhythmless rocking into that overwhelming heat. Nightmare was using gentle suction, and Matty was grateful for it. He already wasn't going to last more than thirty seconds—if Nightmare suddenly pulled some hoover action, it would all be over in an instant, and Matty would probably start crying again.

Matty didn't know what to do with his hands though. He could hold Nightmare's face, but he didn't want to hide any of it. He was so beautiful and scary, and Matty wanted to see it all.

He liked looking at his demon.

"Antlers," Matty finally gasped. "Put them back."

Massive antlers immediately sprouted from Nightmare's head, with barely enough room in the bed to keep them from going through the hotel wall.

Matty grabbed on immediately. Oh fuck, that was better. He started rocking in earnest. Fucking Nightmare's mouth. Oh God, he was *fucking Nightmare's mouth*.

Nightmare seemed to like it. His eyes were glowing so bright, and his hands were gripping so hard, and his shadows were dancing all over Matty's skin, nipping at his neck and cheeks and legs playfully.

It was too much. The hot suction around Matty's cock. The way he was basically riding Nightmare's face. The teasing touches from the shadows.

"Gonna come, gonna come, gonna come," Matty chanted.

And then Nightmare really did suck Matty very, very deliberately, and Matty's soul left his body, straight out of his dick, straight into Nightmare's mouth.

His toes curled behind him, and his muscles trembled, and he maybe went blind for a minute. He fell over, completely boneless, rolling at the last second to keep from falling straight onto Nightmare's face.

"You swallowed." Matty gathered every bit of his strength to raise his head and look downward. "And you're still hard."

Nightmare made a vague sound, a negative to Matty's unspoken question about whether Nightmare would like him to do anything about it.

But Matty couldn't be disappointed this time. Not with the hungry look in Nightmare's eye, or with the way his dark-gray tongue darted out to lick his lips, as if to get every trace of Matty's cum.

Matty flopped onto his belly. "You should jerk off on my back," he offered. "And then rub your cum into my scars."

He had no idea why he said it, other than it felt right. Like something he really, really wanted all of a sudden.

Nightmare snarled, moving quicker than one of his own shadows to straddle the backs of Matty's thighs.

Apparently he really, really wanted that too.

Matty sighed happily, tucking his chin on his folded hands as he listened to the slick, wet sound of Nightmare stroking himself. Matty's belly swirled with warmth again, his dick filling faster than it should have at the thought of Nightmare finding his pleasure right on top of him.

Soon enough something hot and wet hit Matty's lower back. And then Nightmare's hands were on him, massaging upward over Matty's back and shoulders and then down again to massage his ass.

Working his cum into Matty's skin.

Matty moaned as his muscles melted into goo. And then he gasped as long-fingered hands spread his cheeks and held them open.

Oh God. Nightmare was looking at Matty's hole.

Matty forgot how to breathe for a minute. Did Nightmare like what he saw? Was he going to touch Matty there again?

"You could—" Matty swallowed hard. "Just the tip maybe? I promise I won't get scared."

There was a heavy silence. Was Nightmare really considering it? Matty thought of that dark, fat cockhead with its strange petals, and he wanted it desperately. Just the tip would be enough. He'd be so full, even with that.

Matty's alarm blared, breaking the quiet with an irritating chime.

Nightmare released his hold on Matty. "It's time to meet the little chaos demon and his mate," he said, his weight leaving Matty's thighs in the next moment.

Matty tried his best not to pout. He really, really did.

He wasn't successful.

———

THE HOTEL ROOM Ivan had gotten for Matty and Nightmare was incredibly nice. The kind with a separate living room area with multiple comfy chairs and a bathroom big enough for a party.

It also came with a solid door that required a real key and even had a deadbolt.

Which made it doubly alarming when that lock slid back by itself, the door bursting open without warning.

Matty and Nightmare had rinsed off and redressed in the time since Matty's alarm had blared, but Matty still flinched at the surprise, ready to duck into a back corner of the room.

Nightmare laid a soothing hand on Matty's shoulder. "The chaos demon has a way with locks," he explained.

And he was right, of course. It wasn't Dominico's men or some burglar revealed in the hotel doorway. It was Cooper and Chaos, the two of them wearing sort of matching outfits, both in baggy jeans and zip-up sweatshirts that differed only in color. Cooper had a satchel across his chest, and they were holding hands.

As soon as the door closed behind them, Chaos reverted to his demon form, with stubby black horns and a lion's tail and small, feathered wings. His hair was a strange, sparkly black today, but Matty had seen it all sorts of wild colors before.

Chaos's yellow eyes gleamed as they landed on Matty and Nightmare. He released Cooper's hand and threw up his arms. "Nightmare! It really *is* you! I thought Nix might be pranking me." And he lunged forward.

Here was the thing.

Matty had met Cooper and Chaos several times before. He liked them fine. Cooper was reserved but kind, and Chaos was... unpredictable (to say the least) but clearly devoted to his human. And even if Chaos was a little scary sometimes, Matty had decided from the beginning that he was firmly Team Demon. Each one he'd met was better than most humans he'd known, and he was immensely grateful to be included in their small circle.

And yet, when Chaos came bouncing over, his arms held wide open to throw around Nightmare, Matty found himself stepping in front of him, a weird, barking protest leaving his mouth without permission. "*No.*"

Chaos stopped just short of Matty, and all his enthusiasm dissipated in an instant, leaving behind an eerie, predatory stillness. He cocked his head, nostrils flaring. "What's this?"

"Bracchus," Cooper called, maybe in an attempt to bring his demon back to his side.

But Chaos's gaze was fixed firmly on Matteo. "Nightmare is my friend," he said softly. Dangerously.

Matty should back away now. He knew he should. Instead, he cleared his throat. "Yeah, um. I know."

"I was going to give him a hug."

"I saw."

Chaos sniffed the air, little flecks of fire gleaming in his eyes. "Who knew Sascha's little mouse was hiding such sharp teeth?" He snapped his own fanged set in Matty's direction. "Do you really think they can rival mine?"

Matty was shaking now, aware he was leagues out of his depth, but somehow he stood his ground. Nightmare was *Matty's* demon. He'd basically said so himself. And people couldn't go around embracing him without warning. It threw Matty off. It made him do crazy things, like stand up to a demon he knew for a fact had killed men twice Matty's size.

Even if Matty might piss his pants before this confrontation was over.

Taloned fingers settled on Matty's shoulders, warm and sharp and lovely. He was dragged gently to the side. "Thank you, sweet. I'll take it from here."

Nightmare stepped forward and lifted Chaos off the ground by his throat.

Cooper let out a distressed noise, shooting Matty a panicked look, but Matty could only shrug. Nightmare's talons were pressing hard into Chaos's skin, and it looked like they might puncture it.

Chaos's lower lip pushed out into a pout, his feet dangling in the air. "Not the paralysis so soon," he whined. "I only just got here."

"You will not frighten Matteo," Nightmare told him in his quiet rasp. "None of your threats or tricks."

"But I have a gift for you." Chaos's gaze darted to Matty with a wink, and Matty jumped before he could stop himself. "For you both."

At Chaos's words, Cooper hurriedly reached into his satchel and pulled out a small, leather-bound book.

Nightmare's shadows swarmed the thing, and Cooper yelped, dropping it. The shadows plucked it from the air before it could hit the ground, depositing it into Matty's hands instead. Matty quickly clutched it to his chest, although he had no idea what he was holding.

"The Book," Nightmare said, sounding surprised.

Well, that explained that.

Nightmare was still holding Chaos up by the throat, but his grip noticeably loosened, his talons no longer looking like they might slice through the little demon.

"I stole it from Ivan," Chaos said with a manic little giggle, his grin as big as Matty had ever seen it, which was saying a lot. "Again."

Matty caught Nightmare's gaze and held it, unable to look away from that white gleam. They had the Book now. The one with the spell that would allow them to bond together.

Would they do it here? Now? Would Nightmare make Matty wait until Dominico was caught?

Quick as a blink, Chaos was out of Nightmare's hold and back on the floor, his hand once again wrapped around Cooper's. He was still grinning wide, like he hadn't just threatened Matty and been threatened by Nightmare in turn.

"Did I do good?"

12

Nightmare

I n Nightmare's opinion, a subdued and respectful Chaos was barely tolerable as it was.

A gleeful, smug Chaos was something else entirely.

Still, Nightmare inclined his head. "You did very well, Bracchus."

Better than Nightmare could have hoped, really. He'd been expecting the need to take a trip to New York himself to find the Book, and had been dreading leaving Matteo on his own. Nightmare's human was too fragile by half, and it would have meant waiting until Dominico's demise to secure the bond.

But Chaos had solved that little problem. How he'd known Nightmare wished to bond with his summoner was a mystery but not precisely a surprise. Nightmare had learned over their centuries together in the Void that Chaos was wily by nature—he always knew more than he should, for all that he acted like he lived without thought.

Chaos preened at Nightmare's scant praise, glancing to his

mate as if to make sure he'd heard every word. "Aren't you glad you didn't paralyze me?" he asked Nightmare with a sideways look. "You'd be so embarrassed."

Nightmare would have been nothing of the kind, but he supposed it was better that he'd been merciful. Chaos's threat to Matteo hadn't been genuine, anyway. If it had, Nightmare would have already torn one of his little feathered wings off.

Chaos had only wanted to see how Nightmare would react. Too curious for his own good, as per usual.

Chaos tugged Cooper to his side. "Nightmare, this is my puppy," he announced, puffed up with blatant pride as he presented his human.

"Cooper," his mate corrected gently, eyeing Nightmare nervously. "His, um, mate."

Nightmare inclined his head. "I'm aware."

Chaos beamed. "I warned him you could be a bit aggressive. I told him not to worry." He rubbed his cheek against Cooper's. "But you *did* worry, didn't you, puppy? Isn't he perfect?" he asked Nightmare. "Have you seen his eyes? And his lovely fingers? Actually no, don't look at those. Those are mine. But you can look at his eyes. Don't poke them out though. You couldn't anyway—he's wearing glasses."

All Nightmare saw was a human, one like any other. He had tawny hair and mismatched eyes—one green, one brown—covered by spectacles. But his scent mingled contentedly with Chaos's. It appeared Chaos had indeed found a proper mate, one who didn't seem to mind his incessant chatter.

Chaos turned to Matteo, although he wisely didn't step any closer. "Just a little hug, maybe?" he asked hopefully.

Matteo flushed, shuffling his feet and ducking his head, although his hood wasn't pulled up to hide his face properly. "Yeah, of course. I didn't mean to—"

Nightmare laid a hand on Matteo's shoulder, letting his

shadows trail off to stroke Matteo's reddened cheek in reassurance. It wouldn't do for Matteo to feel ashamed of his protective temper. Nightmare had enjoyed it immensely.

"I don't hug, Bracchus. You know this."

It wasn't in Nightmare's nature to enjoy the touch of other creatures. None except his sweet summoner.

And how he enjoyed that touch.

With his extended lifespan, the passage of time was of no concern to Nightmare, but that morning he would have given anything to stop its progress, to freeze that moment of Matteo writhing against him, his sweet cock hard and weeping against Nightmare's leg as he tried desperately to find his release.

And though Nightmare never would have thought he'd enjoy having a human appendage in his mouth without the intent to bite it off, Matteo's cock had fit perfectly, the salty, slightly bitter taste of his copious precum a lovely contrast to the rich, lemony sweetness of his lust in the air.

And when Nightmare had found his own release on Matteo's beautiful back, rubbing his spend into that tender, tortured skin...

It had been satisfying in a way he'd never imagined.

Nightmare had been full of the delicious knowledge that, had they been in the demon realm, every creature near and far would have been able to scent with a single sniff that Matteo belonged to Nightmare. The thought had caused Nightmare's cock to fill again almost immediately, and he hadn't been able to resist parting Matteo's cheeks and gazing at his hole, as tender and pink as the rest of him.

It had been novel, that animal lust. The bizarre need to press his body to another's, to stroke and lick and rub against a second creature's skin.

Nightmare had only experienced one other physical mating in his life, long ago. A fight for territory with a young warrior that had turned into a different kind of battle for dominance. It had been stimulating and not as horrible as it could have been, but Nightmare hadn't sought out the experience a second time.

Touching Matteo was different. Nightmare craved it the same way he craved tearing apart a wicked mind.

More, even.

But now the little chaos demon was pouting again, and Nightmare let out a sigh. They didn't have time for this. "Come here, Bracchus."

Chaos stepped forward—shrewdly keeping his arms to himself—and Nightmare patted his head once. Twice.

"There," Nightmare told him, withdrawing his hand again. "No more."

Chaos cackled his delight and bounded back to Cooper. The two of them clasped hands once more.

Cooper turned to Matteo. "He and Nix hugged for like an hour when they were reunited," he said with a sheepish smile, his cheeks turning pink. "I hated it."

"You never said, puppy." Chaos's lips curled into a sly grin. "But I could feel your jealousy through the soul piece. It was so tasty."

While it was pleasing that this other human wished to reassure Matteo, none of them were meeting for a social call. "You have information," Nightmare pressed.

"Right." Cooper gave his satchel a pat. "Ivan's been monitoring the Carusos that are left. We can go through what I have together." He gave Matteo an apologetic wince. "Sorry I couldn't send it by email. Ivan's really paranoid about that sort of thing. Something about not going to prison so soon after life finally got interesting."

Chaos rolled his eyes. "As if Nix wouldn't break him out immediately. I might even help. Could be fun."

"Th-That's okay," Matteo said shyly, and Nightmare's shirt pulled tightly against his skin as Matteo gripped at the hem, seeking reassurance. His nerves were palpable in the air, his soul piece thrumming with them.

It wasn't because of the other demon in the room. Matteo had been nervous to stand his ground against Chaos, but Nightmare hadn't scented any abject terror. This fear was due to the satchel and the information that might be contained within it.

Nightmare rested his hand on the back of Matteo's neck, stroking the soft skin there gently with his thumb. "I will be right beside you, sweet."

Chaos let out a high-pitched squeak. "Did you hear that?" he whispered quite loudly to Cooper. "*Sweet.*"

"My paralysis has not lost its potency, Bracchus. You will behave."

Chaos gave a salute. "Sir, yes, sir."

It was tempting to incapacitate him regardless, but then this Cooper might not be so cooperative, and they needed the information he'd brought. Nightmare let it go. For now.

They all ended up on the small sofa in the hotel room's living area. Cooper and Matteo sat next to each other, a small, portable computer on Cooper's lap. Chaos sat next to his mate, and Nightmare stood behind the sofa, bent low so that he could rest his hand over Matteo's chest, feeling the steady—if slightly quickened—beat of his heart.

Nightmare had the almost irresistible urge to reach into Matteo's chest and soothe the organ directly, if such a thing were possible. To take it out and swallow it whole and hold it inside himself, keeping it safe within his own viscera.

The impulse was as foreign to him as the impulse to fuck and touch and press together, groin to mouth. How strange, to feel this way for another creature.

But it couldn't be helped, even if Nightmare had wanted it to. Ever since he'd tasted Matteo's soul through the ether, something deep within him had cried out, *Mine.*

Ours, his shadows had echoed.

It was all wrong, of course. A creature like Nightmare was not meant to have a mate, let alone a human one. The darkness was his companion, human pain his sustenance. He and his shadows had no need for anything else.

And yet here he was.

And now that Chaos had brought the Book, it would be official. Permanent.

Perfect.

Cooper cleared his throat. "So as far as we can tell, Dominico has gone underground. We have reason to believe he's still in New York, but he doesn't seem to be trying to take Luca's place and corral the others. He still has a small crew following his orders, but they've been hard to spot. We've only got a few surveillance photos of one of them entering an occult shop. We think maybe because of the rumors about Ivan and his new paranormal enforcers."

"That's me!" Chaos crowed. "A paranormal enforcer!"

Cooper squeezed Chaos's knee. "The only thing we've really got that could be useful is that he's been withdrawing funds from one of Luca's accounts we've been monitoring. I guess he doesn't have enough money of his own?"

"No," Matteo said dully, staring at the computer screen. "Money's not really his vice. He has...other interests."

"The withdrawals are all over the map though." Cooper adjusted his glasses. "Some are in different states and—"

"What's that?" Matteo asked suddenly, pointing at something on the computer. "That transfer. That's super recent."

"Yeah." Cooper nodded. "We followed the account. He transferred it to a man we have reason to believe is still in his employ. Vinnie something. I can look it up."

"Vinnie," Matteo repeated. His hand squeezed at Nightmare's

wrist where it lay over his chest, his short fingernails digging into Nightmare's skin. "We've seen him."

The man Nightmare had killed, then. The intruder who'd met his demise.

Matteo was still staring at the computer screen, but his eyes were unfocused. "That was the day he saw me."

"Who saw you?" Cooper asked. "This Vinnie guy?"

But Matteo seemed to be worlds away. "Dominico knows I'm in Seacliff," he said in a horribly blank voice. "He *knows*."

His heart was racing under Nightmare's hand now, his breath coming in short pants.

He was panicking.

Nightmare crossed around the sofa and knelt in front of him. "Matteo. Sweet."

Matteo's eyes remained unfocused, and his soul piece thrummed with distress in Nightmare's chest, like the heart of a hummingbird struggling to stay aloft.

Nightmare gently took Matteo's hands and placed them on his antlers. Matteo gripped them hard, and Nightmare's shadows raced up Matteo's forearms and over his shoulders, settling around Matteo's neck.

"Look at me, Matteo," Nightmare commanded.

Matteo's deep brown eyes met his instantly.

"We will tear him apart," Nightmare promised. "We will make him hurt. His very last breath will be an anguished scream."

"Hardcore," Chaos whispered.

Nightmare ignored him. He repeated the vow until, bit by bit, Matteo's breathing slowed, his heartbeat following suit.

When Matteo no longer looked or sounded like he was gripped in the throes of unimaginable terror, Cooper cleared his throat. "You think...you think this Dominico is going to come for you?"

"Yes." Matteo's eyes were still locked on Nightmare's. "He will."

"Well, that's perfect!" Chaos cried gleefully.

"How is that perfect?" Matteo asked. He was kneading Nightmare's antlers now, squeezing hard and then releasing the pressure. He seemed to find it soothing.

Chaos laughed. "Little mouse, you have a nightmare demon on his knees for you. What do you think one human creep is going to be able to do? And I bet Ivan would jump at the chance to off another Caruso. *I* definitely wouldn't want to miss anything this fun. " Chaos waved a hand at the laptop. "Let this guy come to Seacliff. We'll be waiting."

It wasn't often Nightmare revised his opinion of a creature, but perhaps now was the time.

Maybe the little chaos demon wasn't so bad after all.

13

Nightmare

"Y ou dislike the food, sweet?" Nightmare asked, glaring at the tiny, offending chicken carcass across from him, with its glazed brown skin and assorted little potatoes.

Matteo glanced up from his task of poking at the chicken listlessly with his fork. "What? No, it's delicious."

"Yet you do not eat it."

Matteo stared at his fork, as if surprised it hadn't made it to his lips. "I'm nervous, I guess."

That much was evident from the way his gaze kept sliding to the side of their table, where the Book lay next to his plate.

Matteo hadn't wanted to leave it in the hotel room. "What if Chaos decides to steal it back just for fun?" he'd asked. And while that outcome was unlikely, it wasn't impossible, so Nightmare had agreed to bring it with them and shroud it in his shadows.

At least the news of Dominico's knowledge of his whereabouts had dampened some of Matteo's twitchy fear of strangers. While that may have been due to shock more than anything else, it made eating in this restaurant less agitating than it could have been for them both.

They'd come to a place recommended by Cooper. Chaos's shy human had told them he'd taken Chaos here on the way to Seacliff before.

The restaurant claimed to be farm to table, though Nightmare saw no barns nor livestock in the vicinity. But it had secluded booths for seating and a quiet atmosphere, and the hostess hadn't frowned at Matteo's casual attire, so it would do.

Cooper and Chaos had bowed out of dinner, much to Nightmare's delight. They'd declared that they'd had other matters to attend to first. Nightmare had no doubt those "matters" included Chaos immediately tattling about Nightmare's intentions to the other demons. But that would work in Nightmare's favor, if there was to be a confrontation in Seacliff. Any backup would be welcome—even the incubus could be useful at times.

Cooper and Chaos would rejoin them in Seacliff instead. Their agreement was to head back in the morning and then have Matteo seen about town as much as possible, to lure either Dominico or his men out into the open.

But first, there was an eternal bond to attend to.

Nightmare nodded toward the Book. "You may ask me questions."

"We'll be together forever?" Matteo asked immediately, like he'd only been waiting for the opportunity for reassurance.

"Yes, sweet. Forever."

Matteo nodded, finally taking a real bite of his chicken. Even after he'd finished the mouthful, he didn't pose another question. Nightmare cocked his head, silently inviting more.

"Oh." Matteo hummed, seeming to think it over. "Will I change somehow?" His gaze darted up to the empty space above Nightmare's head where his antlers would be in his demon form. "Maybe get my own pair of accessories?"

He didn't seem opposed to the idea, a fact that made Nightmare smile.

"No accessories. Though your lifespan will increase drastically and your aging will slow," Nightmare explained. "You will gain access to demon strength and healing, to call upon when needed. You will be very hard to kill."

"But not impossible to hurt?"

It was a reasonable question for Matteo, who'd been hurt so thoroughly and so often by those around him in the past.

"Demons and their mates can be harmed, yes," Nightmare conceded. And that may have been true for demons in general, but it wouldn't hold true for Matteo; Nightmare would make sure of it. "But you will have me."

"Always," Matteo prompted, a new ferocity in his voice. "That's what the bond means. I'll have you always."

"Yes."

Matteo smiled for the first time since they'd sat down for dinner. He slouched back in the booth with a contented sigh. "Okay."

"Is that really all you have to ask?"

Nightmare knew, somewhere in the deep recesses of his soul where his reason lay, that he was asking for far too much too soon. It made sense that a rational human might have many questions and reservations for him.

Did Matteo really care so little for his life as to enter such a bargain so hastily?

The thought had Nightmare gritting his teeth, his rage suddenly overwhelming. Not toward Matteo, but toward the world. This realm. For failing to protect him. Failing to nurture his tender spirit.

A small hand covered Nightmare's clenched fist, squeezing lightly.

"I want to keep you," Matteo said clearly, looking straight into

Nightmare's eyes. "The rest is extra. I'm not hopeless, Scary. I'm hope*ful*, for the first time in my life."

Nightmare allowed the words to soothe his anger. He unclenched his fist and turned his hand, clasping Matteo's fingers with his own. "We'll be linked, our souls tangled together. You may feel my emotions at times, which could be...disturbing for you."

Matteo shrugged. "I doubt that."

"Matteo," Nightmare chastised, the flippancy beginning to concern him again.

"Scary," Matteo countered in a singsong tone.

They were interrupted by the arrival of their waitress, who began refilling water Nightmare hadn't been drinking, leaving his glass close to overfilling. She had short dark hair, equally dark makeup, and enough tattoos to rival Nightmare's own (though his were not human ink but the evidence of his magical contract etched onto his flesh).

She'd commented on Nightmare's marked skin when she'd first arrived to take their orders, and Matteo had growled at her, disguising the sound poorly with a contrived cough when she'd looked at him in alarm.

Now, as she leaned over their table to take away the small plate Nightmare hadn't used, Matteo stabbed into his chicken with alarming force, his gaze on her all the while. He savaged the animal's flesh with his teeth as she scurried away.

Nightmare let out a soft huff of laughter. "You know where my interest lies, little human."

Matteo gave him a sheepish look as he swallowed his oversize bite. "I can't help it. Everyone's always ogling you."

"I stand out."

Matteo ran an assessing gaze over Nightmare's human visage. "We should put you in something with a hood."

"I prefer my vision unimpaired."

Matteo pushed his plate away with a huff and grabbed the Book. "Can we do it here? Now?"

Nightmare's blood ran hot at the sudden enthusiasm, and his shadows itched to come out to play, to reward Matteo for his eagerness. Even Nightmare's cock twitched with interest, with the knowledge of what was to come. Still, he shook his head. "You would not appreciate the location, I think. The bond requires...consummation."

Matteo's tongue darted out to wet his lips. "We get to fuck?"

"Your body will demand it," Nightmare explained. "As will mine."

Matteo's dark eyes shone across the table. "I'm done with dinner," he said firmly.

"You have taken but two bites."

"I'm *done*. We can get a box if you want."

"So eager," Nightmare murmured, unable to keep his sharp smile contained.

Matteo nodded, unashamed. "Yes."

When the waitress arrived to drop off the bill, Matteo did not so much as look at her. His gaze was locked on Nightmare, his eyes full of promise.

They would wait no longer.

———

Nightmare followed as Matteo rushed through their hotel room door, the Book clutched to his chest.

"Okay!" Matteo yelled as soon as the door was shut, whirling to face Nightmare. "We recite the verse, right? Is that how we do it? And—and blood. We exchange blood, right?" Before Nightmare could confirm, Matteo bit down hard on his lower lip, splitting the skin anew. "I'm ready," he said, his lip shining red.

Nightmare stepped forward, cupping his mate's eager face with both hands. "Matteo."

Matteo's face fell. "No. No waiting. No—"

Nightmare ran his thumbs over Matteo's cheeks, shushing him gently. "The bond will require penetration, sweet. And you have yet to be penetrated by more than my fingers. You will allow me to prepare you before we begin." It was not a negotiable request for Nightmare. He would not allow himself to harm his summoner. Although, perhaps he was assuming...

"Unless you'd prefer to do the penetrating?" he asked.

Matteo's big, pretty eyes widened. Had he not considered the possibility? "Oh. Oh wow. Maybe—maybe later? But this time I want you to—I need you to—"

Nightmare nodded his understanding. "Then you will be patient and you will allow me this."

"Yes," Matteo agreed, licking the blood off his lower lip.

Nightmare's cock ached at the sight. Soon enough that blood would be used to bind them together for eternity. Any essence belonging to Matteo was precious, but that fact made it even more so. "I'll undress you now, shall I?"

"Yes."

Nightmare's shadows rushed out to strip Matteo of his clothes, and soon he was standing before Nightmare clad only in the few shadows still teasing at his collarbone.

He was so beautiful, Nightmare's summoner. Scarred and slender, narrow of shoulders and hips, with sharp lines and wiry muscles usually hidden by his baggy clothes. And graced with a substantial cock, already filling with blood.

Nightmare nodded to the bed. "On your stomach, sweet."

Matteo seemed to need no further encouragement. He scrambled up onto the bed, and Nightmare tucked a hotel pillow under his hips.

Matteo shot him an imperious look over his shoulder. "Now you though. With the undressing."

Nightmare let his clothes fall back to the ether. Matteo eyed his naked form hungrily, from the top of his antlers to his toes, then back to his groin. "No hair," he said softly.

"No."

Matteo licked at his lip, where small drops of blood had welled again. "I'm gonna rub all over you after this. All. Over."

Nightmare grinned. "Yes, sweet."

Matteo turned his head back and rested his chin on his folded hands. Nightmare gave in to temptation and placed a knee on the bed, leaning in close, petting along the bare skin in front of him. He traced his taloned fingertips over Matteo's shoulders, his scarred back, his bottom. He kneaded the flesh there hungrily, unable to stop his grip from firming. There was a dark urge whispering inside him, telling him to hoist Matteo up and claim him with all the full, terrible ferocity inside him.

But there were also Nightmare's shadows, murmuring in his ear. Reminding him. *Soft. Sweet. Gentle.*

Nightmare parted those round cheeks, revealing Matteo's furled pink hole to his gaze. Nightmare let hot saliva gather in his mouth and spat.

"Oh," Matteo gasped, squirming in Nightmare's hold.

Nightmare pressed with his thumb—his talons blunted short for the occasion—coaxing and rubbing his offering into that tender spot.

He leaned in closer, breathing in Matteo's lemon scent.

Nightmare knew what he must look like, crouched and looming over Matteo's supine form. A monster of the dark, here to devour an innocent, unsuspecting victim.

But while innocent Matteo might have been—in Nightmare's eyes if not his own—he was in no way unsuspecting. He was possessive and greedy and perfect, and Nightmare was finally stealing him for his own.

Nightmare blunted his sharp teeth and pressed his face in close, tonguing at that precious, hidden spot.

"Ohhh," Matteo sighed. "Oh. Oh *fuck*."

Nightmare groaned into the flesh surrounding him. Matteo's skin was musky and rich, the perfect pairing with the lemony sweet of his arousal. Perhaps Nightmare should have let Matteo bathe before bonding, but he was being selfish, letting himself enjoy the full breadth of Matteo's humanity as he licked along that furrow, paying special attention to that tender hole.

He was patient as he worked his tongue through the tight ring of muscle. It was easy to be patient with Matteo panting and whimpering his pleasure, mumbling into his hands every now and again, little happy, breathless murmurings of, "Ohh, I like that. I like that so, so much."

Nightmare's cock was hardening rapidly, his so-called petals unfurling, allowing his smoky essence to leak from the tip. Nightmare gathered the natural lubricant with one hand, coating his fingers.

He pressed one of those fingers to Matteo's hole, working it in. Then another.

Nightmare groaned again. He was going to be inside this tight passage soon. His aching cock was going to be sucked and caressed by Matteo's inner muscles. Nightmare was going to fill his summoner with his demon seed, again and again and again, until Matteo was overflowing with it.

Nightmare growled, his tongue lengthening alongside his fingers, growing longer and searching deeper.

"Oh my God!" Matteo's whimpers and groans turned to desperate babbling. "Please, please, please! My cock, Scary. Touch it. Make me come. You're going to make me come. You are, you are, you are."

Nightmare slid his free hand under Matteo's hips, circling Matteo's erection with his fingers, letting him rut against his hand.

Matteo's hips moved frantically, and he erupted with a high keen, his channel pulsing around Nightmare's fingers and tongue.

Perfect, so perfect. So responsive to Nightmare's touch, able to find his release with the slightest bit of coaxing.

Nightmare rumbled his approval directly into Matteo's skin.

He lifted his head and released Matteo's cock, licking the salty, bitter essence off his hand as Matteo trembled beneath him.

"Now we do it?" Matteo asked, looking blearily over his shoulder. "The bond? It's time?"

Nightmare grinned at his human's naivete. Somewhere along the way, his teeth had sharpened again. He no doubt looked feral.

"Oh, sweet summoner," he crooned, pressing his thumb to that wet and softened hole, breathing in Matteo's gasp at the unexpected touch. "I'm not nearly done. Be good and stay right as you are. We have a long way to go."

14

Matty

Matty was living in an alternate dimension. One where time made no sense and nothing ever felt bad. Only good.

Only very, very good.

Nightmare had been playing with Matty's ass for what felt like hours. Maybe it really had been. Hours of lips and fingers and a tongue that was *not* a normal human length. Matty may not have had much experience, but even he could tell that much.

Matty's cock had hardened again a long time ago, but there was no urgency to come again yet. It just felt amazing, having his hole played with while he occasionally humped lethargically at the mattress, at other times just lying puttylike under Nightmare's ministrations.

He whined as that hot mouth left his entrance for the first time in forever. "Put it back," he mumbled petulantly, pushing his ass up in the air.

But then Nightmare's hand was on Matty's head, stroking his hair with nimble fingers. "Are you ready, Matteo?"

Ready for what? For fucking? Hell yes.

"Yes," Matty slurred. "So ready, Scary."

And then the Book appeared in front of Matty's face. The shadows had fetched it, and now they turned it to the last page.

"Repeat after me," Nightmare commanded, a dark, raspy voice in Matty's ear.

Oh, right. The bonding. They were bonding before they were fucking. Matty never would have forgotten, except Nightmare had been relentlessly eating his ass for the last eternity, and Matty had apparently lost quite a few brain cells along the way.

Maybe that was good though. With all the blood in his dick and none left for his brain, Matty couldn't even be nervous.

It was strange doing this lying on his stomach, Nightmare crouched above him where Matty couldn't see. Strange but also perfect. His eerie shadow demon, coaxing vows from Matty in the dark.

Nightmare began reciting foreign words above him, and Matty repeated them mindlessly. A thready voice whispered a translation in his ear. Was that one of Nightmare's shadows? Did they talk?

"I am bound to you, by body, heart, and soul. To be parted only briefly in death, and then together forevermore. Two souls made one, my mate's and my own. My soul for my mate, and my mate's soul for me in turn."

Matty barely had time to marvel at the vow he'd made when a shadow nipped at his lip, reopening his wound. Nightmare's finger swiped at the fresh drops of blood, and then his hand returned in front of Matty's mouth.

Even in his foggy state, Matty knew what to do.

He found the base of Nightmare's thumb, and he bit as hard as he could. Smoky copper swept over his tongue, and Nightmare's hand was gone again.

Black smoke filled the room.

And then Matty's body was on fire.

The languid feeling he'd been reveling in evaporated, and he was all static electricity, every muscle inside him twitching and trembling. The bed was shaking from the force of it. Or maybe Nightmare was shaking too? It was hard to tell. Matty was too overwhelmed by this new jittery, buzzing need. He could feel Nightmare's warmth, but it wasn't enough. Nightmare was over him but not *in* him. That was wrong. So wrong. Every part of them should be touching. Merging. Joining.

"Scary," Matty whined.

"I've got you, sweet."

Slender fingers covered Matty's where they were clawing at the bedspread. A large hand on his. Matty clenched at it desperately.

"I need—"

"I know."

Something broad and blunt pressed at Matty's entrance. Bigger than fingers. Much wider than a tongue.

Matty arched his back and pressed his ass up, desperate to get at it.

"Push out, sweet. Bear down. Let me in, Matteo."

Matty did what Nightmare said, and that impossibly thick head breached him. Pushed in. Filled him.

Matty moaned.

Every inch that Nightmare gained, that fat head pressed against everything good inside Matty, and when Nightmare bottomed out, that buzzing electricity finally calmed.

What was left was hot, perfect arousal.

"Oh fuck," Matty cried, clenching hard around Nightmare's cock, groaning at the sensation of being perfectly filled. "Fuck, fuck, fuck."

It was going to be his favorite thing, wasn't it? Getting fucked by his demon.

Nightmare didn't pause, didn't make Matty wait for more. He withdrew in one long, fluid motion and then drove right back in. Again. And again. His hands were still clasped with Matty's, their clenched fists pressing into the mattress.

When Matty caught the rhythm, he somehow found the strength to start pushing back into it, pressing his ass up to get Nightmare even deeper. The angles Nightmare reached made Matty's belly clench and his cock jerk. It felt good to move, to follow that rhythm, his cock sliding against the bedcovers whenever Nightmare pressed him down again.

"I love it," Matty moaned. "I love it so, so much."

He did. He loved the way Nightmare filled him, the way his big body covered him. He loved the way their bare skin pressed together. Loved the way Nightmare's body was hotter than it should be, the way it made sweat prickle and gather on Matty's skin. He loved the growling, grunting noises Nightmare made above him, Matty's calm and eloquent demon somewhere beyond words now.

Matty was so lost in his new love of fucking that it took him a minute to recognize the change within him. A dark presence in his chest. It was steady and strong and...*hungry*. So hungry. A hunger that was deeper and darker than anything Matty had ever felt.

A coveting hunger. A need to claim.

Matty froze, and Nightmare stilled above him, his cock still nestled deep within Matty.

"You want me," Matty said with wonder. "You want me so bad."

"Yes," Nightmare confirmed in his low, husky rasp. It was the first time he'd spoken since their bodies had joined. His shadows gathered at Matty's lips and cheeks and neck as he started rocking his hips into Matty again, driving that hot length into him. "And now we have you."

The shadows traveled down from Matty's neck to his chest, over his belly, all the way to his cock, where they stroked and squeezed.

The new pressure around his cock had Matty's muscles clenching tight around Nightmare's dick, and a low, dark rumble left Nightmare's chest. And then he was slamming in even harder, pressing Matty deeper into the mattress with every thrust.

Matty had lost his own rhythm—the pressure inside him and the shadows rhythmically sucking and squeezing at his cock had him frozen. He was afraid to breathe, afraid that if he let himself relax even the tiniest bit, he was going to come again and it was going to be too much to bear. The pleasure would tear him into a million tiny pieces and scatter him to the winds.

But Matty didn't have a choice as that big, bulbous cock filled him again and again. His spine was already tingling, his fingers and toes curling tightly in desperation.

"Ah, ah, ah!" was all he could say, over and over. He couldn't find the words to warn Nightmare that he was about to dissolve.

And then it was too late. Matty was coming again, too overwhelmed to even cry out this time, only barely able to press his face hard into the bedspread and whimper as his muscles trembled, his channel clamping down again and again, milking Nightmare for all he was worth.

He was pretty sure Nightmare was coming too, his strokes stuttering as his big body pressed Matty down, down, down. He cock felt even bigger somehow, or maybe that was just from Matty's spasming as the pleasure racked through his body.

It felt like another eternity before Matty came back to himself.

He was panting into thick fabric, half-suffocated, and he had to lift his head to the side to breathe properly again. Nightmare was still inside him, and when Matty tried to move out from under him—he wanted to see his demon's face now—a dull pain ached, right where Nightmare was lodged.

Matty yelped at the unexpected sensation.

"Stay still, sweet."

Despite Nightmare's warning, Matty wiggled his hips just a little. He took stock of what he was feeling. "Scary, are you—" He wiggled again, and then he was almost sure of it. "Are we...locked together?"

"What you call my petals," Nightmare said, and was it just Matty's imagination, or was there an almost sheepish note in his voice? "They have...expanded."

"Um." Matty tried to think of something reasonable to say in response to that. "For how long?"

"For some time, I believe."

Matty squirmed again, testing the give between them. It didn't hurt unless he pulled too suddenly or too hard. "Is that what you thought would scare me?"

"Perhaps. I can dislodge if you wish. Though it will take some...effort."

"Oh." Matty considered as he relaxed back onto the mattress, done with his experimental writhing for the moment. "I don't mind," he finally concluded.

Actually, other than the not getting to see Nightmare's face part, it was kind of perfect. Matty had not only bound Nightmare to him, but he'd trapped Nightmare *inside* him, and without even meaning to. He was surrounded by his demon in every way: Nightmare's scent bathing Matty's body, his solid weight resting on him, and his big demon cock lodged deep within him.

Matty started giggling, suddenly finding the situation unbearably funny.

Was this what that manifestation stuff people were always talking about was about? To be so insanely needy that Matty had created a universe where his demon mate physically couldn't leave his body?

Nightmare let out an amused huff, and then he was rolling them over onto their sides without breaking the connection.

Oh, that was nice. Spooning with extras. Matty reached back and tugged Nightmare's arm around his middle, shifting his legs until their limbs were entwined together.

He turned his head, and Nightmare caught on to the unspoken request, capturing Matty's lips in a perfect, possessive kiss, his tongue fucking deep into Matty's mouth.

Matty sighed into the claiming, and he couldn't help wiggling again, playing with that fullness inside him. There was enough leeway for him to pulse his hips a little, and it felt surprisingly good. Like an internal massage. Nightmare took over the gentle rocking, and then Matty's cock was filling again, a slow, nonurgent arousal building within him. He kind of wanted to touch himself, but his limbs were too heavy to manage it.

"What's it for?" Matty broke the kiss to ask with languid curiosity. "The petals expanding like that?"

Nightmare spread his palm over Matty's belly. "Breeding, I suppose. I wasn't sure if it would take—it didn't in my only other experience. But you'll be full by the end; perhaps that's the intent."

Full of Nightmare's cum, he meant. Matty shivered. He could feel it, now that Nightmare had mentioned it—a hot warmth inside him. There'd be more of that, then.

"I will bathe you afterward. And my...secretions have healing properties. You won't be sore, sweet."

Nightmare almost sounded apologetic, like he was worried Matty was going to be angry with the situation. And underneath his words, thrumming between them, Matty was getting little glimpses in the new bond too. Kind of like fear, or some quieter version of it. Fear that Matty would get scared. That he'd regret.

Poor Scary. Matty didn't regret anything, except that he was so weirdly tired.

"I'm getting sleepy," he murmured with a pout. "You can keep going though." He pressed Nightmare's hand harder to his belly, where he could almost swear he felt the bulge of Nightmare's cock from the outside. "Fill me up, Scary."

There was a hitched breath behind him. Matty craned his neck to find Nightmare's white eyes were glowing.

"Would you like that, sweet?" Nightmare rasped, his gaze intent on Matty's. "For me to take my pleasure while you slumber?"

It sounded perfect to Matteo. To fall asleep with Nightmare as close as he could physically be. For Nightmare to pump him full and claim him while Matty lay dead to the world.

Maybe Matty would dream about it. Maybe for once in his life, his sleep would be a place for sweet things.

He rested his head on his arm, letting his eyes fall closed, even as heat swirled low in his belly, his cock full between his legs. "Yeah, Scary. Like the vows said: I'm all yours."

15

Nightmare

recious. Perfect. Sweet, sweet, sweet.

Nightmare knelt on the floor by the foot of the hotel bed, holding Matteo's lax thighs open with his hands, watching his spend trickle from Matteo's open hole.

It had taken longer than Nightmare had imagined for his petals to constrict. Whether that was due to the power of the bonding or the covetousness that ran through his very bones, he didn't know. He'd caressed and scented and ground deep into Matteo's limp form, his cock pulsing out more and more cum, and then he'd turned Matteo onto his stomach and rocked against him until finally Nightmare's hunger had abated enough for his cock to unlatch.

Matteo had slept through it all.

The trust he'd shown in Nightmare—in allowing himself to slumber while Nightmare surrounded him in every way possible —was a heady drug indeed. Nightmare had gotten immense pleasure from stroking his mate's cock just to watch him sigh and shift in his sleep, his eyelids fluttering but never opening entirely.

Nightmare hadn't needed to siphon any fear from Matteo at all. His mate had slept peacefully, his lemon scent rich with arousal. Perhaps his lack of dark dreams was due to his new link with Nightmare's soul, or perhaps it was due to the fact that he'd had Nightmare's body wrapped so firmly around him. *Inside* him.

Nightmare regretted the loss of that closeness already, even as he experienced immense pleasure watching his release drip from Matteo's sleeping form. He'd sensed it would be this way. Sensed that once he got a taste of burrowing inside his mate, he'd never want to leave. He'd been cautious for this very reason.

He placated himself by massaging the firm, supple muscle of Matteo's thighs. For once, Nightmare's shadows were resting in Matteo's presence, tucked deep within Nightmare, exhausted from the bonding.

Nightmare had his summoner to himself.

He ran his nose along the tender flesh under his hands. He opened his mouth and gently—carefully—bit down, tonguing the salty skin. Matteo was soaked with sweat from being wrapped up with Nightmare's inhuman warmth for so long. Nightmare had the strange urge to lick every drop from his body.

Perhaps he would.

He slid his hand up Matteo's inner thigh and thumbed at his mate's hole. More spend trickled out, dark and smoky. A quiet rumble of satisfaction left Nightmare's chest. The tender pink skin might have been red and puffy except that Nightmare's ejaculate —like his saliva and his blood—held healing properties, if he wished it to. A tool for demons to tend to their human summoner's needs. A tool now to keep his mate without pain, unharmed by Nightmare's immense, immeasurable hunger for him.

Matteo's muscles shifted under Nightmare's palms, and a soft sigh came from above him.

Nightmare glanced up to find Matteo awake, looking down the length of his torso to Nightmare. "Scary?" Matteo frowned, his dark eyes still foggy with sleep. "You got out." His hand drifted down to his entrance, as if to verify, and his lips pushed into a pout. "I missed it?"

Nightmare couldn't help his smile. "There will be other opportunities, sweet."

Matteo's pout shifted into a shy little grin. He rose higher onto his elbows, although he didn't attempt to close his legs, didn't try to shield himself from Nightmare's hungry gaze. "What are you doing down there?"

"Admiring."

"Oh." Matteo's cheeks flushed pink, and he shifted on the bed. His cock—still hard from Nightmare's attentions—bobbed in the air. Matteo wrapped his hand around it with a sigh. "I'm so turned on. It's weird to wake up like that." He gave himself a stroke, then let his hand drop. His expression turned sweetly beseeching. "Will you suck me, Scary? Please?"

"Mm." Nightmare pressed a palm on Matteo's belly. "Lie back, sweet."

Matteo shook his head. "No, thank you." His flush deepened. "I want to watch."

He was a terror, this one. And Nightmare was ever at his disposal. He blunted his teeth and took Matteo's cock in his mouth, tonguing at the salty, bitter precum at the tip.

Matteo curled up into his touch with an almost pained cry. "Oh!"

His thighs came up around Nightmare's head, and his hips started moving, fucking into Nightmare's mouth without hesitation. He was so eager to mate, so responsive to any touch. Primed for pleasure in a way that must have been innate to his nature, given his lack of experience.

Nightmare hollowed his cheeks and sucked. He was in a mood

to be merciful, given how long he'd been playing with Matteo's pliant body already. And sure enough, the poor thing didn't last long at all. He only managed a few more frantic pumps of his hips before he curled up into a ball around Nightmare's head—his hands grasping desperately at Nightmare's antlers—and shot into Nightmare's mouth with a cry.

Nightmare swallowed. Licked his lips. Swallowed some more.

This was even better than Matteo's sweat.

Eventually Matteo started pushing at Nightmare's head, forcing it off his tender member. When Nightmare released him, he flopped onto his back with a sigh, reaching his arms up without looking. "Come here."

Nightmare climbed onto the bed and crawled over him, laying his chest down on top of his mate, careful not to let his full weight fall.

Matteo wrapped his arms around Nightmare's back, welcoming his touch as he always did. "I can feel you in me still."

Nightmare nuzzled against his neck. "We mated for a very long time."

Matteo laughed brightly. "Not your cock. Your soul. Our bond. You feel things differently than I do, so the emotions are...odd." Nightmare lifted his head to look at him, and Matteo's dark eyes were shining. "But I've never felt safer. You're here. You're filling up all my little cracks and empty places. You're making me stronger." His brow furrowed. "What do I give you?"

"You," Nightmare rasped. "All of you."

Matteo's frown deepened. "And that's enough?"

"Always." Nightmare slid off the bed. He picked Matteo up in a bridal carry. "Time to bathe, sweet."

"Okay." Matteo wrapped his arms around Nightmare's neck. He glanced back at the bed. "Where are my shadows?"

"Resting."

"But they'll be back?"

"They'll be back."

Nightmare took Matteo into the large hotel shower. He pressed Matteo's hands against the tiled wall and began helping him empty himself of every last trace of Nightmare's essence. He didn't want his summoner left sticky and uncomfortable because he'd been careless.

Matteo looked over his shoulder at Nightmare kneeling behind him. "Should this be embarrassing?"

"No."

"Okay," Matteo said easily. "It isn't." He shifted on his feet, pushing his ass out against Nightmare's helpful fingers. "It's kind of hot, actually. Should it be hot?"

Nightmare bit at Matteo's bottom with blunt teeth. "Insatiable."

"Am I?" Matteo laughed. "That's funny. I never thought so before."

Nightmare carried him to the tub next, where Matteo insisted Nightmare join him. It was cramped, Nightmare's knees jutting out from the sides, but Matteo didn't seem to mind. He snuggled against Nightmare's chest, his soul lemon-bright with happiness.

"Maybe we could just run away," Matteo eventually said, tracing his fingers lightly over Nightmare's belly under the water.

"No more running, little human. We will battle your monsters first."

Matteo let out a sigh. "Bossy."

Perhaps. But Nightmare was also certain in his course of action. He could taste it now, through the full bond they now shared: the corner of Matteo's soul that Dominico had claimed with his torture and his threats, one where the bright lemon had been replaced with bitter despair and ash.

Dominico would not be allowed to keep it.

Matteo's soul was for Nightmare and his shadows. No one else.

———

NIGHTMARE once again found himself on human public transportation.

He and Matteo were meeting Chaos and Cooper in Seacliff, the other pair arriving by way of rental car. Cooper had informed them that he'd only recently received his driver's license, and Nightmare wasn't willing to leave Matteo in the hands of an inexperienced human driver. And knowing the little chaos demon, it would be just like him to take over the wheel and drive them all off a cliff, if only for his own amusement.

The bus was safer for Nightmare's summoner.

Matteo was alert but far less twitchy than on the voyage over, his surveillance of their fellow passengers more purposeful and less paranoid.

"Maybe it's a good thing we're taking care of things," Matteo mused after giving a burly, bearded man a remarkably thorough once-over.

"It is, sweet."

"Because then we can go somewhere private and just fuck and fuck and fuck for days."

A woman across the aisle from them coughed loudly.

"If you like," Nightmare said evenly, as if he wasn't salivating behind his fangs at the thought of such a thing.

Matteo gave the coughing woman a look and lowered his voice. "And when Dominico comes, you're going to make him suffer? Make him hurt?"

"Yes, sweet. He will suffer greatly."

Nightmare knew now that Matteo liked hearing things said out loud for reassurance, often more than once. And while by no means verbose by nature, Nightmare would tell his mate what he needed as many times over as Matteo required.

And for once in his long existence, Nightmare could perhaps use a little reassurance of his own.

He didn't like that Dominico's men had been found in an occult shop. Demons weren't the only inhuman creatures roaming this realm. And while the likelihood of those mobster humans finding anything of substance was unlikely, it wasn't impossible.

But that wasn't for Matteo to worry about. The sweet contentment he'd been radiating since their bonding needed to be maintained at all costs. And perhaps that was selfish of Nightmare, but so be it. It fed something in him, that sense of well-being emanating from his mate. Nourished some deep, dark place he'd never known needed filling. He ached to keep it.

Nightmare had known the taste of Matteo's soul already, but he hadn't realized how the whole of it would feel. That it would be like a bright bit of light in his sternum, nestled somewhere that had never once seen the sun. A place for Nightmare's shadows to feel the heat of that blaze, a warm caress Nightmare had never known they craved. Even now they kept diving in, basking in the glow of it—a small bit of recompense for being denied the pleasure of wrapping around Matteo in public.

Nightmare had been sure of his course ever since he'd come across Matteo in the dream realm, but this was confirmation.

Matteo was Nightmare's purpose, his answer to an existence that went beyond mere survival. His destiny. His perfect, soulful mate.

And Nightmare had claimed him for eternity.

So Nightmare kept his worries to himself, and soon enough their bus arrived at their destination, the depot in Seacliff.

Once they were off the bus, Matteo glanced around warily, then tucked his hand into the crook of Nightmare's elbow. "Let's walk to the house. You want me to be seen, right?"

Nightmare didn't. He wanted to keep the sight of his beautiful summoner all to himself, for him and his shadows alone.

But the plan said otherwise. So they walked, Matteo's thick hoodie in place despite the heat of the summer sun.

Perhaps Matteo was not feeling completely carefree, then. He was still hiding, in his way, even with Nightmare at his side.

They didn't come across anyone who seemed likely to have been working for Dominico. They mainly came across families Matteo identified as tourists, swarms of them taking photos and devouring the local treats while they visited the quaint shops of the town. The few solo travelers they saw were mostly women, and none of them smelled like nefarious intentions. There was no one Matteo seemed to recognize, other than familiar townspeople he still shied away from.

At least not until they arrived at the house. Because there on the porch was a large, muscular figure, his burly arms crossed in front of his chest, a slim blond man standing beside him.

The warrior Kaisyir and his human mate.

Nightmare halted their progress on the sidewalk, keeping Matteo at his side. "Did the chaos demon spill so soon?" he called out. "Who would have thought the little menace was such a telltale?"

"It was the incubus, actually," Kaisyir told him in his low rumble. "As soon as he got off the video call." He sent a severe look Matteo's way. "Matteo. Come stand by Sascha, over here."

Matteo nibbled at his lip, looking up at Nightmare with a furrowed brow. Nightmare didn't need their soul connection to know his human was torn. Nightmare even knew why: the loyalty and gratitude Matteo held toward this couple, the ones who had saved him from his old life of pain and misery.

And for that reason alone—the part those two had played in saving Matteo's life—Nightmare would quell this dark surge of possessiveness and allow Kaisyir to keep all his limbs, despite the warm smile Matteo had displayed upon seeing the other demon.

"Kai," Matteo called softly, a note of pleading in his voice. "You remember your friend Sarkaron."

Kaisyir grunted. "I can remember him with you over here."

And there. That was enough protectiveness from the warrior toward a mate that didn't belong to him.

Nightmare tugged Matteo into him, wrapping an arm around his chest, his front to Matteo's back. He watched the way the gesture made Kaisyir's eyes narrow. And maybe centuries spent with Chaos's mischievous nature had infected him, because Nightmare lifted a hand to cup Matteo's fragile throat, pleased beyond measure when Matteo relaxed into the touch.

Kaisyir growled.

Nightmare grinned, and the gesture was all sharp teeth. "You're aware I can't harm him, warrior. Not with a contract in place."

"I know that he's a sweet soul," Kaisyir ground out. "And that you're trickier than Chaos when you want to be." The warrior stepped forward—even in his human form, he was a massive presence—and then he froze, sniffing at the air. His brutish face fell, and he gave Matteo an oddly imploring look. "What have you done, little chick?"

"Why?" The warrior's mate—Sascha—looked between them all, his pale eyes wide with panic. "What happened to Matty?"

"They've bonded." Kaisyir turned toward the house, shepherding a gaping Sascha in front of him. His parting words held a dark finality. "We're already too late."

Nightmare watched them go, his arm held secure around his mate.

His grin never faltered.

16

Matty

Matty watched Kai stalk off with Sascha in tow, something heavy sinking in his stomach. Those were his friends. His *only* friends.

With some effort, Matty loosened Nightmare's hold across his chest enough to turn around to face his demon. He peered up at Nightmare's severely handsome human face. "Is everyone mad at me?"

Nightmare's sharp grin dropped immediately. "No one's angry with you, sweet."

"It feels like everyone is." Matty craned his neck to frown at the open doorway behind him. "Kai *definitely* is."

A vaguely sinister rumble left Nightmare's chest. He set long fingers on Matty's chin, turning his head back to face him. "I will speak to the warrior."

"But you won't hurt him."

There was a suspicious pause before Nightmare's answer. "No."

Matty narrowed his eyes, wishing for the first time for a little less of a height imbalance between them. He felt like maybe he needed to really get into Nightmare's face for this one. "Or paralyze him," he pressed. "Or stomp his psyche into mush."

Nightmare let out a long, put-upon sigh, although his lips twitched up at the corners. "He will remain unharmed."

"He saved me," Matty reminded him.

A muscle ticked in Nightmare's jaw. "I'm aware."

Matty cocked his head, studying his demon. He was getting a little more used to this human form of his. And it was easier to read Nightmare's expressions this way too, especially without the shadows shrouding his face. Plus, Matty could feel it through the bond, this vague air of discontent and itch for violence.

"You wish *you* had saved me?" Matty guessed.

That muscle ticked again. "Yes."

"You did." Matty stood on his tiptoes, tugging Nightmare's face down to his for a kiss, murmuring happily as he was enveloped in the scent of smoke and shadow. His demon smelled the same like this, at least. "You are, all the time."

Apparently not satisfied with a chaste press of lips, Nightmare pulled Matty off the ground, claiming his mouth more thoroughly. He kissed the same in his human form too. Possessive and heated and hungry, like all his careful restraint left him the moment he had Matty in his clutches.

Matty was panting and a little lightheaded by the time Nightmare let him go.

"We should...head inside?" Matty asked, no longer sure which direction that even was.

"Mm."

Nightmare set Matty down, and Matty grabbed his demon's hand. He stood there for a second too long, and Nightmare very thoughtfully turned him by the shoulder toward the house's porch.

Ah. Right where Matty had left it.

Matty pulled Nightmare through the door, where Sascha was waiting for them inside the entryway. Matty's friend looked concerned. "Kai's out back," he said quietly, his fair brow furrowed as he looked Matty over.

Nightmare released Matty's hand, turning to presumably head out back after Kai. Matty tugged at his shirt before he could get too far. "A conversation only?" he reminded.

"Mm."

Sascha sidled up to Matty as Nightmare walked away. "That's Nightmare?" he whispered. "I didn't think he'd be so...hot."

Nightmare whirled in the hallway to face them, twisting back into his demon form. Matty realized why a second later, when Nightmare's shadows swarmed his way.

Sascha let out a loud yelp as the shadows whirled past him. "Agh! Fucking fuck!" He lowered his voice again as Nightmare stalked out of sight. "Okay, well... Those antlers. Yeah. And—and those eyes. The whole— He just—" Sascha shuddered dramatically. "That's more what I was expecting."

Matty didn't have anything to say to that. He thought Nightmare's demon form was lovely.

Sacha stared at one of the shadows, which was making a pretty good smoky impression of Nightmare's skull mask about a foot in front of his face. "Those are his shadows."

"Yes." Matty smiled at his little friends. "These are them. But don't touch." Matty eyed Sascha's hands, making sure they stayed right where they were. "They're cute, but they're shy."

Matty might have been lying a little bit. It was more like they were his, and he didn't want anyone else pawing at them, even if it was his extremely generous and good-hearted friend Sascha. But he didn't know how to say that to Sascha without sounding unhinged, so he kept it to himself.

Sascha's gaze tracked the shadows' swirling movements. He shuffled a little further away from Matty, since the shadows were mostly congregating in front of him. "Chaos said they were incorporeal, but Kai said they can touch things. Hurt people."

Matty shrugged. "They can be both, I think. Like, they can get inside someone and stir their mind up from the inside. But also I'm pretty sure they can consume a dead body."

"And you think they're cute." Sascha gave him an unreadable look. "And also shy."

"I do." The shadows came to wrap around Matty's neck, settling like a scarf around him in the way they sometimes did, and he grinned. "See?"

Sascha pinched the bridge of his nose, a move Matty had seen Ivan make when he was getting overwhelmed with the idiocy of the masses. "I'm starting to understand Kai's concern."

The front door burst open, and it was Matty's turn to yelp, the shadows sliding off his neck and rushing to the door to fend off whoever was arriving.

But it was only Chaos and Cooper.

Chaos bounded through the shadows like they were nothing, tugging Cooper with him, completely ignoring Matty's scowl at their disregard for the shadows' personal space.

"Was there violence?" the chaos demon asked eagerly. "Did I miss it? How many arms does Kai still have? Or did Nightmare rip off one of his wings instead? Do you think he'd let me keep it?"

"Congratulations on the bonding," Cooper said when neither Sascha nor Matty answered Chaos's questions. He gave Matty a smile that was a little awkward but seemed kind enough.

Sascha's brow furrowed as he looked between the three of them, his gaze lingering especially long on Chaos, who was now snapping his teeth at the stray shadows that kept trying to cover his eyes. "This whole time I've been worried about my own family, but I didn't quite understand the family I was marrying into."

"Aw," Chaos crooned, his eyes flashing through different colors before settling on a painfully bright pink. "Please let me be in the room when you tell Kai you consider us his brothers."

———

BY THE TIME Nightmare came back inside the house to lurk in the living room doorway, the four of them—Matty, Chaos, Cooper, and Sascha—were crowded on the couch, oohing over photos of Alexei's vampire den.

"Why's the pretty one wearing a fur coat in summertime?" Chaos asked, pressing his face to Sascha's phone.

"Oh, Soren? I think just because he can." Sascha shrugged. "You know. Fashion."

Chaos's eyes gleamed. "Fashion," he mused, straightening and giving Cooper a glance.

Cooper flushed, tugging on his hoodie strings. "I'll stick to my sweatshirts, menace."

"But don't you think *I'd* look good in a fur coat?" Chaos asked, snuggling into him and rubbing his head against Cooper's shoulder like a cat asking for scratches.

"You would," Cooper agreed, patting at Chaos's head. "You can wear whatever you want, in whatever season you want to wear it."

"A tiara? I saw a woman wear one at the ballet that one time. It looked ridiculous. I loved it."

"Ten tiaras." Cooper pressed a kiss to Chaos's shimmering hair, which had gone kind of rainbow at some point. "Go nuts."

Matty beckoned to Nightmare, and his demon left the doorway, stalking over to the couch. He didn't exactly look happy, but he wasn't covered in blood either, and nothing too murderous was coming down the bond. His white eyes were flat too, and not glowing with any sinister intent.

"You talked?" Matty asked when Nightmare was in front of him.

"We talked."

Matty grabbed hold of Nightmare's outstretched hand and used it to stand from the couch. Nightmare didn't move back when he did, so Matty ended up with his face basically pressed into Nightmare's chest. He tilted his head back. "I'm going to chat with him too."

"Mm."

"Scary?"

"Yes, sweet?"

"You're holding my hand very tightly."

"Yes."

Matty wiggled back and used his free hand to tug on Nightmare's shirt until he was bent low enough to press their foreheads together. "A little conversation," Matty murmured, staring kind of cross-eyed into Nightmare's white gaze. "Because he kept me alive long enough for you to find me."

A low rumble left Nightmare's chest. He pressed a hard kiss to Matty's lips, and then he straightened, his shadows rushing out to drape over Matty's neck, shoulders, and arms, all the way down to his wrists.

There sure were a lot of them.

Matty grinned. "Thank you, Scary." He pushed Nightmare toward the couch. "Why don't you take a seat and look at Sascha's pictures. I'll be right back."

Sascha made a little strangled sound as Nightmare sat next to him, but he didn't move away. He didn't move at all, really. He seemed kind of frozen.

He'd probably warm up to Nightmare eventually, right?

Matty made his way through the back of the house and into the backyard. It was lovely in the summertime, with its lush grass and the big tree in the corner and the overgrown flowers left behind from the previous owner. Matty didn't spend nearly enough time in it—he'd been too busy hiding on the couch under his blankets.

And there was Kai, standing with his arms crossed, kind of glowering at the tree trunk. He turned at Matty's arrival, his scowl deepening at the sight of the shadows swirling over Matty.

"Possessive bastard," he growled.

Matty kept going until he was right next to the demon. He crossed his arms in solidarity, and they both stared at the tree.

"You're angry with me," Matty finally said, eyes locked onto the bark in front of him.

Kai made a vague grumbling noise. "Not with you, little chick."

With Nightmare, then.

"He didn't do anything wrong though," Matty argued. He didn't know why everyone kept acting like Nightmare had stolen him from his bed in the middle of the night and whisked him away to some hell dimension. It was Matty who'd summoned him. Who'd asked for his help.

"He came here with the express purpose of keeping you."

Matty shrugged. "I know. He's been pretty up front about that."

"It's permanent, Matteo. The bond."

"I know that too."

There was a long silence, and Matty let it ride. Kai wasn't big on words unless he was with Sascha, and Matty wasn't going to rush him.

"We would have protected you, Sascha and I," Kai eventually said.

"Kai." Matty waited until Kai turned to face him, his dark brow furrowed. Matty placed a hand on his arm, meeting his blue gaze. "I *know*."

Matty turned and walked over to sit on the porch steps, and after a moment, Kai followed. He barely fit next to Matty on the step, and maybe it wasn't wise of him to be out and about in the backyard like this—where a neighbor or two could potentially see him—but Matty liked him in his demon form.

This was how Kai had looked when he'd freed Matty from his old life. Huge and muscular with his blue skin and black horns and spray after spray of blood gushing in his wake.

Matty cleared his throat, staring down at his clasped hands. Even if Kai wasn't big on words, Matty felt like he owed him some.

"I'm so grateful to Sascha, you know. Because he wanted a friend, and that's why you kept me. But I used to get jealous too. Because he had you." Kai made a quiet sound of surprise, and Matty clarified, "He had someone who was his and his alone. Someone who kept him safe and made him whole. I wanted that so badly." Matty nudged Kai's knee with his. "And now I have it."

Kai let out a harsh breath. "That demon—"

"Is everything I've ever wanted, deep in the darkest corner of my heart. He makes me feel safe and wanted and—and *alive*."

Kai let out a growl of frustration, and Matty made one back at him.

"You trust him. I know you do."

"And why do you know that?"

Matty waved a hand back at the house. "Because you left Sascha alone with him. You'd never do that if you thought he'd hurt him."

"Because he's on a leash now," Kai said, speaking more harshly to Matty than he ever had. It was only Matty's deep, bottomless trust in the warrior demon that kept him from flinching. "Because you're already bonded, and he knows what Sascha means to you. I wouldn't have otherwise."

"If you know he's leashed"—and for some reason, saying that out loud made Matty's cheeks heat—"then why are you still so upset?"

Kai rubbed a hand over his face. "I'll tell you a story, shall I?"

Demons and their stories—apparently that was a thing. Matty settled in.

"We were summoned at the same time once, Sarkaron and I. I'd been called first, by a clan chieftain who needed powerful aid in battle." Kai's brow furrowed. "He didn't realize one of his closest men was set on betraying him. That man stole the Book and summoned Nightmare for his own ends."

Kai stared off into the distance, as if remembering. "I was guarding the chieftain when Sarkaron came for him. But there was nothing I could do to stop his shadows." He grimaced. "The anguish on that man's face. The noises he made. He took his dagger and stabbed it into his own chest, trying to dig out his heart. That's what killed him in the end—his own hand." Kai turned to face Matty again. "I saw Sarkaron's face, lurking in the dark. I saw the way he enjoyed that man's suffering. And when he'd fulfilled his contract and mine had dissolved with my master's death—in the split second before we were pulled back to the Void—he sent his shadows after his own summoner. The man was left a husk." Kai met Matty's eyes. "There's violence in battle, and then there's...that."

There was a long silence while Kai stared at him, and Matty realized Kai was expecting him to speak. Was he supposed to be horrified? "It sounds like two violent men met violent ends."

Kai's features twisted into a look of pure disbelief. He shifted forward on the step. "You don't speak of it, Matteo, but we know you escaped a life where you were tyrannized by terrifying, cruel men. I did not wish for you to be chained to a terrifying, cruel demon."

Matty straightened, narrowing his eyes. "He's not cruel, Kai. Not to me. He's wonderful."

Kai only huffed, and Matty toed at the grass at the bottom of the steps. "I don't know why he wants me," he admitted, since they were sharing truths and he didn't really have anyone else to tell. "I don't know what I give him in return."

The sigh Kai let out was weary beyond even his ancient years. "Your soul speaks to him. It's a possessive, possessing kind of love compared to what humans are used to. But it's powerful."

Matty was too startled by the word *love* to think before he spoke. "I like powerful."

Kai's lips twisted into a strange smile. "I'm realizing such."

"You think it makes me a bad person," Matty guessed.

"No, Matteo. I think it makes you human. You're not a damsel in distress, and you're not a lost little boy. You're a grown man, and you have the desires of one. You wouldn't be the first to lust after power."

Matty frowned, wondering if he should be offended. "That's not a very flattering picture."

Kai shrugged. "Because I imagine it's not the whole picture, is it? How does his soul feel to you?"

Matty considered the dark presence inside him, that pulsing vortex that was so strange and so familiar at the same time.

"Strong," he said after a moment, aware that maybe that specific adjective wasn't helping his case. "And...mysterious. And comforting." He pressed a hand to his chest. "It's like—like it's no wonder I was so scared before, or that life felt so hard. It's a miracle I was surviving at all, with such a vital piece of me missing."

Kai let out another long, weary sigh, then slapped his thighs before standing. "He's not the mate I would have chosen for you, but it's done. I'm glad you finally feel safe, Matteo. Between you and Nix..." He let out a mirthless laugh. "Well, I'm no matchmaker."

"Who *would* you have chosen for me?" Matty asked, curious despite himself.

"Some steady human, I suppose." Kai placed his hands on his

hips, looking out into the distance again as he considered. "An accountant named Benjamin, perhaps."

Matty couldn't help his peal of laughter. "What on earth would I do with an accountant named Benjamin?"

"Probably nothing, I see now." Kai tilted his head toward the back door. "Come, little chick. Let's rescue Sascha from your terrifying mate."

17

Matty

Matty hadn't realized he'd gotten used to having the house all to himself until suddenly it was full again.

In reality, Matty hadn't even had an entire week on his own before Nightmare had appeared, but so much had changed since then that it felt like ages ago since he'd had house-mates to contend with.

So it was an odd sort of relief to be wrapped in a fuzzy blanket on his own bed, cuddled up to his demon as *Scream* played on the TV Sascha had gotten for him.

Nightmare was half-reclined against the headboard, and Matty was lying on his side, resting his head on Nightmare's stomach.

And they were alone. Finally.

Although, first they'd had to kick Chaos out of Matty's bedroom—apparently he'd sneaked in and hidden under the bed. Nightmare had found him immediately and tossed him out, despite his screeching protests. ("But a nightmare demon mating is incredibly rare! You're depriving me of novel entertainment!")

Nightmare hadn't even tried to paralyze the mischievous demon, so maybe he was just as worn out from company as Matty was.

Things had been...tense between Nightmare and the other residents. Not terrible, but not exactly a light and fluffy reunion either.

"Is it really so rare?" Matty asked now, thinking back to what Chaos had said. "A nightmare demon bonding with a mate?"

"Mm," Nightmare confirmed. "We are not ones for the touch of others."

"But you like *my* touch?" Matty clarified.

"Yes, sweet," Nightmare rasped, his voice a little rougher than usual.

It was a good thing Nightmare liked Matty's touch, because Matty had been groping Nightmare pretty shamelessly for the last twenty minutes. He'd meant to be on better behavior—there were so many people around, and Matty wasn't really any good at staying quiet when he and Nightmare got intimate—but his cuddling position made it so easy to fondle. And it was *fun*. Nightmare's cock was kind of like an erotic stress ball, hardening or twitching depending on how Matty brushed or kneaded it. And he got special pleasure in finding the spongy head and massaging it through Nightmare's pants, listening to Nightmare's breaths quicken above him.

It was hard to stick to just fondling though.

Now Matty worked on undoing the ties of Nightmare's pants, plucking and rearranging the fabric until Nightmare's cock was mostly freed. It was fully hard now, the black veins bulging. Maybe Matty really had been teasing him.

"Are you having fun, sweet?" Nightmare asked, amusement lacing his roughened tone.

"Yeah." Matty craned his head up to catch a glimpse of Nightmare's glowing white eyes. "Are you?"

"Mm."

Matty wrapped a hand around the head of Nightmare's cock, swirling his thumb over the tip and gathering the precum before sliding his fist down, the petals bunching under the head like they had for Nightmare. "Very cool," Matty praised. "If I blow you, is this going to latch onto my face?"

Nightmare let out a huff of amusement. "No."

Well, then.

Matty escaped his blanket cocoon and shuffled until he was lying fully between Nightmare's spread legs, resting his weight on his forearms. He tugged at Nightmare's pants again until Nightmare was freed all the way to the root.

Matty had never given a blow job before, and while with anyone else that might have made him self-conscious, this was his mate. His demon. Nightmare had never made Matty feel anything less than wonderful in bed, and Matty trusted him with all his firsts.

So Matty didn't overthink it. He shoved his head right in there, rubbing his cheek against the soft skin of Nightmare's groin, his nose brushing against Nightmare's cock. Nightmare smelled good here—smoky and intense. Matty breathed in deeply for a while and then moved on, rubbing his lips and nose and cheeks against the whole solid length.

With the amount of precum Nightmare leaked, it didn't take long for things to get pretty messy. Nightmare didn't seem to mind though. His breathing only grew heavier and faster above Matty's head.

Matty rose onto an elbow, grasping Nightmare's cock in his hand. Nightmare grunted.

"Be good," Matty crooned at the dick in his hand, staring at the fat, dark head, rubbing his thumb along the bunched petals underneath. "No *Alien*-esque face hugging, please."

Another huff from above him. "I do not understand the reference. My cock doesn't either."

"That's okay."

They could rectify Nightmare's horror movie ignorance later. For now, Matty worked on fitting that fat head in his mouth. It was surprisingly doable—there was a spongy give to it that Matty liked. That must have been how it fit inside him in the first place. Matty sucked experimentally. It tasted good too. Like a rich, smoky treat.

Matty tried to take it deeper and immediately coughed, gagging around the mouthful.

Nightmare's hand settled in his hair, stroking lightly. "Careful, sweet."

Matty popped off with a glower. "*You* be careful," he muttered before trying again.

He went slower and had more success this time fitting that rigid length deeper in his mouth.

It didn't take him long to decide he liked sucking Nightmare's dick. Matty liked it a lot, in fact. He liked the noises Nightmare made—the huffs and grunts and harsh, inhaled breaths. He liked that when his lips got sore from the stretch, he could take a break and rub his face along it—mouthing and tonguing along the black veins—and Nightmare seemed to enjoy that just as much. He liked that Nightmare's thighs and belly got all tense and hard, the muscles trembling as he took the pleasure Matty gave him.

Matty had to look a mess, his face all streaked with gray precum and his own saliva. But he couldn't find it in himself to care, and his cock was heavy and full as he humped it against the mattress.

When Matty's jaw grew weary, he went back to sucking on the head, tonguing hungrily at the fleshy, bunched petals, using both hands to massage and stroke the rest. Nightmare's hands were roaming everywhere now—Matty's hair, his cheeks, his chin—and he seemed to be fighting to keep his hips in place.

That was thoughtful of him. Matty didn't think he was ready to have his face fucked.

Eventually there was a tug on Matty's ear, either Nightmare's fingers or his shadows, which had been swirling more and more frantically the longer Matty worked. "Do you wish to swallow, sweet?"

Matty moaned around his mouthful, grinding his hips harder into the mattress, his balls drawing tight. Yes, he wanted that. He *needed* that.

Nightmare hissed out an incomprehensible sound, and then a burst of something hot flooded Matty's mouth. He swallowed as best he could, choking and coughing as he only half succeeded at his task. He shoved a hand down his pants and grasped his cock, shudders racking his body as his dick spurted before he could do anything but grab it.

Matty kept sucking and coughing and dribbling cum out of his mouth until Nightmare finally pried him off gently.

Matty smiled up at him, aware he had to look completely undone. "I came in my sweatpants," he said dazedly.

Nightmare's white eyes gleamed. "Show us."

Matty scrambled onto his knees and pulled down his sweats enough to reveal his sticky, softening cock.

Nightmare let out a low rumble of approval. "What a mess you've made, little human." He sounded pretty pleased about that, and his eyes hadn't lost their glow.

"I'll go clean up. I think I might need actual water for this one." Matty reached over Nightmare and grabbed a washcloth from the drawer of his bedside table, doing a quick, probably useless sweep of his face. Then he toddled on trembling legs to the hallway leading to the bathroom.

He heard frantic whispering and looked to the left to find

Chaos's yellow eyes peeking out from a crack in the guest bedroom's doorway.

Then Matty felt the warmth of Nightmare at his back, and that open door shut quickly, though the sound of Chaos's gleeful cackle was perfectly loud and clear.

Maybe Chaos had gotten his novel entertainment after all.

———

Sascha kicked Matty out of the house in the morning.

Well, not permanently, but still.

It had been the plan for Matty to be seen around town anyway, but also Matty had been looking forward to cuddling Nightmare in his own bed until he got his fill. Maybe he would have ventured out three or four days from now?

It was Kai who'd banged on Matty's bedroom door with all his might, yelling that they needed to come down for waffles immediately. And then Sascha had politely but firmly told Matty he needed to be seen out of the house as much as possible. "I want to get the guys after you, but I don't want it to go down here. This is my home. My safe space. Is that—is that okay?"

And of course it was okay. Matty didn't want Dominico stepping into his safe haven either. But it had meant he'd kept his mouth shut about the intruder Nightmare had caught. The shadows had cleaned up all the evidence, anyway. No need to worry his friends.

And now he and Nightmare were outside in the bright sunlight, surrounded by tourists. Matty was staring at a flyer pinned on a billboard outside the town's most popular diner. It was for the next dance night at the Lighthouse, Seacliff's one and only gay bar.

"You think we could lure Dominico out with something like this?" Matty asked Nightmare.

Matty didn't exactly want any innocent bystanders involved, but Dominico was wily—he wouldn't do anything in public that could get him caught by authorities. He would try to get Matty out. Get him alone. And a confined bar at night would be easier to manage than out in the town during the day, with kids and families running around.

"Yes, sweet. We can manage."

Matty swallowed. The flyer was for Friday. Five nights away.

He shivered, suddenly cold despite the summer sun, but then something warm pressed against his chest. He pulled the collar of his sweatshirt out and peered down. It was one of Nightmare's shadows, about the size and shape of a handkerchief, plastered to Matty's T-shirt.

Matty grinned down at it. "Oh, hello. What are you doing out and about?"

The shadow didn't answer, of course, but it didn't seem like it was going anywhere either.

"Are you ready to return?" Nightmare asked.

"No." Matty shifted his sweatshirt back into place, patting at the shadow hidden there. Now that they were already out, it didn't make sense to retreat so soon. "We should walk around a little more."

He grabbed Nightmare's hand, and they wandered further along the main street. It wasn't long before they found Chaos standing on top of one of the benches, a group of older children huddled, rapt, in front of him.

Chaos held out his hand, his fingers bent into an imaginary claw. "And then I sliced him with my talons!" he cried. "All the way through!"

Cooper was on the sidelines, looking on with amused fondness, and Matty approached him. "Um, what's he doing?"

Cooper's grin grew wider. "He's reenacting a deadly Mafia meeting for these innocent children."

"And is he...allowed to do that?"

"They think it's a made-up story."

Matty watched Chaos slice through the air with vengeful glee. "Isn't it a little violent?"

Cooper shrugged. "Have you seen the movies these kids watch these days?"

It was true that the children were all smiles as they stared up at the cackling chaos demon. One of them was holding an ice cream cone, and Matty gazed at it longingly. He hadn't had ice cream in ages.

Nightmare gave Matty's hand a squeeze, then let it fall. "I will fetch you some, sweet."

"Um." Matty tried to think of a polite way to ask his question and came up short. "Do you even know how to use human money?"

But Nightmare was already gliding away in the direction of the small ice cream shop on the corner. Matty frowned after him.

"Chaos and I will watch out for you," Cooper reassured him.

"It's not that." Matty narrowed his eyes at a group of women in their twenties, whose attention was fixed on Nightmare's retreating form already. "What if someone tries to touch him?"

"Then I think he'll probably bite their head off. Possibly literally?"

"Oh. Right." That had Matty feeling better, actually.

There was a burst of flame from the bench, followed by oohs and aahs from the children. Cooper ran forward. "Bracchus! Not the—the special effects, please."

It must have been tough keeping up with a chaos demon. Matty was lucky to have gotten Nightmare. He was so...calm. Steady. Murderous but in a refined way.

A large figure approached, and Matty tensed, if only for a moment. The man was broad and muscular, with dark hair freshly grown out from a buzz cut.

And then Matty recognized him, and his tension melted. He grinned shyly. "Benny!"

"Little dude!" Benny lifted his huge palm for a high five, and Matty gave it to him.

Benny was Seth's older cousin who did odd jobs around town. Matty had a hard time keeping track of them all, but he knew Benny was a regular bouncer at the Lighthouse.

But Matty had gotten to know him from his side job of delivering food for the apps.

Matty liked him. It was easy to like Benny. He was friendly without being pushy, and he was never offended when Matty didn't have the stomach for people and selected the "leave it on the porch" option for delivery. Benny would just rap on the front door, yell, "Dinner's on, little dude!" and walk away.

Matty trusted him, and he couldn't say that for many humans. Benny had been gone for weeks already this summer, and Matty had kind of missed him.

A throat cleared pointedly, and Matty realized there was someone else with Benny, standing a little behind him. A stunning man with wavy dark hair, aristocratic features, and shockingly bright turquoise eyes.

Bright, *cold* eyes, and they were narrowed on Matty.

Matty took a step back, the shadow on his chest vibrating against him.

"Oh." Benny clapped his companion on the shoulder. "Right. Matty, this is my boyfriend, Helio. He's a little shy."

The guy didn't look shy. He looked...mean. "Oh. Hi. I'm—"

A pale, tattooed arm wrapped around Matty's middle, pulling him against a warm chest. "Do not give him your name, sweet."

"Benny already knows my name?" Matty couldn't help phrasing it like a question. Nightmare seemed tense, and Matty wasn't socially adept enough to navigate whatever was going on here.

"The fae," Nightmare rasped. "No names. No favors."

Was he talking about the cold-eyed man, Helio?

Helio, who was now tugging at Benny's arm, whispering furiously in his ear.

Benny's eyes widened. "Oh, that guy's a devil too?" he asked, pointing at Nightmare, his voice at a completely regular volume, like he wasn't even attempting to lower it. "Like Kai?"

Matty gaped. "You know Kai's a demon?"

Helio sneered in Matty's direction. "If he didn't, you would have just confirmed it."

A rumble left Nightmare's chest—a clear warning.

Benny only laughed. "Be nice, babe," he said to Helio. He grinned at Matty. "I deliver at your house a lot. You all seem to forget that people can see through the windows when the curtains are open." He gestured to the top of his head. "Those horns, you know."

"Have you...told anyone?"

"Um, no." Benny scratched at his chin. "It's a secret, right?"

"Yeah, it is." Matty didn't know what to do in this situation, and he found himself giving Benny a thumbs-up. "Thanks."

The two supernaturals seemed to be in a strange staring contest now, both of them vibrating with tension as they glared at each other.

"This is Nightmare," Matty told Benny while they waited it out. "You can call him Night. He's—" Matty paused. *Boyfriend* didn't seem right. And *husband* wasn't technically correct either. "He's mine," he concluded.

"Right on." Benny raised his hand for a fist bump, only to have Helio tug it back down again immediately.

But he and Nightmare seemed to have come to some sort of unspoken truce, because Nightmare finally spoke again. "There will be danger," he said, apparently talking to Helio. "Take your mate."

"Oh! Take Seth too," Matty added. He wanted to be sure his friendly neighborhood baker was safe.

Helio gave a stilted nod and began pulling Benny away. Benny waved as he was tugged in the other direction. "Nice to see you, little dude!"

Matty watched him go, patting at Nightmare's arm around his chest. "That's Benny. We like him, just so you know."

"Is Benny short for Benjamin?"

"What?"

"The accountant?"

Who the fuck? It took Matty a minute to catch up. "Oh. You heard Kai? Benny's just Benny. There's no Benjamin the accountant. Kai was just—"

"Meddling," Nightmare finished for him.

"He wasn't meddling." It wasn't like Kai had actually tried to steer Matty away from Nightmare after he'd realized they were bonded. Or maybe he had, but he hadn't done a very good job. "He was just...adjusting."

Nightmare released his hold, turning Matty to face him. His dark human gaze bore into Matty's. "There will be no accountants for you, Matteo."

It sounded like a threat, but it only made Matty grin.

"I know." He rose onto his toes to kiss his demon, then stopped when he saw what was in Nightmare's other hand. "Oh! My ice cream! Thank you, Scary."

Maybe it wasn't so bad after all, being out and about in town. Not when Matty had Nightmare at his side.

_____

18

Nightmare

It was on the third day of Nightmare escorting Matteo around town that Matteo finally saw another familiar face, this one not so welcome.

Nightmare had just finished fetching his mate his ice cream cone for the day, and they were sitting on one of the town's benches as Matteo discussed the local wildlife.

"I don't think I'd mind being a seagull," he mused, watching one of the birds in question dive to the sidewalk to snatch an errant french fry. "They get to live by the coast and steal human food, but they don't get the bad reputation of, say, a pigeon." His brow furrowed as he considered. "But there's something lonely about birds, I think. Maybe because they don't have anywhere cozy to go. Bird nests are just so open to the elements. If I were a fox, I could have a little den." He took a lick of ice cream, turning to Nightmare. "What do you think?"

Nightmare had no interest in being any earthly creature at all, but he'd play the game for his mate. "One of the big cats in the mountains," he said after a moment. "Solitary, with a large territory. I'd protect your fox den from intruders."

Nightmare was rewarded with a huge, beaming grin from his mate.

And then, a moment later, the soul connection between them thrummed with shock, and the ice cream fell from Matteo's hands.

Nightmare's shadows caught the dessert before it could hit the ground.

They were always close at hand now, his shadows. Where once they hadn't ever deigned to emerge while Nightmare was in his lesser human form, they now tucked themselves into his clothing, waiting for any opportunity to rush out in secret to swarm their mate.

But Matteo didn't reach for the little cone suspended in air, and eventually the shadows let it drop to the sidewalk.

Nightmare followed Matteo's dismayed gaze to a wiry blond man who was pretending to read a newspaper in one of the outside seating areas of the local café.

"Dominico?" Nightmare asked, though he didn't think Matteo's reaction was in keeping with his greatest fear come to life.

"No," Matteo said dully. "But...one of his."

The man rose unhurriedly from his seat, tossing cash on the table before walking off, the newspaper left behind.

"Is that it?" Matteo asked. "Just let him see me? He *did* see me, right?"

Nightmare sent one of his curious shadows after the man to make sure they didn't lose his trail, then rose from the bench, holding out his hand. "Come."

The two of them followed Nightmare's shadow, which led them away from the downtown area and into the surrounding neighborhood. They came around the corner to find the man had stopped under a tree and was digging his phone out of his pocket.

About to report to his master, no doubt.

Swifter than a breath, Nightmare strode forward, letting his human nails extend into talons and pierce the man's neck, his venom seeping out eagerly. Nightmare kept it to a light dose—this man wasn't meant to meet death so soon. Not when he still had a role to play in their plans.

Nightmare pulled the man's slack form into a dark patch of grass hidden by the trees and let his shadows pour forth, delving in through the cracks and crevices of his mind. The shadows found the man's recent memories, and Nightmare began to twist them.

"Are you— What are you doing?" Matteo asked. He'd crept up to Nightmare's side, huddling into him in a way where he didn't come into contact with the man Nightmare held.

"He'll remember seeing you," Nightmare explained. "But he'll also remember you speaking about exactly where you'll be Friday night. You said you didn't want Dominico finding you in Sascha's home."

"And he won't remember this moment? You attacking him?"

Nightmare grinned at his shadows, busy in their work. "No."

The man would be lucky to have the majority of his wits left when Nightmare was done with him. His shadows weren't being particularly careful, and Nightmare wasn't in the mood to admonish them—not when this man's very presence had cast such a pall over their day.

"Make me happy in the memory, when he sees me," Matteo requested, a mere whisper in Nightmare's ear. "Make sure I'm smiling and laughing. Dominico will hate that."

Nightmare hummed his agreement, but he didn't share his second task as he delved into the man's mind. Didn't share that he was searching deeper into those recent memories until he came upon a face. A man perhaps in his mid-fifties, with graying hair and a thin-lipped sneer. He was tall and broad-shouldered, with a butterfly knife he kept flicking through his fingers as he barked out orders to the group surrounding him.

Dominico Caruso.

Nightmare couldn't scent the man's soul through memories, but he knew it would be vile, rotten to the core in every sense. He kept the vision of the human in his mind's eye.

He'd know who to search for now.

"He looks uncomfortable," Matteo said after a moment.

"It's very painful to have your memories tampered with." Or perhaps it was only Nightmare's methods. It mattered little to him. This stranger had pledged his allegiance to the wrong man—pain was his due.

But Matteo didn't chastise or balk. He cocked his head, eyeing the agonized expression on the blond's face. "Good," he said quietly. "I'm glad."

And Nightmare realized in an instant that, for his mate to be so bloodthirsty, Matteo must have been hurt by this cretin, either directly or by way of this man delivering him to Dominico.

It was more difficult than Nightmare could have imagined, not killing the man that very second.

But Matteo was counting on Nightmare. So when his task was done, Nightmare released the man, letting him fall to the grass in a tangled slump. He'd sleep off what had been done to him and wake up with the memories Nightmare had created. He'd report to his leader, as intended, and Dominico would come.

And then this man would die.

Nightmare toed at the sprawled form with his booted foot. "I look forward to ripping your heart out of your chest," he hissed.

He turned, wrapping an arm around Matteo. "Shall we get you another dessert?"

"No." Matteo shook his head, his gaze still fixed on the unconscious man. "Take me home, please."

———

WHEN THEY ARRIVED at Sascha's home, Matteo tugged Nightmare past the living room, where the warrior and the chaos demon were playing some card game that had Kaisyir glowering and Chaos cackling.

"Do not disturb until further notice!" Matteo yelled out as he hurried Nightmare up the stairs.

His words only made Chaos cackle all the harder.

Once in the bedroom, Matteo began shedding his clothing at an alarming rate, coming much too close to falling on his face as he attempted to tug his pants off before removing his sneakers.

Nightmare's shadows began helping him as Nightmare switched back to his demon form, stretching his neck in relief as the weight of his antlers settled into place.

Matteo sent a glare Nightmare's way as he climbed naked onto the bed. "No clothes."

Nightmare sent his clothes off into the ether.

Matteo lay on his belly over the covers, tugging a pillow under his hips. "Like before," he said. Demanded, really.

"I assume you refer to our mating?" Nightmare asked, his voice laced with amusement and no small amount of arousal. As rushed as this seduction was, it was impossible not to feel desire with his mate splayed before him, his perfectly round globes of flesh propped into the air.

They hadn't had a chance to repeat their act of penetration yet, much to Nightmare's dismay. There were too many people in this damned house, and Matteo was often impatient to find release in other ways when they finally had time to themselves.

Apparently today Matteo's impatience ran in another direction.

"I want you to fuck me, and I want your petals to do their thing, and I want you to keep fucking me while they do, and then I want to fall asleep tonight with you still inside me." Matteo looked over his shoulder to Nightmare looming at the foot of the bed. "Is that too much?"

It would never be too much—not in this lifetime or any other —but Nightmare climbed onto the bed, pulling gently at Matteo's shoulder until he was flat on his back. Nightmare pressed Matteo's thighs up and back and settled himself between them, cupping Matteo's fretful face. "I won't let him harm you," he promised.

"I know you won't." Matteo blinked large brown eyes at him. "But I need—" He bit at his lip, shaking his head. "I just *need*."

"And you will get what you need, little mate," Nightmare soothed, rubbing his thumb over Matteo's cheek. "But I would look at you while I claim you."

"Oh." Matteo's gaze softened even as he pouted. "Okay."

Nightmare dipped his head, stealing a kiss from those pouting lips. He couldn't help but slip his tongue inside, and Matteo groaned, sucking eagerly as he always did. Nightmare let his heavy cock slide up and down along Matteo's hardened member, teasing them both.

Nightmare knew this pliant state wouldn't last long, not when Matteo was so desperate for physical reassurance. So he gathered the viscous precum from his cock, using blunted fingertips to work the slick substance into Matteo. Nightmare didn't take his time with it, not this time. Matteo was too impatient—too unsettled— and Nightmare wasn't cruel enough to make him wait.

So Nightmare did the best he could, distracting Matteo with gentle nips and fevered kisses, and he managed to get two fingers in before Matteo started biting at Nightmare's tongue and pressing up his hips, wordlessly demanding his due.

Although, he didn't stay silent for long.

"Fuck me," Matteo panted when Nightmare growled at him in reprimand for knocking away Nightmare's fingers. "You promised."

And since Nightmare intended to keep each and every promise he made to his little human, he notched the fat, spongy head of his cock to his mate's entrance and pressed in.

Matteo moaned in eager abandon, wrapping his legs tightly around Nightmare's hips as he bore down and let him in. Nightmare hissed at the tight squeeze, the way Matteo's inner walls sucked in the head and pressed at his so-called petals, urging him ever deeper.

Matteo wound his arms tight around Nightmare's neck as he bottomed out. "Yes," he sighed, some of the tension melting from his frame. "Yes, yes. More of that, please."

Nightmare rocked his hips back and drove in again, battling Matteo's body for dominion. The slick of his precum eased the glide as he fucked into him, biting at that tender neck with blunted teeth. He allowed his shadows free rein, letting them swarm and caress and squeeze until Matteo was crying out in no time at all, splattering his own sweet belly with creamy white cum.

Nightmare sped up his pace, a growl erupting from his throat. The shoddy human bed banged against the wall again and again.

Matteo whimpered and whined and urged him on, lifting his hips again and again despite the shudders that racked his frame from his drawn-out release. "All of it," he ordered, biting savagely into Nightmare's pec. "You promised."

His display of sweet, tender viciousness spiraled through Nightmare like a flame, setting his nerves alight. He could feel Matteo's need through the bond, the ache of his want. The way he coveted being surrounded by Nightmare in every way. The hole inside him that the usual mechanics of sex weren't enough to fill.

Matteo needed to be bred and locked in place, claimed by Nightmare inside and out. Consumed by him until nothing was left but the bond they shared with each other.

Nightmare groaned, and as he spilled inside his mate with one last hard press of his hips, he could feel the sweet relief of his petals expanding, making a home within Matteo's tight passage.

Apparently Matteo could feel it too.

"Yes, yes, yes," he chanted, digging his heels into Nightmare's ass as he clawed at his back, rocking and writhing until those petals had locked into place and he was forced to still.

Nightmare stroked every bit of skin he could reach. There was nothing like it in this world or any other, to be lodged so deep inside his mate. To have his cock squeezed like a vise as he emptied his seed into such a welcoming vessel.

Matteo's sigh was pure relief as he smiled up at Nightmare, still wrapped tight as a limpet around him. "Thank you, Scary." His smile fell immediately into a concerned frown as he took stock. "You're all hunched though. Did you really think this position through?"

In answer, Nightmare rolled them with ease until his mate was on top of him, his thighs to either side of Nightmare's hips.

"Oh." Matty pressed his hands to Nightmare's taut stomach, regaining his balance with a small giggle. "Hello."

"Better, sweet?" Nightmare stroked his hands down Matteo's thighs, and Matteo leaned down until he was plastered to Nightmare's chest, his cheek to Nightmare's sternum. He wiggled his bottom, and Nightmare groaned as his cock was massaged by the move, spurting weakly inside his mate.

"Oh yes," Matteo sighed. "This is good."

He relaxed in Nightmare's hold, trusting Nightmare to keep him comfortable and safe and free of pain, and Nightmare accepted it for the gift it was.

19

Matty

The room was dark and quiet, and everything was still. And yet Matteo already knew who was there beside him.

Maybe his body had registered the new weight on the bed, or maybe his brain had realized there should still be a light shining from the TV. He'd fallen asleep with it on, hadn't he?

But there was no light when Matteo opened his eyes. Someone had turned it off.

"Matteo," a familiar voice called in a crooning whisper. "Matteo, Matteo, Matteo."

Matteo could just make out the dim outline on the edge of his bed. Close enough that they were almost touching. The man had his back turned, Matteo was pretty sure.

It didn't matter. Matteo knew who had come to haunt him.

"Dominico," he said. The one time Matteo had refused to acknowledge the apparition, he'd been made to regret it. "You're back."

"I heard you misbehaved while I was away."

Matteo swallowed with difficulty, his throat dry. Of course

Dominico had already been told. One of his spies had probably reported everything the moment it had happened. Dominico had no doubt hurried back early to ensure he'd be the one to mete out punishment.

"Maybe Luca will let me take something this time," Dominico mused. "You don't need all ten fingers to be such a wretched disappointment. Or toes, for that matter."

All ten of Matteo's digits curled in on themselves without his permission, but he tried not to move otherwise. Quiet and still was always the best option.

"You should have just done what the old bastard wanted."

But Matteo couldn't have. He'd been ordered to execute the wife of a traitor—a bloody message to deter any other defections. But the woman had been innocent; she hadn't known anything about what her husband had done. She hadn't done anything to warrant pain or death.

Dominico clucked his tongue. "Well, she's gone now anyway. Begged and pleaded and wept for hours. Would've been quicker if you'd done it."

Matteo bit back sudden tears. He'd known his refusal was a stupid, meaningless gesture. But even with a gun in his hand and Luca at his back, he hadn't been able to pull the trigger. He'd never been able to. Not once.

The mattress shifted as Dominico turned to face him. Matteo's eyes had adjusted to the dark now—enough to see that there was blood on the older man's face. Probably on his hands and his clothes too, judging from past experience. Most likely Matteo's sheets would be covered with it in the morning.

"He's growing tired of you, Matteo." Dominico rested a hand on Matteo's face, and Matteo had to swallow down bile at the wet, sticky touch. "But don't worry." Dominico started rubbing a calloused thumb over Matteo's cheekbone. "I won't grow tired. I'm going to keep you alive for ages, Matteo. I'm going to find every tender spot you never knew you had and make it bleed. I'm going to take off bits and pieces so slowly you'll forget you ever lost them."

Matteo didn't dare move. He hardly dared breathe.

Dominico grinned at him, white teeth flashing in the dark. "How's your back, hm? Has it healed yet?"

It hadn't. Matteo's skin was still raw, the cuts scabbed over in places that kept breaking open and bleeding when he moved in the wrong way.

Dominico leaned in close, looming over Matteo, his breath hot in Matteo's ear. "So quiet in the dark," he whispered, the soft croon of a lover. "But don't worry, Matteo. We'll fix that. You're going to scream and scream and scream."

With a final pat to Matteo's cheek, Dominico rose from the bed. "Time to make my report to dear Luca. But I'll be seeing you soon."

A crack of light illuminated the room as he opened the door. Enough for Matteo to see the bulge in his pants as he made his way out.

He did so love to make Matteo afraid.

Matteo stared into the dark of his silent room, feeling each second slip away. Dominico would make his report, and then Luca's men would come for Matteo. They'd take him down to that horrible basement and tie him down, and Dominico would meticulously reopen all Matteo's wounds, no doubt adding a few more to the collection.

It would hurt. Matteo would cry.

He always cried.

Luca might watch, or he might let his psychotic dog do it all on his own. It didn't seem to matter much to Luca either way. All that mattered was that Matteo had refused to do what he was supposed to do. Refused to kill a weeping woman who hadn't done anything wrong except choose a stupid husband.

And in the dark, with his back still burning from the last time he'd disobeyed Luca's orders, Matteo couldn't even decide if it had been worth it. Couldn't figure out if it was morals or cowardice that stayed his hand each and every time.

It was probably cowardice.

And that made him just as bad as any of them.

———

MATTY BLINKED AT THE WALL. He didn't know why he'd let his mind go there, back to that dark time. He couldn't even blame the influence of sleep. He hadn't been dreaming; he'd been remembering—one night like so many others.

Nightmare's arm tightened around him. "You think of dark things, little mate."

Matty shuffled to face him, peering up at his demon in the midmorning light. Nightmare had done exactly what Matty had asked the night before: he'd fucked and fucked him until Matty had fallen asleep with Nightmare still inside him. Matty had woken up in the middle of the night to Nightmare withdrawing carefully from his body, his shadows trailing over Matty to clean up the mess.

It had been the exact kind of comfort Matty had needed—or, more accurately, demanded. And yet the morning still seemed bathed in foreboding now that he was awake.

"Dark memories," Matty told Nightmare.

It was obvious why they were bubbling up, even if Matty didn't want to admit it. Because tomorrow night was the night Dominico would come for him. Matty was sure of it, despite the fact they didn't have any confirmation. He could *feel* it.

"I could take them from you," Nightmare offered, his white eyes flat as they bore into Matty. "The dark memories. I could do it with very little pain."

Matty considered for only a moment before shaking his head. "Too much of myself is wrapped up in them, I think. I wouldn't be me without them."

"Who you are has nothing to do with that scum," Nightmare hissed, his shadows swirling around him, as if in agreement.

Their ire had Matty feeling weirdly calm despite the dark memories. "Maybe. Maybe not. But one day, a long time from now, they'll be so distant they won't mean a thing to me. They'll have no power." He scooted up in the bed until he could plant an easy kiss on Nightmare's frowning mouth. "It's something to look forward to."

Nightmare stole another, deeper kiss from Matty before letting out a sigh. "The incubus is here with his mobster. I can hear them all chattering."

Matty wanted to sigh too. He was loath to leave this cozy cocoon they'd made, one that was full of Nightmare's warmth and his smoky scent. Loath to let time move on and take him that much closer to tomorrow.

Because one day, yes, those memories of the pain he'd suffered would be distant. But Matty had to face Dominico first, and that thought still made his throat dry and his palms sweat, even with his demon close at hand.

But staying in bed wouldn't actually stop time, would it?

"Okayyy." Matty dragged himself out of bed, tugging Nightmare by the hand up after him. He whirled with a sudden thought before they reached the door. "He doesn't flirt with you, does he? Nix?"

Nightmare's lips twitched up at the corners. "He doesn't dare."

Matty let out a breath, his shoulders slumping with relief. "Good."

Nix was basically a gorgeous supermodel of a demon, and Ivan was incredibly protective of him. Matty didn't want to make any moves that would piss Ivan off, but he also might not have been able to stop himself from snarling if Nix acted all flirty and seductive with Nightmare in front of him.

Matty led them down the stairs to find everyone gathered in the living room. Sascha and Ivan were sitting next to each other on the couch. Nix was next to Ivan with his legs slung over his mate's lap. Kai was standing at the arm of the couch by Sascha, his big arms crossed. Chaos and Cooper were on the other side of the room in one of the armchairs together.

Everyone seemed to be getting along, although Ivan was

eyeing Chaos warily. But Chaos was too busy nuzzling Cooper in his lap to take notice.

Nix's eyebrows rose at Matty and Nightmare's appearance in the doorway. "Well, well," he purred, shooting Matty a wink. "We were told not to disturb you. I wonder why?"

Matty's cheeks went hot, and Chaos let out a taunting, "Ooh! You're asking for it, Nix!"

All eyes were on Matty and Nightmare now, and Ivan's gaze was particularly appraising as he took in Nightmare's tall, antlered form. "*That* is what I was hoping to summon," he said after a moment. "That air of menace."

"Vanya!" Nix scolded. "You'll hurt my feelings." He dug his toes into Ivan's thigh. "And I guarantee Nightmare wouldn't let you bend him over any office desks, even at your most charming."

Sascha let out a disgusted noise. "When is Ivan ever charming?"

Nix graced him with a catlike smile. "Oh, you'd be surprised."

Ivan wrapped a hand around Nix's foot, his gaze molten. "There's only one demon I'll be bending over anything, and he's already mine to have."

For some reason, Matty couldn't make himself take a seat in their midst. He was suddenly frozen there in the doorway, unsure of himself. Everyone here had so much history together, related by blood or a bond. And they were so beautiful, the demons and humans both. He felt small and inexperienced and wholly inadequate.

But then Nightmare's arms wrapped around him, lifting Matty with ease until Nightmare was sitting cross-legged on the floor, facing the others with Matty tucked in his lap.

The room went silent, even Nix's purple eyes widening in surprise.

"Comfortable, sweet?" Nightmare asked quietly.

"Yes." Matty snuggled deeper into Nightmare's lap, his

momentary uncertainty gone. These were his friends, Sascha and Kai at the very least. And this was his mate. And Matty belonged. "Thank you, Scary."

Nix choked on air, the opposite of his usual elegant poise, and Chaos cackled.

"I tooold you," he sang.

Nix seemed to take a moment to get his bearings, and then he cocked his head at Ivan. "Well, maybe if you were Matty, Nightmare *would* let you bend—"

"Incubus," Nightmare warned.

Nix immediately held his hands up in a placating gesture. "Sorry, sorry. Shutting up now."

"Are we clear on tomorrow night?" Ivan asked, and Matty realized with a start that the mobster had directed the question at him.

He took comfort in Nightmare's warmth as he answered, "Um, yes. Sascha and I will go out with Kai and Nightmare. Presumably Dominico has already realized I'm staying with Sascha, so it's not like we have to be discreet. Cooper and Chaos will arrive separately—Dominico won't know about them yet. And you and Nix...?" Matty trailed off.

"We'll be close enough to help out if necessary but not be seen," Ivan finished for him. "My presence poses too much of a risk of Dominico pulling out."

"What if Dominico doesn't show?" Nix asked, looking at Matty with what might have been concern. "What if he just sends one of his men to grab you?"

Matty let out a breath, reminding himself he was safe. He and Nightmare had discussed this already, and he knew the answer.

"Then we let me be taken," he said. "Nightmare will sense if you need to intervene before we get to him. And I won't be alone." He pulled down the collar of his T-shirt just enough to show where one of Nightmare's shadows was nestled. Matty wasn't sure if it was the same little guy as before or if they'd switched out. It kind of *felt* like the same one though.

Sascha frowned, twisting his hands in his lap. "Let's hope it doesn't come to that. I don't like the idea of you getting taken elsewhere. And if this Dominico *does* show...?"

"Then he's mine," Nightmare rasped, and the naked violence in his voice sent a shiver down Matty's spine.

He gathered himself just in time to see Nix pinch Ivan's thigh viciously. "Stop ogling him. You got what you got, and you should be *grateful*."

Huh. Maybe it wasn't Nix's attention Matty needed to worry about. His demon had so many admirers—Matty just hadn't expected Ivan to be one of them.

20

Matty

Matty turned his head to the right, then to the left. He wrinkled his nose. Pursed his lips. Stuck out his tongue.

"What do you think?" Sascha asked.

They were in Sascha and Kai's bedroom, and Matty was sitting on a little padded stool in front of Sascha's vanity, taking stock of what the mirror showed him.

Matty kind of thought a lot of product had been used to make his hair do what it always did—fall messily wherever it wanted—but Sascha had spent a lot of time on it, so Matty settled on, "It's nice."

Sascha frowned at him in the vanity mirror, then sighed. "I'll take it." He held up a small dark pencil. "How do you feel about eyeliner?"

"I have no feelings about eyeliner whatsoever," Matty answered truthfully.

Sascha put his hands on his hips, which kind of made Matty

think it had been the wrong answer. "We don't have to do this, you know. Doll you up."

"I don't mind," Matty told him. After a moment, he shifted in his seat. "But, um, why *are* we doing this? Dolling me up?"

Matty had been coming out of his room with Nightmare in tow when Sascha had basically dragged Matty into his bedroom, declaring they only had a few hours to get ready and needed to get "straight to work."

Matty had planned to go to the Lighthouse just as he was, so he hadn't realized there was work to be done in the first place.

Sascha adjusted a few of Matty's wayward strands. "Because you've never really come out with us before, and I thought we could make the night a little fun and not just all doom and gloom. Plus, Seth's shown me some makeup stuff and I've never gotten to practice on anyone else."

Matty *had* gone out with Sascha and Kai the one time, but in his fearful state, he'd convinced himself he'd seen a familiar face dancing in the crowd, and he'd run right out of the Lighthouse and basically sprinted home, hiding under his covers for the rest of the night.

Apparently Sascha didn't count that time.

"Oh." Matty smiled at his friend. "That's really nice." He nodded to the pencil Sascha still held. "I'll try it."

Sascha bent low and started swiping the pencil along Matty's lash line. After a few minutes, he leaned back, narrowing his eyes to assess his work. He nodded once, seemingly satisfied, then leaned back to let Matty take a look.

Matty blinked at his reflection in the mirror. His big eyes seemed...even bigger. And maybe a little sultry?

He turned on his stool to face Nightmare, who was sitting silently in the corner, wreathed in shadow. Sascha had sent him wary glances every few seconds in the beginning, but he seemed to have gotten used to the demon's presence by now.

"What do you think?" Matty asked.

"Pretty," Nightmare rasped.

Sascha clapped his hands. "So! For clothes. Our styles are...not aligned, you could say."

That was true enough. Sascha had once told Matty that he was detoxing from all the whites, blacks, and grays he'd been made to wear as a representative of his Mafia family. Now he favored bright colors and—when the weather permitted—as little clothing as possible.

But Matty didn't mind whites, blacks, and grays. And he didn't mind being covered head to toe either. He supposed his style could be defined as both cozy and boring.

"But," Sascha mused, wandering over to his closet, "I do have this black mesh thingy I wore to one of the Lighthouse's themed parties." He held up what seemed to be a very small scrap of fabric, one with tons of tiny little holes. "What do you think?"

"Oh." Matty considered. "Um..."

He looked to Nightmare, who remained expressionless in the corner. Then Matty raised the bottom of his shirt enough that Sascha could see some of the crisscrossed white lines that ran along his skin. "I usually prefer to keep these covered. My chest and my back. Mesh might not work."

Sascha blinked. He blinked again. Then suddenly his pale-blue eyes were swimming with tears. "Oh, Matty."

Matty had never heard his name sound so sad.

"It's okay," Matty reassured his friend, lowering his shirt back down. "They don't hurt or anything."

Sascha wiped at his eyes. Luckily he'd done Matty's makeup first—if he'd been wearing the same eyeliner, it would have smeared everywhere.

When he'd scrubbed the tears away, Sascha's face twisted into a surprisingly fierce look. "You know, I was annoyed at the time, having to do Ivan's dirty work. But I'm glad Kai killed Luca. He should have made it last longer." He sniffed once, then turned back to his closet. "Okay. So what are you comfortable showing? Do you want long-sleeved?"

"My arms are fine."

Sascha dug around and then came out with a sleeveless black shirt with a high neckline. "This and jeans, then. I have a loose-fitting pair. Comfy and very *in* right now, the oversize look. With your coloring and that black eyeliner, you're going to look hot as fuck." He winced in Nightmare's direction. "You know, objectively speaking."

Matty grinned at him. "That sounds nice." He reached out and grasped Sascha's wrist gently. "*You've* been nice. Thank you for taking me in. And for being so patient. You've been very good to a stray."

Sascha glared at him. "You're not a stray, Matty. You're family. Fuck the Carusos. As far as I'm concerned, you're a Kozlov." He handed Matty the shirt and dug out a pair of jeans. "Okay, I'm going to find something bright and slutty for myself." And he disappeared fully into his closet.

Matty rose from his stool and walked over to Nightmare. His demon stayed seated, but he wrapped his big hands around Matty's hips, his face hidden by his shadows.

"Come with me to get changed?" Matty asked.

"Of course."

"Wait!"

Matty turned to find Sascha had returned, and he swiped something wet across Matty's cheeks.

"A little glitter. I can't resist. There!" And he walked away again.

Matty tilted his head at Nightmare. "What do you think?"

Nightmare's lips curled up at the corners. "Like the night sky."

Matty let out a long breath. "I'm nervous, but not as nervous as I could be. Because you're here." He tapped his chest, at the spot he could feel Nightmare's soul connection the strongest.

It had been Matty's one comfort throughout this long, tense day: his connection with his demon, and the emotions that had been filtering through their bond. Not just the dark devotion that was always there, wrapped around Matty like a blanket, but the bloodthirsty rage that had been growing by the minute.

Nightmare's rage.

"You're going to kill him for me," Matty said now. He wanted to hear it once more from his shadow-wrapped demon.

Nightmare didn't hesitate. "Yes, little mate."

Matty felt words bubbling up inside him. Important words. Words he wanted to say out loud more than anything. But he held them back.

For now.

There were ghosts and monsters to put down first.

————

MATTY WAS a little surprised to see the town's regular bouncer at the door to the Lighthouse.

Mostly because the town's regular bouncer was Benny, and Matty was fairly certain Nightmare had been a real bro and told Helio to take him and flee.

But here was Benny, in a sleeveless shirt he filled out very differently from how Matty filled out the one Sascha had given him. Helio was lurking beside him, glowering at every single person Benny let into the bar.

Benny's eyes lit up when he caught sight of their group. He pointed to Sascha and then Matty. "Little dude and little dude!"

So, yeah, maybe his nicknames weren't the most original in the world. Matty liked him anyway.

"You finally came to dance!" Benny held his fist up for a bump, and this time Matty got one in before Helio tugged his boyfriend's arm back down.

"Hey, um, Benny?" Matty stepped closer and lowered his voice to a whisper. "Weren't you supposed to be gone by now? You know, for the danger?"

"Oh, is that tonight?" Benny asked.

When Matty nodded, Helio hissed, "I knew it!" and Benny scratched at his head. "Well, I'm supposed to be the bar's protection. It would be kind of shitty of me to leave right when things got rough." He crossed his arms, his biceps bulging kind of obscenely. "Helio and I can make sure everyone gets out if things go down."

"I will do no such thing," Helio sneered.

Benny turned to him, and he didn't seem at all put out by Helio's unwillingness to help. "But think of how grateful people will be. You'll be owed, like, tons of favors."

Helio's eyes gleamed, and he seemed for a moment to...shift. Like he grew taller and brighter and a little more than human. "Mm. That's true..."

"And I'm the one asking you, so I'll owe you, like, extra."

Helio hummed in thought, looking at Benny in a way that made Matty feel like they should definitely be giving the two some privacy.

"Get rid of your friends," Helio said, echoing Matty's thoughts. "I want to start taking payment now."

"Okaaay." Matty sidled past, pulling Nightmare with him, Sascha and Kai following right behind. "We'll just... Bye, Benny!"

"Have a rad night!" Benny yelled after them, seemingly unconcerned that Helio was already squeezing at his pecs with deranged fervor.

The bar wasn't too full yet, but there were some people dancing already, grinding together to a pop remix Matty didn't recognize. Matty didn't see Seth in the crowd, so hopefully he'd either gotten out of town or, at the very least, stayed in for the night. Matty knew Sascha had texted him to keep his distance.

Cooper and Chaos were already stationed inside, both of them standing at the bar. Chaos had just been poured some shooter that had flames dancing on it, and he was laughing in delight as Cooper looked on fondly.

Sascha threw his arms up as the lights flashed. "Let's dance!"

"Oh." Matty sidestepped to the wall, where a high-top table with stools to sit at was open. "I'll just—" He gestured vaguely. "Over here."

Nightmare stayed standing beside him while Sascha and Kai made their way to the dance floor.

"I don't really dance," Matty admitted, peering up at his demon. Nightmare still looked disturbingly handsome in his human form, but at least he was covered up in a long-sleeved shirt. "Did you want to?"

Nightmare shook his head. "No, sweet."

They sat at their table and watched the dance floor. It was kind of nice, even. Although, the bartender kept bringing over drinks that one pretty man or another had sent for Nightmare. It was hard to tell who the culprits were as the crowd grew, with so many people checking Nightmare out, so Matty glowered in everyone's general direction to be safe.

They returned the drinks, telling the bartender to give them to whoever he pleased. Nightmare wasn't interested in human liquor, and Matty didn't want his mind impaired in any way. Not with what was at stake tonight.

Still, Matty could almost convince himself it was a fun night. Or at least, he could see how it might be in the future. The music had a good beat, and Sascha and Kai's version of dancing seemed to be mostly Kai standing still and pawing at Sacha while Sascha ground against him. Matty could probably manage that sometime —with Nightmare, not Kai, of course.

It had been almost an hour when Matty saw the first familiar face in one of the bar's dark corners. After that, it was only a matter of seconds before he spotted another. And then another.

Matty didn't see Dominico yet, but he suddenly knew it, deep in his bones.

Dominico was here.

Matty turned to let Nightmare know and saw that his demon had gone completely rigid.

And then Matty felt it through the bond: shock and dismay, or what Matty thought might be Nightmare's version of them. He looked to the dance floor to see Kai had stopped dancing and was standing just as stiffly, holding Sascha tightly to his side, as if to protect him from something.

And then Nix burst through the bar's entrance, with Benny and Helio right behind him. Benny started calmly directing confused patrons out the door as Nix made a beeline for their table. Matty saw Cooper and Chaos at the back entrance, letting out a small crowd of patrons there as the fire alarm went off.

"Sarkaron," Nix said, a desperate edge to his voice.

Nightmare nodded, scanning the crowd. "I know."

"What's going on?" Matty asked. He didn't think this reaction was just from Dominico's presence, if he really was on site. They'd planned for that contingency, and it didn't make sense that the demons were panicking. "What's happening?"

It was Nix who answered him, wringing his hands as Kai and Sascha ran up to their table. "There's another demon here. We can sense him."

"One of yours?" Matty asked. He didn't remember hearing about anybody else in the Void, but maybe—

"Ours isn't the only Book in the world, sweet."

Matty nodded uncertainly. He'd known that, he thought. Or maybe he'd only assumed.

And then the truth of it hit him, sudden and sure. The reason everyone was so upset.

Dominico hadn't just brought his men here to Seacliff.

Dominico had summoned a demon of his own.

21

Nightmare

Nightmare felt it a moment before the others: a sharp, electrical impulse in the air. It was oddly familiar, though Nightmare knew he'd never met a demon of this kind before. Familiar because this demon's powers, like his own, were rooted in suffering.

A pain demon.

Nightmare had heard of them, lurking in the depths of the demon realm. Other demons avoided them, so as not to become their next meal. They were known for being particularly ravenous, struggling to find a balance between keeping their prey alive long enough to feed and inadvertently killing them with the pain they inflicted.

Perhaps Nightmare should have felt some sort of kinship at its presence, solitary as his own existence had been in the demon realm. But this demon had been summoned to harm Matteo. There would be no kinship for it here. No mercy.

Nightmare kept watch for it as the bouncer and his fae mate

began shepherding humans out, as Nix and Sascha and Kaisyir all came to the table where he and Matteo sat. Nightmare couldn't find the creature, but he could feel its energy growing closer. Stronger.

Nightmare tried to break it to Matteo gently, that there were other demons that roamed this realm. And he watched as terrible understanding washed over Matteo's face, the knowledge that Dominico had a new kind of weapon with which to torment him.

Nightmare would never let that happen. This demon would not touch Matteo. It would not disturb one hair on his mate's head.

Nightmare would make sure of it.

Cooper and Chaos joined them, and even Chaos was remarkably subdued, throwing concerned glances toward his human.

"Protecting our mates comes first," Kaisyir growled.

As if there was any question.

"I'll get Matty, Sascha, and Cooper out," Nix offered quickly. "We'll meet with Ivan and get as far away as we can."

Nightmare inclined his head in agreement. As much as he was loath to let Matteo out of his sight, that was for the best. He couldn't have Matteo within reach of an enemy demon, and fighting and battle weren't in Nix's nature; the incubus would be particularly mismatched against another demon. Running was best.

"There are men here too," Matteo said, and Nightmare felt a fierce pride run through him at the steadiness in his mate's voice, quiet though it was. "Dominico's men."

Nightmare surveyed the bar. It was true that, now that the other patrons had run—the masses growing quickly panicked at the fire alarm and forced evacuation—a number of men remained glued to the walls, clutching at poorly hidden human guns. They weren't approaching the table or attempting to fire any shots. It was clear they weren't the main cavalry.

And there was a wiry blond Nightmare recognized.

"Kaisyir," Nightmare rasped.

Kaisyir cracked his knuckles. "I will handle the humans and their weapons. You and Chaos attend to the demon until I finish."

Chaos rubbed his hands together, his brown human eyes finally flashing with fire. "It's a pain demon, isn't it? It feels all prickly in the air. This is going to be fun."

Nightmare felt Matteo tugging at his sleeve. He lowered his head to his mate. "Nightmare," Matteo whispered, and his voice was no longer so steady.

"Go with Nix, sweet," Nightmare coaxed. "I will be with you as soon as I can. We will regroup."

Matteo was trembling now, tears welling in his big brown eyes. "I'm scared. Really scared."

Nightmare cupped his mate's cheeks. He could feel that electrical signal growing stronger. Nearer. They didn't have much time. "I know, sweet," he soothed. "But after tonight, it will be over. Dominico has contracted with a demon, and such a contract leaves a trace. Even if he were to escape, I'd be able to track him. We'll end this, with blood and pain. Just as I promised."

And then Nix was tugging Matteo away, and Nightmare had to allow his mate to be pulled from his side.

They hadn't been parted since Nightmare had been summoned to this realm. Nightmare hadn't realized how painful it would be to watch him go, only a single shadow on his person to keep him company in Nightmare's absence.

It was wrong. All wrong.

The human mates had only just escaped when the back door of the bar burst open to reveal a demon only slightly larger than Chaos, with glowing red eyes and elongated arms almost reaching the floor. He was bald but for two red horns jutting from his scalp, and his skin was a mottled, stony color.

And he was alone, no Dominico in sight.

There was no more time to mourn Matteo's absence. Nightmare, Kaisyir, and Chaos reverted to their demon forms instantly. Discretion was no longer their main concern, and only Dominico's doomed group of humans remained, anyway. Nightmare distantly registered their murmuring at the shift, but his focus was on the pain demon in front of him.

"Where is your summoner, demon?" Nightmare asked.

The creature's only answer was a snarling screech, loud enough to shatter glasses at the bar.

"Oooh, I like him," Chaos whispered, his skin smoldering with banked flames.

Kaisyir was already off, dispatching the screaming men with guns with practiced ease, even as bullets began sinking into his skin. It would take him only a few minutes to complete his task. Nightmare noted with particular satisfaction when a certain blond human man had his throat sliced by one of Kaisyir's knives. It wasn't quite the same as Nightmare ripping the man's heart out himself, but it would have to do.

The pain demon screeched again. Chaos, eager for violence as ever, leaped into the air with his talons outstretched, his small wings giving him the momentum to land at their visitor's feet.

But Chaos didn't get a chance to land.

He was immediately thrown back by a burst of energy from the enemy demon, engulfed in red light that crackled with electricity. The bar filled with a pungent scent, like burned rubber, as Chaos cried out.

The red light dissipated, and the little demon sat slumped on the floor for a moment, a hand to his chest. "Ouch," he said clearly, though he didn't sound too put out by it.

The pain demon let out another horrendous screech.

Nightmare sent his shadows toward it, letting them writhe through the available crevices into the creature's mind. But there was nothing to twist or manipulate there, no desires or fears or regrets. The creature was a void inside, its only imperatives the distribution of agony and the aims of its contract: capturing Matteo for its master.

Nightmare didn't know if that emptiness was in his nature or a twisted side effect of his particular contract, but the result was unsettling, even to Nightmare's shadows.

They swarmed out of the demon's mind and returned to Nightmare's side, chittering with unease.

Then Chaos was up in the air once more. His flames erupted in front of him, clearing a path, and he was able to get close to the pain demon this time. Close enough to slice deeply through the pain demon's arm, but also close enough for Chaos to be wounded in return. The pain demon got his talons into Chaos's side, and he used his bloody hold to toss the little demon away from him.

Chaos landed on the ground again, his wings crumpled underneath him.

This time, Chaos didn't rise. He didn't cackle in delight at his unexpected defeat. He only slumped onto the floor, twitching and moaning weakly.

The pain demon must have had venom in his talons, as Nightmare did.

The creature screeched and stalked over to Chaos.

Nightmare let out a warning growl, allowing his limbs to lengthen and his skull mask to appear from the ether to protect his face.

Whatever poison he'd been given, Bracchus would recover or he wouldn't. But either way, this pain demon wasn't going to live long enough to deliver a killing blow.

Nightmare approached the two of them. The pain demon sent a burst of its electrical energy his way, and Nightmare's shadows swarmed to take the hit.

They shrieked with pain, their cries operating at a frequency higher than a human could register, and Nightmare mourned their suffering. His devoted companions, his weapons and his friends.

But it was for Matteo, this pain. Nightmare and his shadows would take any amount of suffering for that.

Nightmare could feel it now, his mate's fear and anxiety, brought to a boil by the wretch who had summoned this new monster. They would pay for making Matteo go through such anguish again, this demon and its master.

Nightmare stretched out a spidery limb, and the pain demon swiped at him with its talons. Nightmare didn't attempt to dodge them. They caught in Nightmare's skin, and fire licked up Nightmare's veins—the poison trying to achieve its aims—but he kept going, straight into those mad red eyes, locking his talons in and letting his own venom flow.

The pain demon screeched and flailed, clawing at Nightmare's arms with all the fervor of a caged animal.

More venom. More poison. That fire spread through Nightmare, and his muscles twitched and jolted with agony. His shadows roamed inward, racing through his veins, trying to combat the venom as best they could.

It didn't matter if they were successful. Nightmare would not falter.

Too much was at stake.

Eventually the demon in his clutches went still—paralyzed by Nightmare's venom—and Nightmare dropped it to the ground, clenching and unclenching his fist as his muscles continued to spasm.

He turned to find Kaisyir cradling a limp Chaos in his arms.

"You have your knives?" Nightmare asked.

Kaisyir possessed demon steel, and its use would be necessary here. A demon couldn't be killed by human weapons, and even sharp talons were no match for demonic bone and sinew.

"I do," Kaisyir said darkly.

"Allow me five minutes to search. Then decapitate it. Have Chaos burn the remains."

Perhaps Nightmare should have mourned the need to end the life of one of his own, but he couldn't find the empathy to spare. This creature had made its choice, and its soul would return to the realm from which it had come, dispersing there.

It was a better fate than it deserved.

Nightmare crouched down, breathing in the scent of the demon on the floor. Its essence itched Nightmare's nostrils, and Nightmare's muscles were still spasming from the poison inside him, but he kept at it, marking the tendrils of the contract this creature had made.

He stood, keeping his beastly shape. If a townsperson saw him, so be it.

Nightmare had a human to hunt.

22

Matty

Everything was chaos outside the Lighthouse, and Matty didn't mean the demon.

Most of the patrons who'd been shepherded out by Benny were milling around, in various stages of drunkenness and annoyance. Helio looked about ready to strangle anyone who dared speak to him, but Benny was just gently and cheerfully pushing people in the direction of the main street, trying to clear the area without causing a panic.

Matty had his hand in Cooper's, and he was grateful for the reassuring touch after having to leave Nightmare's side. They were being guided by a determined Nix through the crowd, but it was slow going with how tightly everybody was packed.

Matty was in a sort of daze. He couldn't help but focus inward, on the feel of Nightmare through the bond. Matty might have been imagining it, but he thought he could catch a sense of Nightmare's dark focus and deadly intent.

The pain demon must have been something really vicious, for Nightmare to be so engrossed.

And it was that thought that was sending Matty spiraling. What if Nightmare got hurt? Could he be *killed* by this demon?

He couldn't be—Matty wouldn't allow it. He'd been promised forever. They'd made a magical vow and everything.

Forever, he started chanting in his head to calm himself as he followed Cooper and Nix through the crowd. *He promised me forever.*

There was a little sting at Matty's chest, followed by a warmth that started surface-level at Matty's skin and seemed to bleed inward. A nibble from a friend. Matty patted at his shirt, at the spot where the little shadow still lay between the fabric and his skin.

He was grateful for the reminder that he still had a piece of Nightmare with him, even if it was a small one. The rest of the shadows had stayed with Nightmare at the bar, and Matty was grateful for it, even if he missed them. He wanted his demon to have all the help he needed.

Matty could be calm. He could be brave.

He took a deep breath.

BANG.

Matty's big, calming breath couldn't have been more poorly timed if he'd tried. He inhaled just as a flash of light and a bloom of smoke filled the air. Matty started coughing immediately, choking on the smoke as people started panicking.

Was that smoke from Chaos, or had someone set off a firework? Everything was too frenzied—Matty couldn't tell what direction things were coming from.

Matty's hand slipped from Cooper's as he bent forward, racked with coughs he couldn't stop. The connection was immediately replaced by a strong grip on his bicep—Nix must have found Matty in the smoke—and Matty was tugged away through the mess of now screaming people and smoke-filled air, the long, quick strides of his companion leading him down the street.

Matty wiped at his eyes with his free hand, but they wouldn't stop streaming with tears, irritated by the smoke. He was blinded by it, unable to see his feet in front of him. He didn't think it was painful enough to have been tear gas, but it seemed like it was something close to it.

Yet the hand guiding Matty was sure, unaffected by the streams of people running past, and soon they'd made their way off the street and into the door of a building, Matty wasn't sure which one.

"Is this where Ivan is hiding?" he asked, keeping his head ducked down and his eyes shut tight, hoping that resting them would help them recover faster.

There was no answer as the door slammed behind them.

And that was...wrong. Even the few times Matty had seen him frightened and unsure, Nix was never quiet for long. He wouldn't leave Matty to guess and wonder when Matty had asked him a direct question.

Matty finally looked up as he was pulled further inside, to the back of the building. The air was clear here, and Matty's coughing had eased now that he could get a decent lungful. His eyesight still wasn't great, but he could see now that it wasn't Nix leading him at all. The form was wrong, much too broad, and whoever they were, they were wearing black.

Nix had been wearing red, hadn't he?

And the hand on Matty's bicep wasn't hot enough to belong to a demon anyway.

Matty jerked his arm away, and his movement was sudden enough that his captor didn't fight it. "Who—"

The words froze in his mouth as the man turned to face him. He was wearing a face mask with a respirator, presumably to breathe easily through the smoke bomb that had gone off.

But Matty knew who it was even before the man lifted the mask off his face.

He should have known the second that hand had touched his bare skin. He should have recognized the grip, the painful pull of it.

But Matty had let himself feel safe for just a moment, even with the chaos—had let himself believe he had people watching his back against the threats that surrounded him—and he'd allowed his worst nightmare to come to life without realizing it.

The face that met Matty's when the mask was off was clean-shaven and olive-skinned. The man it belonged to was somewhere in his mid-fifties, and he might have been considered handsome if not for the lack of humanity in his dark eyes.

"Hello, Matteo," Dominico purred, leering at Matty like a long-lost lover. "Did you really think you could hide from me forever?"

23

Matty

When Matty had been alone and friendless in a world of monsters, he hadn't been able to exist in Dominico's presence without shaking.

It had been like his body hadn't been able to help itself, trapped in a mixture of acute fear and PTSD from all the punishments that had come before.

Matty would always stumble on clumsy feet and choke on his words, and the more he'd dissolved, the more pleased Dominico had been with his reactions.

It had disgusted Luca, that weakness of his.

Matty was different now. He wasn't alone or friendless, and he knew without a doubt that Nightmare was coming for him. That he would sense Matty was in trouble and he wouldn't let any man, demon, or mobster stand in his way.

Dominico was no longer the biggest monster in Matty's life.

But Matty's body remembered.

It remembered every cut of Dominico's knife, every broken

bone, every startled wake-up in the middle of the night, pulled from sleep into acting as a monster's plaything. It remembered every mangled body they'd seen, dead boys who'd served as a warning of Matty's intended fate.

So Matty still shook as Dominico tied him down to the metal gurney, his muscles weak and treacherous. He was bonded now, and Nightmare had told him that meant he had a demon's strength to call on, but Matty didn't know how. He barely knew how to move his lungs to breathe.

Maybe the bonding hadn't gone right. Maybe Matty was too weak of a vessel to be a real demon's mate.

The shadow at Matty's chest pinched at his skin, as if in retribution for his disparaging thoughts.

Right. Matty choked in a breath, his throat still sore from the earlier smoke. Weak or not, he wasn't alone. Nightmare would come for him. Matty didn't have to be strong in the face of his worst fears come to life. He didn't have to be deadly and vicious like another demon might have been. He only had to survive. That was all Nightmare would ask of him.

To survive.

Matty tried to focus on practicalities. He didn't know exactly where they were, but they hadn't walked far; they still had to be in the downtown area. Matty's shadow hadn't made a move against Dominico, which probably meant one wasn't enough to do the damage a group of them was capable of. In which case Matty was glad it was staying close—he didn't want it to get hurt.

"That's better, isn't it?" Dominico asked in a false croon as he got Matty's ankle tied down, the last of his limbs to be trapped against the gurney. He stroked a hand over Matty's cheek, and Matty bit at his lip to stop from retching. "Just like old times."

"Shouldn't you be t-taking me back to New York?" Matty asked, and he wasn't sure if he should be proud that his voice only trembled a little.

Dominico sighed, looking toward the door they'd come through. "I'm waiting for my driver. I didn't expect you to have so many bodyguards around you, Matteo. It's been all hands on deck." He stroked Matty's cheek again, and then he was hinging at the hips, pulling a familiar bag out from underneath the gurney. The one that held Dominico's favorite knives. "But we can have a little fun while we wait, can't we?"

Dominico caressed the bag like a lover, the same way he'd caressed Matty's cheek. "Although, the real fun will begin when my new friend gets here. So many things I've learned since we last saw each other, Matteo. You can thank your friend Ivan for leading me in the right direction." Dominico leaned in close again. "My demon is going to make you *scream*."

At his words, a jolt of searing pain ran through Matteo, sharp and vicious. For a second, he thought it was his body reacting to those words, to the sight of that bag, to all the memories those knives held for him. But then Matty realized it had come through the bond. From Nightmare.

His demon had been hurt.

Dominico pulled out one of his boning knives, one Matty knew all too well. Matty's shaking intensified, even as he tried to tell himself that knife wasn't going to touch him. That, even injured or delayed, Nightmare wasn't going to allow it.

That felt real. That felt like truth.

It was strange. Now that the buildup of fear was over and the worst was already happening—Matty captured, Nightmare struggling, Dominico holding a knife—Matty was able to breathe again, to find the tiniest shred of inner calm deep inside his shaking, traumatized body.

Dominico was only a man. An evil man, but a man nonetheless. He had indents on his face from the pressure of his mask, and he smelled of bad cologne that was failing to mask the rank scent of stress sweat.

And he could hurt Matty, sure, but he couldn't get at what mattered. He couldn't get to the core of him, where Nightmare's soul lay entwined with Matty's, nestled within his very being. Dominico's knives couldn't cut that deep.

Nothing could.

The shadow against Matty's chest grew warmer, as if in agreement, and Matty focused on that heat. That comfort.

He was grateful for the distraction, because Dominico took his time setting up his station. He kept his boning knife in hand but laid all the others out carefully on a little table he'd pulled from somewhere. Dominico's precious tools. The only things he really cared about other than himself.

And then eventually—sooner than Matty would have liked—Dominico turned his attention back to Matty.

"Can I a-ask you a question?" Matty asked. He was glad for the tremble in his voice now. Dominico liked to hear it, demented asshole that he was. And Matty would keep him happy, keep him occupied.

And Nightmare would come.

Dominico cocked his head. "Am I going to fuck your corpse after I kill you? Why yes, Matteo."

Matty's flinch was just as involuntary as the shaking, but Dominico seemed to like it, so oh well. The shadow on Matty's chest grew even warmer. Maybe its heat was a gauge of its rage. Or maybe it was just comforting Matty in the face of that vile promise.

Matty's swallow tasted of bile. "Why did Luca choose me? What d-did he see in me? He would never say."

"You don't remember?" Dominico's dark eyes gleamed as he leaned against the wall, toying with the knife, testing its edge against his thumb. He'd always liked the buildup, the anticipation of incoming pain, and that was working in Matty's favor tonight. "One of his men tried to hurt your mother, back when the bitch was still around. You bit him. Practically straight to the bone even with those baby teeth of yours."

He grinned, condescension in his gaze. "I suppose you did it to protect her. And then she sold you for nothing before leaving you behind, and you never showed any bit of spirit ever again. Luca hated that." Dominico straightened from the wall, stepping up to the gurney. "But I like how soft you are, Matteo. How weak."

Without warning, he sliced the point of his knife straight down Matty's chest, from sternum to belly, cutting through Matty's shirt. He wasn't careful with it, but the shadow covering Matty cushioned him, and Matty wasn't cut by the blade. Dominico didn't seem to notice, his gaze intent on Matty's face.

"Some people think it's no fun, breaking something that's already broken. But you can always smash a person into smaller pieces." Dominico cocked his head, gauging how well his threats were landing. He must have seen something he liked, because his lips curled into a cruel smile. "Why, Matteo, have you gone and grown a backbone while I've been away? I could almost swear I see a little life in those big eyes of yours. That's a first."

Matty blinked, but his eyes were dry. He had the answer to his question, and it was just as meaningless as he'd thought. His life of suffering with Luca had basically been random. He'd tried to protect someone who hadn't cared for him enough to deserve it, and he'd been traded for nothing. It wasn't surprising news, and he wasn't going to be broken by it.

"My friends are coming for me," he said quietly, without the slightest tremble in his voice.

"You have no friends, Matteo. You have no one. You've always had no one." Dominico leaned closer, his breath hot and rank against Matty's face. "From the day your worthless mother pushed you out of her cunt, you've been unwanted and alone." Another caress to Matty's cheek. Matty would need to take a hundred showers after this, just to wash off the stain of this man's touch. "You should be grateful for my continued interest. It's the only proof you even exist. There's no one else who cares to remember."

The shadow still hiding under Matty's torn shirt shifted and wiggled, as if to remind him that Dominico's words weren't true.

But Matty already knew.

Dominico had been so turned on by his own slimy voice that he'd missed the room around them growing darker, the shadows in the corners lengthening and stretching, merging together. He'd missed the spiderlike limbs coming out of the darkness, and the white skull hanging three feet above his head.

Matty grinned, and maybe he had a bit of Nightmare in him after all, because for the first time in Matty's life, he saw fear in Dominico's eyes, even as the horrible wretch had no idea what surrounded him.

"*He* cares," Matty said fiercely, just as Nightmare's talons pierced Dominico's neck.

Nightmare was the most massive and monstrous and wonderful thing Matty had ever seen as he lifted the six-plus feet of Dominico off the ground, easy as anything.

His eyes were glowing, his skull was grinning, his fangs were flashing. If Dominico could see what had a hold of him, he'd piss himself with fear.

But Dominico didn't get a chance before Nightmare dropped his limp body to the ground.

Matty twisted in his restraints to frown down at the slumped form. "He's not dead already, is he?"

"No, sweet." Nightmare glided forward, slicing through the ties so Matty could sit up on the gurney.

"Okay, that's good." And for some reason Matty was shaking again, his teeth chattering loud enough to be heard in the quiet. "You s-said he w-would hurt. You p-promised."

Nightmare's limbs were still eerily long, his talons more claws than fingers, but his grip on Matty as he lifted him off the gurney was the gentlest touch Matty had ever felt. "And he will."

There was something in Nightmare's voice that Matty had never heard before: a barely contained rage that in anyone else would have sent Matty scrambling. But this was Nightmare, so it only made Matty cling tighter.

"You're trembling, little mate."

"I kn-know. I c-can't stop. B-But I knew you w-would come for me. I *kn-knew*."

Nightmare's shadows draped around Matty like a cloak, and suddenly Matty was so perfectly warm. His shaking didn't cease entirely, but it lessened. Nightmare set Matty on a chair, and then that skull face was pressed to Matty's, forehead to forehead. His demon smelled like smoke and safety and the faintest hint of death.

Matty breathed in deep. "Where are we?" he asked.

"Some business for sale. In the back room."

"Will we be interrupted?"

"No, sweet."

Matty let out his breath, then leaned back in the chair. He watched as Nightmare set Dominico on the gurney where Matty had just been strapped. Watched as Nightmare shrank back down to the tall, slender demon form Matty knew best.

"Is he just...asleep?" Matty asked.

"He passed out." Nightmare returned to Matty's side. "I may have been overzealous with the venom."

"You were hurt," Matty said, suddenly remembering that flash of pain.

"Just a touch."

Matty glared at him, relief and some other overwhelming emotion making him tetchy. "It was more than that. I felt it."

Nightmare slipped his hand into Matty's, squeezing tightly. "I'm unharmed."

So they waited, their hands clasped together. They didn't speak anymore, at least for now. Nightmare seemed to sense Matty's need for silence, wrapped in this little pocket of time before his long-awaited retribution.

Finally, Dominico stirred. He groaned, his eyelids fluttering. He turned his head toward them, his gaze widening almost comically as he took in the sight of Nightmare at Matty's side.

And while Matty might not have been able to eat fear like Nightmare did, he could almost swear in that moment he tasted it on the air.

"Dominico, this is my Scary," Matty said, as pleasant as could be, making his introductions. "Scary, this is the man who tortured me. The one who wanted to own me. The one who thought he could take my life in the most painful way possible and then desecrate my corpse."

Dominico jerked, his entire back lifting off the gurney with the effort to escape. But there were shadows on each of his limbs, holding him in place. "My demon—"

"Your demon is dead," Nightmare interrupted in a deadly rasp. "Your men are gone. There's only you, Dominico Caruso. Friendless. Powerless." He stretched and lengthened again, back to his spidery nightmare form, his sharp fangs bared in a vicious grin. "Doomed."

Matty watched the pulse throb in Dominico's neck as Nightmare approached the gurney in a silent glide. He watched that same pulse skitter and skip beats as Nightmare began Matty's retribution, neatly and carefully slicing into Dominico's flesh.

Dominico didn't scream at first, not even when Nightmare began using his talons to recreate every single one of Matty's many scars. He whimpered, yes. Grunted. Groaned. But he didn't yell out. Matty could even give the man credit for that, if that sort of meaningless display of toughness meant anything to him.

But when the shadows came into play? When they flooded

Dominico's senses and began playing with his disgusting mind in the same way Nightmare played with his disgusting body?

Then Dominico screamed loud enough to wake the dead.

———

It TOOK hours for Dominico to die.

Matty barely blinked at all during that time, his eyes so dry by the end that it was starting to get painful. But he didn't want to miss a moment.

And he didn't, did he? He watched every single second of Nightmare's torture.

But then the last scream turned to a gurgle, and that gurgle turned to silence, and finally Matty closed his eyes, tears slipping out from beneath his lashes.

It was done.

His ghosts were finally gone, sent back to the wretched hell they'd come from.

Warmth and smoke enveloped him.

Matty opened his eyes to find Nightmare kneeling in front of him. He'd returned to his usual demon form, the skull mask gone away again to the ether. Matty could just make out his shadows behind him in the dark, cleaning up the blood and gore.

And until this moment of overwhelming, debilitating relief, Matty hadn't realized the fear still hiding in his mind. The fear that Nightmare really would disappear when Dominico was gone and their contract ended, even with the bond in place.

But he was still here, Matty's demon. He was still Matty's.

Nightmare pushed back a lock of Matty's hair. He stroked his cheek with his lovely, warm hand.

Maybe Matty wouldn't need a hundred showers to feel clean again after all.

"Time to go home, Matteo," Nightmare rasped, the bridled

rage finally gone from his voice. He'd worked it all out on Domini-co's bloody body, Matty supposed.

"Okay, Scary."

Matty was feeling strong enough to walk now, but Nightmare made a move to lift him from the chair anyway.

Matty held out a hand. "Wait."

And Nightmare waited.

Matty had been thinking during these many hours together, making the man who'd hurt him so badly hurt just as badly in turn. He'd been thinking, and he had something to say, and he wanted to say it now, before the exhaustion of the night caught up with him.

Matty clasped his hands in his lap, meeting Nightmare's glowing white gaze. "I don't know what makes a person good or bad or evil, exactly. That compass in me—if I ever had one—got messed up a long time ago. I know I don't like seeing innocent people hurt. And I know you don't feel the same. You don't care, which is maybe supposed to worry me. But you care if *I* hurt. You care about that more than anything else. And I'm selfish enough to want that."

"Good," Nightmare told him immediately. "Be selfish. Take all of me."

"I will," Matty said. "And I know that's enough for you. That you'd be happy if I took and took and never gave you anything in turn. But I still want you to know that I love you."

Matty placed a hand on Nightmare's chest, right on the spot where he felt the bond strongest in his own. "Maybe you can already feel that. And maybe you already know the way I feel when I'm with you. Safe and whole, like you patch up my little broken bits, and they're not suddenly fixed, but they're not falling through the cracks anymore either. But I wanted to say it anyway." Matty dug his fingers harder into Nightmare's chest—hard enough to hurt. "I think I've loved you since that very first time you caught me in my dreams, back when I thought you were a figment of my imagination. When I had no idea you were coming to keep me."

Nightmare's white eyes weren't just glowing anymore—they were shining. The shadow blanket tightened against Matty's skin, and Nightmare pressed his hand against Matty's chest in turn, his touch as gentle as ever. "You are my soul, Matteo, and whatever heart I have is yours to own."

Matty slumped his head forward, pressing against the back of his hand on Nightmare's chest. "Good. I meant it. I want it all."

"And you have it." Nightmare's arms came around Matty, lifting him in a bridal carry. "Come, sweet. Let's wash away this night."

24

Nightmare

The unfortunate drawback to claiming a sweet, wounded soul was that sweet, wounded souls inevitably attracted devoted companions.

And while Nightmare wanted nothing more than to carry Matteo upstairs to the bedroom and surround him with nothing that wasn't Nightmare or his shadows—to go over every inch of Matteo's tender skin and reassure himself it remained intact—there were obstacles in Nightmare's way.

Living obstacles. And they were Matteo's people, so Nightmare wasn't allowed to murder them all for delaying him in his goals.

For Matteo, Nightmare would tolerate them. Even if Nightmare was currently...less steady than perhaps he should have been.

It didn't matter that they'd planned for the possibility of Matteo being taken. That knowledge hadn't done anything to quell the bottomless rage and agony Nightmare had felt at finding Matteo in Dominico's hold once again, that vile man's hands and knives and the stench of his rotten soul surrounding him.

If it wouldn't make Matteo cry, Nightmare would eviscerate Nix this very moment for losing him.

The other demons and their mates were gathered in the living room off the house's entryway. Chaos was grinning maniacally from his position on the couch, for some reason wrapped in a multitude of blankets while his mate fussed around him, adding and removing pillows seemingly at random.

Kaisyir had cleansed himself of any traces of blood and was resting in one of the room's oversize armchairs, holding Sascha in his lap with utmost tenderness. Ivan and Nix were standing off to the side, Nix clasped tightly in his human's arms, the tears running down the incubus's face doing little to ease Nightmare's ire with him.

The room was silent as Nightmare and Matteo entered. Matteo shifted in Nightmare's arms, moving as if to climb down, and Nightmare tightened his hold.

Matteo looked up at him. "Scary, can I have a few minutes?"

Minutes were nothing to Nightmare. They were inconsequential segments of meaningless time, drops in the bucket of his extended lifespan. But he found himself requesting, "Five minutes only, sweet."

Matteo pressed a cool kiss to his cheek. "Thank you."

Nightmare lowered him gently to the living room floor. Matteo was still draped in Nightmare's shadows, at least. They wouldn't be leaving him anytime soon; they were just as unsettled by the events of the night as Nightmare was.

Because while it was true that, with the bond, Matteo hadn't been in life-threatening danger from Dominico, the vision of him on that table...

It had been a glimpse of what might have been. What *could* have been, if fate hadn't played out differently. If Nightmare had never found his Matteo in the dream realm. If Sascha and Kai hadn't found him first, rescued a stranger without knowing what they were doing.

If none of that had happened, it would have been Matteo tied down in some dark room just like that, dying friendless and alone and in wretched, overwhelming pain.

And that thought, even hypothetical, was agonizing in a way Nightmare had never felt. It was ten times more excruciating than the pain demon's venom, and Nightmare was just as helpless to fight against it.

He couldn't take his eyes off Matteo. Couldn't stop reassuring himself that his human was here and whole and brimming with life.

Matteo walked over to Sascha and Kaisyir first, grabbing Sascha's hands and murmuring to them both. He seemed to be apologizing for the mess he'd brought into their town, and Nightmare had to bite off his offended growl. Matteo was shaken from his ordeal—if he wanted to make unnecessary apologies to undeserving parties, Nightmare would have to allow it.

Nightmare focused his gaze on Chaos, even as his attention remained on Matteo. "Aren't you healed already?"

Chaos's grin widened. "Of course," he said happily, accepting a mug of something hot from Cooper. "But my puppy's taking such pleasure in pampering me. I should get hurt more often."

"*No*," Cooper said fiercely, tucking the blankets tightly around Chaos's legs. "You shouldn't."

Chaos laughed brightly, his head thrown back like Cooper had said something hilarious. "You see? He never tells me no. But he was so worried for me, he can't help it."

Nightmare watched as Matteo moved on to Ivan and Nix next. Nix was blubbering, apologizing for losing him, and Matteo was patting at his arm. "It was always the plan B, me getting captured," he said softly. "It just happened in a different way than we expected."

Ivan tucked Nix under his arm again, murmuring something in his ear, so softly that Nightmare couldn't hear it, though it made Nix finally wipe away his tears as he leaned into his mate.

Ivan glared out at the room at large. "Nix did nothing wrong. It was chaos out there—we're lucky he was able to get the others to safety. They might have been grabbed for extra collateral."

No one argued—the others perhaps because they agreed, and Nightmare because he didn't care enough to form the words. Not now that Matteo was back in his clutches.

Ivan's cold gaze landed on Nightmare's. "He's gone, then? Dominico?"

"Bits and pieces," Nightmare told him, unable to stop the curl of his lips at the thought. He'd be reliving the memories of Dominico's screams over and over again in the coming days.

Ivan gave him an appraising look. "You could come in handy sometimes."

Nightmare had no interest in being a mobster's pet. He turned his attention to the wall, irritated by everyone's presence all over again. "I serve at my mate's pleasure."

"And was it *Matty's* pleasure to cut that man into bits and pieces?" Kaisyir asked with a decided note of hostility, rubbing Sascha's back in soothing strokes when his human made a gagging noise at the question.

Nightmare sneered in the warrior's direction. Kaisyir had always struggled with foes he couldn't vanquish with his fists or knives. Had always been leery of Nightmare's shadows and thirst for unconventional violence. Surely that discomfort had been exacerbated tonight, with the pain demon's arrival and the threat to his own mate.

"It was," Matteo countered fiercely. Loudly. "It *was* my pleasure."

All eyes turned to him, the little human draped in shadows from neck to ankle. He looked tired and lovely and vicious, and Nightmare wanted to kiss him until their mouths were bruised with the force of it.

"I wanted him to hurt," Matteo said, each word deliberate. "I wanted him to die screaming. I'd ask Sarkaron to do it again a hundred times over if I could."

He was met with silence, and then Chaos cackled. "I told you," he said gleefully to the room at large. "Hardcore."

No one else said a word.

"My five minutes are up," Matteo announced, lifting his arms into the air. Nightmare swooped in and lifted him, heading to the house's staircase without another thought to the rabble.

The weight of Matteo in his hold again soothed something in Nightmare. He hitched him up even higher, until his chin was brushing Matteo's dark hair. "Did I live up to my promises, sweet?" he asked as he stepped onto the stairs.

Perhaps Nightmare should have let Dominico linger for days. He'd wanted the deed done and had extended it as long as his impatience had allowed. But perhaps it hadn't been enough.

But Matteo let out a happy sigh. "You did, Scary." He tucked his head into the crook of Nightmare's neck. "Every single one."

———

IT DIDN'T TAKE LONG for Nightmare to have a clean and naked Matteo tucked into bed.

Naked but for the shadows, that was, who refused to give up their tight hold on Nightmare's mate.

Possessive little beasts.

"I'm not actually sleepy," Matteo grumbled, glaring out from under the covers at Nightmare.

Nightmare didn't call him out on the lie. "It is I who needs rest," he said instead. "We'll watch one of your films."

He turned on the TV in Matteo's bedroom and chose a horror film with *Nightmare* in the title, because doing so made Matteo laugh. Nightmare set the remote on the little bedside table, sent his clothes away to the ether, and curled up behind Matteo on the bed. He wanted as much of their skin pressed together as possible while Matteo slumbered.

"Could he have killed you?" Matteo asked after the opening scene of a knife-embedded glove being made had played out. "The pain demon?"

Nightmare scoffed, his breath stirring the wayward hairs at the back of Matteo's neck. "A mere pest."

Matteo clutched Nightmare's arm tighter to his chest. "And he's gone?"

"Kaisyir removed his head with a demon blade," Nightmare confirmed. "He's gone."

"Good." Matteo relaxed again. After a few more minutes of filmed terror, he yawned. "Scary?"

"Yes, sweet?"

"If I fall asleep, I want you to be inside me." Matteo hitched his leg up in front of him, making his invitation clear. "You don't have to be, like, locked in. But I need that—to have you in me. There's lube in the bedside drawer."

Nightmare's cock stirred, and his belly warmed, his hunger for his mate immediate.

One of Nightmare's shadows—eager as ever to get their mate exactly what he wanted—peeled off Matteo and returned with a little bottle. Nightmare pushed the covers down and traced a finger over Matteo's bottom, parting his cheeks to reveal that furled pink hole.

After the many unpleasantries of the night, such a gift as this seemed almost outside the realm of possibility.

But Nightmare's summoner had made a request.

So Nightmare used the little bottle, coating his fingers and rubbing and petting and coaxing those muscles open, drinking in Matteo's little huffs and groans as his human pretended to watch the slaughter on-screen.

It didn't take long for Nightmare's cock to fill adequately, not when Matteo was so soft and sweet and pliant against him. As soon as he was able, Nightmare slipped his cock inside with surprising ease, a rumbling sigh of pleasure leaving his chest at the tight fit.

"Is that better, sweet?"

"Mm," Matteo hummed, wiggling back until every inch of his body was touching Nightmare in some way.

His eyes fell closed almost immediately, as if having Nightmare's cock inside him was all he'd been waiting for to drift off into dreaming.

It may well have been. It was almost dawn already, and they'd both been through an ordeal.

Nightmare hadn't been lying when he'd said he was drained—even nightmare demons needed sleep occasionally—but he found himself wide awake still. He couldn't stop touching Matteo's skin, the shadows that coated it dispersing in the path of his fingers and resettling in the wake.

The touch was for reassurance at first. A reminder that Matteo's scars were the only wounds marring his skin—that no fresh marks had been opened. A reminder that Matteo was here, and he was whole, and any monsters who had sought him were long gone.

And then Nightmare's hand brushed down Matty's chest, his talon edging one of Matty's nipples, and Matty sighed in his sleep, shifting. The movement added sweet pressure to the firm grip around Nightmare's cock, and then he couldn't resist sliding a hand down to Matteo's lower belly and pressing in, feeling the swell of his cock from the outside. The proof of his presence.

Matteo let out a soft, panting moan, his hips shifting again.

Nightmare should wait to slake his urges. He should let his mate rest.

But maybe this was why so many humans felt such a strong urge to rut against each other at every given opportunity. Maybe it was the fleeting nature of their lives, the slippery edge to their continued connection.

Matteo and Nightmare had brushed up against that edge tonight, and Nightmare couldn't stop caressing his human. Couldn't stop the slow drag of his hips back and the sharp push forward. Couldn't stop exploring the way Matteo's body welcomed him and pressing his blunted teeth into Matteo's shoulder, just to feel the give of his flesh.

And maybe he was too rough, because eventually Matteo's eyes fluttered open.

"Wha—?" Matteo groaned as Nightmare pressed his cock in deep. "*Ungh.*" He lifted his arm, hooking it around Nightmare's neck. "Oh fuck, Scary," he slurred. "H-Hand. Put your hand—"

Nightmare wrapped a taloned hand around Matteo's cock. Matteo moaned his approval, bending his leg back and over Nightmare's thigh. He was spread open now, speared on Nightmare's cock.

At his mercy.

"Oh fuck. Fuck. *Fuck,*" Matteo kept chanting with each snap of Nightmare's hips. He turned his head with his eyes shut again, searching blindly for a kiss, sucking on Nightmare's tongue hungrily when Nightmare granted it to him.

Nightmare thumbed at the tip of Matteo's cock as he drove in again and again, unable to stop seeking that tight warmth around his cock, unable to stop spearing into his mate like a demon possessed.

Matteo's moans only grew hungrier. "Give it to me," he whined, biting sharply at Nightmare's lip. "Your cum. Give it, Scary."

Nightmare growled, turning them over until Matteo was on his belly. Nightmare reared back and tugged Matteo's hips up, driving in with determined fury until he could feel himself getting close to giving Matteo what he wanted. The heat in his belly tightened and spiraled, and then he was filling his mate, the release so sweet he shuddered with the pleasure of it.

Nightmare let his petals latch without fighting the connection. He knew Matteo would want them to remain linked when he fell asleep again.

Matteo's whine was high-pitched and desperate, and then he was wrapping his hand over Nightmare's on his cock, encouraging Nightmare to stroke him until he was spurting into Nightmare's fist with a wail.

They remained as they were, Matteo's head on his forearms, panting in the aftermath. Eventually he twisted, peering at Nightmare with heavy-lidded eyes. "Is it morning already?"

"No, sweet." Nightmare carefully turned them onto their sides again, coaxing Matteo to bend his knees and curling his own behind them. "Go back to sleep."

Matteo yawned, his lashes fluttering down once more. "Mmkay."

Nightmare's own eyes were growing heavy now. The shadows would have to clean up the mess tonight.

Nightmare would join his mate in the dream realm.

25

Matty

Matty woke up warm and rested and...light.

He'd never felt so light, not once in his life.

And maybe he shouldn't have felt that way after having his life threatened and watching a man get sliced slowly and painfully into pieces just the night before, but he did. Like there was a giggle at the back of his throat, just waiting to come out.

He kept it in for now. Nightmare was sleeping, and Matty had never seen him do that. Maybe he needed the rest. And he deserved it, after making every single one of Matty's dreams come true.

They'd separated again at some point in the night, and Matty had turned in his sleep so they were facing each other, one of his legs slung up over Nightmare's hip. The shadows must have cleaned Matty up, because he didn't feel sticky anywhere.

One of them tickled his cheek now, and Matty pursed his lips, a silent good-morning kiss hello.

"I'm awake, sweet," Nightmare rasped, barely above a whisper. "Only resting."

"Oh." Matty glanced up to find Nightmare's eyes already open, his flat white gaze focused on Matty's face. "Good morning, Scary," Matty said with a grin. "The rest of our life begins today."

Immediately, Matty's cheeks warmed. That had to have been the cheesiest thing he'd ever said in his life.

But Nightmare's lips twitched, his fangs peeking out in a small grin. "That it does, little mate."

The giggle that had been threatening finally came out, and Matty tucked his head into Nightmare's chest, laughing at absolutely nothing, except for maybe how wonderful he felt.

When he'd gotten it out of his system, Matty let out a happy sigh. He was safe and warm in their little cocoon together, and he found himself saying, "I think I might want to go back to school. Luca pulled me out of high school, and he never let me get my GED. I'd like to now."

He hadn't realized it was something he wanted until the words were already leaving his mouth. But it was true. He'd had so much taken from him, and Matty wanted to take a little of it back, if he could. It was a start, at least.

"A noble pursuit," Nightmare told him.

"I can do that part online, I think. But maybe—maybe one day I'll want to go to college? If they'll have me. I could study film or— or something like what Cooper does with computers?"

His sentences kept ending in question marks, and some of the lightness left Matty as he considered. Shouldn't he know by now what he was interested in? Shouldn't he have had some secret yearning for a vocation lingering in the back of his mind all this time?

Nightmare rubbed a soothing hand along Matty's spine. "You'll be able to study many, many subjects in your lifetime, Matteo. You don't have to choose now."

Matty bit at his lip, scratching his nail lightly down Nightmare's chest. "I might not be a good student."

Nightmare scoffed, but it was a nice kind of scoff. "There's no need for you to be. But you're curious and brave and determined. You'll do well."

Matty frowned. "I'm not sure I'm any of those things."

One of the shadows pinched his cheek as Nightmare told him, "I'm certain enough for the both of us."

Matty snuggled even closer, although it was barely possible with how hard he was pressed against Nightmare already. It was a nice reminder that they were naked, and wonderful things could happen when they were both naked together.

But then Matty's stomach grumbled loudly enough to startle the shadows, sending them spinning off the bed.

Matty glared down at his stomach. "Maybe we should go down for breakfast."

"Mm," Nightmare agreed, his lips pressed tightly together, like he was fighting off a smile.

They dressed quickly and headed down to the kitchen. The whole crew was gathered around the table there, with assorted mugs in front of them and a plate of pastries that had clearly come from the Bakeshop on the table.

"Does anyone know if Seth's okay?" Matty asked as he and Nightmare walked in. He couldn't believe he'd forgotten to check the night before. "And Benny?"

Sascha swallowed his bite and cleared his throat. "They're both fine. Seth stayed in last night, and Benny's the one who dropped off the pastries this morning. I don't know if he even knows what really happened last night. He just gave me a fist bump and told me to pass one onto you while his creepy boyfriend glared at Kai like he was the devil."

There was a sort of tense silence after his announcement, and it took Matty a moment to remember that he'd basically admitted to being a bloodthirsty murderer at heart last night.

Maybe he and Nightmare were no longer welcome here, in Sascha's safe place. Maybe they were too broken and twisted for family and friends.

But then Sascha stood from the table, walking quickly over to Matty and enveloping him in a hug, not even hesitating with the fact that Nightmare and his shadows were within touching distance.

"Everyone's got their issues," Sascha murmured in Matty's ear before releasing him. "Come eat something."

And then Cooper was making space for Matty at the table, and Nix was patting gently at his shoulder, and Kai was placing a Danish in front of him.

"Blueberry lemon," the big demon said gruffly. "Sascha saved it for you." He looked over to Nightmare, arching a brow. "We don't have any virgin blood or children's tears on hand, but the coffee's hot."

Nightmare scoffed, scooping Matty from his chair and placing him back down on his lap. "As if I would have anything to do with children, crying or otherwise."

"We won't ask you to babysit the hatchlings, then," Chaos said nonsensically, ducking under Kai's massive arm to steel his mug of coffee, seemingly for no other purpose than to hear him yell in rage.

Matty sat very still for a moment, until he was certain he wouldn't burst into tears at the table. Until the happiness in his chest was contained enough for him to move steadily.

Then he ate his breakfast, surrounded by his friends.

———

By late afternoon, the other couples had left to go back to New York—with a promise to return to Seacliff later in the summer for an extended stay—and then it was only Sascha and Kai in the house with Matty and Nightmare.

The other two had sojourned to Sascha's office to rebook their flights and reschedule their travel plans, so there was plenty of space for Matty and Nightmare to be on their own, but Matty had gotten kind of accustomed to his and Nightmare's new routine of strolling around the town every day.

"Should we go for our walk?" he asked a little before sunset, and Nightmare agreed.

The evening was warm, and now that they didn't have to make an effort to be seen by lingering mobsters, they had the option to explore more of the residential neighborhoods, so Matty took them down a new route.

And there, on a street Matty had never been down before—near enough to the coastal path that he could still hear the sound of the waves breaking against the rocks if he listened closely—was a little house.

It was a single-story clapboard cottage, painted a cheerful pale yellow, with a covered porch and a large, overgrown yard. The sign said it had two bedrooms and one bath.

The sign said it was for sale.

Matty stood there staring at the apparition, Nightmare's hand clasped tightly in his. He looked up at his demon. "You believe in fate, right?" Matty asked. "You think we were, like, meant to be together?"

Nightmare had never said as much, but Matty didn't know how else to describe Nightmare's very singular obsession with his mortal soul.

Nightmare's dark human eyes flashed white in the twilight. "I believe you're mine."

Matty grinned up at him, even though it wasn't a real answer to his question. Or maybe it was.

And then Matty couldn't stop staring at that sign. He'd loved living with Sascha and Kai—as much as he'd been able to love anything with how scared he'd been of Dominico's return—and he knew he wanted to stay close to them. But also...

A place of his own. Matty had never had that. Not once.

"I don't have any money," he pointed out quietly, more to himself than anyone else.

Nightmare huffed, sounding almost offended. "I can get you money, sweet."

"You can?" Matty tilted his chin to peer down at the shadow nestled between his pecs, the one who'd become his more or less permanent companion. "Are you all robbing banks now?"

"I've found my way into endless dreams over the centuries, little human. I've seen buried gold, hidden riches. Not all of it was imagined. I know where to find these things."

Well. That was... Matty didn't know what to say to that, actually. Those things—buried treasures haunting someone's nightmare—didn't sound real to him. But then again, neither had demons, once upon a time.

"Enough for a little cottage?" he eventually asked, unable to keep the hope from his voice.

"Many times over," Nightmare told him, pulling Matty closer to him and wrapping his arms around Matty's chest so Matty was still facing the house. He seemed content enough to stay there, staring, for as long as Matty liked.

Matty bit at his lip. "It's not too small for you, is it?"

"I like cramped, dark corners. All the better for looming over my prey."

Matty laughed, delighted. Everyone thought Nightmare was so serious all the time, but he had some great jokes, if people ever bothered to listen to them.

"A place of our own," Matty mused.

"A place of our own."

"We'll have a lot of them, I guess. Over time."

"We will."

"Because we'll be together always."

"Always," Nightmare repeated.

They stood there as the sun set fully over the horizon, the light around them growing dim.

A year ago Matty had thought himself doomed for pain and death, unwanted and unloved. Unlucky, definitely. He'd always thought that. Maybe less than some but surely more than most, was what he'd decided.

But now, with his demon at his side, the future an endless road of infinite possibilities before them, Matty thought he might be the luckiest human alive.

When the world was dark around them, Matty tugged on Nightmare's hand, pulling him to the empty house. "Come on, Scary. Let's look inside."

He wanted to see what the start of the rest of their life looked like.

EPILOGUE

Matty

Matty was stuck in a long, narrow hallway again.

There was a light at the end of it, but as he walked down along it, each step only seemed to get him further away, that little light he was heading toward never getting any closer.

There were doors lining the wall along either side of him. They were quiet and still, although Matty had learned that if he listened closely, he could maybe make out what was behind them.

He pressed his ear to one now. It sounded like a litter of puppies on the other side, whimpering and snuffling and letting out cute little barks.

Matty grinned. That was sweet to hear, although he wouldn't want one for keeps. The shadows might get jealous if he picked up any other pets.

Matty pressed his ear to another door, one on the opposite side of the hallway. There was the dull throb of pulsing music, the kind that played at the Lighthouse on dance nights. Matty would bet his friends were behind this one, writhing under those flashing lights, waiting for Matty to join them.

But Matty kept going, and before long he crashed into a familiar warm body, the force of it sending Matty to the ground, though his landing was anything but harsh.

He looked up and up, past elongated, spiderlike limbs, to the toothy, grinning skull miles above his head.

A rush of affection ran through Matty at the familiar sight, and then a rush of...*pleasure,* a tightening swirl of heat in his belly.

Matty cocked his head. "What are you doing to my body out there?"

The skull mask grinned wider, its fangs dripping some dark, viscous substance.

"Delicious things," it rasped. A long-fingered hand came up to cup Matty's face. "Time to wake up, Matteo."

———

MATTY WOKE UP MID-MOAN, his back arching off the bed. There was hot, wet suction around his cock, and he managed to crane his neck enough to see Nightmare between his legs, his mouth on Matty's dick and three fingers stuffed inside Matty's ass.

"Mm," Matty moaned again. "'S'nice."

Nightmare must have been playing with him for a while already, because Matty's whole body felt flushed and heavy and already too close to coming.

Way too close.

"Scary," he whined, clutching his fingers into the bedspread.

Nightmare let out a low growl, the sound vibrating along Matty's sensitive, overworked cock. At the same time, he mercilessly crooked those long fingers, petting along Matty's inner walls.

"F-Fuck!" Matty curled up with a cry, shooting his release into Nightmare's waiting mouth.

His orgasm lasted forever—Nightmare swallowing every last drop—and Matty was left panting, trying to get his bearings, only to find his legs folded up against his chest and a broad, blunt cock pressing at his entrance.

"Yes, Scary," he sighed, not caring that he'd just emptied his load ten seconds ago. He was a horny little beast in his early twenties—there was always more where that came from. "Fill me up."

And Nightmare really must have been doing delicious things to Matty for ages already, because he slid in so easily, all the way to the hilt.

And then Matty was surrounded by his demon in the way he liked best: Nightmare's thick cock filling him and his broad form pressing Matty's legs to his chest, those glowing white eyes hungry above him, Nightmare's warmth and smoke and shadows hiding the morning light from Matty's eyes.

"G-Good morning," Matty managed to say between breathless little pants. He wrapped spaghetti-noodle arms around Nightmare's neck and drew him in for a kiss. The price of Nightmare waking him up with sneaky blow jobs was dealing with Matty's morning breath.

Not that Nightmare ever seemed to care about that.

He started driving into Matty as Matty sucked on his tongue, not bothering with a slow build or teasing strokes. He must have been getting impatient out here, to have invaded Matty's dream just to wake him up.

"No—no latching," Matty reminded him, rocking his hips to meet every thrust, desperate for the way that fat head rubbed inside him. "We have to be at the docks."

Nightmare let out an exasperated, grunting huff, but he started placing hungry, hot kisses along Matty's neck and chest, so he couldn't have been all that put out.

It was a sloppy, rushed sort of fuck, and it was Matty's very favorite way to wake up. He loved that Nightmare got hungry for him while he slept, that his demon could never seem to wait until Matty woke up on his own to start toying with Matty's body. Loved that he craved him as badly as Matty craved him in turn.

The shadows seemed just as impatient this morning, squeezing and sucking at Matty's cock as Nightmare drove into him, getting Matty hard and then beyond hard, to the point where he was going to come before Nightmare did. Again.

Or maybe not.

Broad palms slid to the backs of Matty's thighs, folding him into a little sex pretzel, and then Nightmare was grinding his hips against Matty with all his substantial weight, his rhythm stuttering as he growled loud enough for the whole block to hear.

Matty clenched around the incoming heat, his own cock spilling into the shadows, crying out in protest when Nightmare withdrew too soon.

But right. No latching. They had plans today.

Nightmare rested his forehead against Matty's, panting into his mouth in a way that Matty enjoyed immensely, and then he rolled off him. Matty immediately curled onto his side, grinning at him. "Puppies and besties? Really?"

Nightmare smirked at him. "That was *your* dream, little human. I merely interrupted."

Matty snuggled closer, tossing a leg over Nightmare's hip. "Should we cancel? See what other interruptions you can come up with?"

Nightmare's white eyes gleamed. "Yes, sweet. Let's cancel."

Matty immediately sighed, shaking his head. "No. We can't."

He hopped out of their king-size bed before he got too tempted by Nightmare's nude, sexed-up demon form. He scurried to the bathroom, hastily cleaning up what the shadows hadn't gotten to, and then brushed his teeth, the shadows nipping around him, clearly feeling playful this morning after their little sex romp.

It wasn't long before the biggest shadow of all loomed behind him in the mirror, and then Nightmare was there, wrapping his arms around Matty's chest, bending to rest his chin on top of Matty's head, his antlers jutting out beyond the mirror's reflection.

It was a good thing the cottage had high ceilings.

But of course it did because it was perfect. Almost as perfect as Matty's demon, and Matty loved it almost as much. His first real home, one without any bad memories or ghosts to haunt it. Only Matty's creature of the dark lurking in its shadowed corners, as he should be.

When Matty was as freshened up as he was going to get, they dressed for the day.

They were supposed to meet everyone down at the docks soon. Cooper and Chaos and Ivan and Nix were all visiting at the same time for once, and Sascha had decided this was the year he was learning how to sail. He'd commanded they be there for his first solo excursion, as was their duty as his family.

Matty was pretty certain they were going to capsize by the end —by Chaos's hand if no one else's—but he supposed that was what life jackets were for.

The morning sun was lovely, the days getting warm again as they approached another summer, and Matty was comfy enough in only his T-shirt, his hoodie left at home today.

The change of season meant ice cream and sunshine and more time at the beach, but Matty had learned this year that winter was his very favorite, and he was a little sad to fully let it go.

The town had emptied out like it always did come fall, and the days had been short and dark and cold. Matty and Nightmare had holed up in their cozy cottage, fucking and snuggling and watching every horror movie ever made. More than once, Sascha and Kai had been forced to come banging on their door to get them out of the house.

It had been perfect.

Matty had even come out of it with his GED, and next fall he was going to start taking a few college courses online, just to see what sparked his interest.

Matty was no longer Matteo Caruso either. Ivan had procured documents for Nightmare, and ever since the courthouse wedding, Matty was Matteo Night, married to Sarkaron Night. And if anyone thought it was weird he called his husband by their shared last name, no one said anything about it.

It was a small town, after all. There were bigger kooks than Matty and Nightmare running around.

Matty had worried a little bit about Nightmare managing with such prolonged domesticity, but it seemed it was basically impossible for his demon to get bored. If Nightmare ever got restless within the confines of Seacliff, he stepped into the dream realm and fed on human terror. And when he returned, he'd share the weird, horrific visions he'd been part of, if Matty was in the mood for them.

It was like having new horror stories always on tap, whenever Matty wanted them.

Matty's favorites were when Nightmare found particularly vile, rotten souls, ones who were a danger to all the innocents around them. Then Nightmare would ask Matty for his desired retribution, and he and the shadows would deliver it the next night.

So maybe Matty was still a little bloodthirsty at times, even with Dominico long gone. Nightmare didn't seem to mind.

Not every day started out perfect. Some mornings Matty woke up and forgot Dominico was dead, old terror vibrating through his bones. But on the rare occasion Nightmare wasn't already in bed to soothe him, the shadows were, a perfect reminder of everything that had changed since Matty had been that sad, scared, lost boy.

"I love you, Scary," Matty said now as they walked together in the sun. He liked to say it every day when he was at his happiest, and right at this moment, he was feeling pretty damn happy.

Nightmare pressed a kiss to their clasped hands. "My heart," he crooned.

Maybe one day Matty would want to travel as often as Cooper and Chaos did. Or perhaps he'd want to try living in a city again like Ivan and Nix. But for now, he was content to finally have a home that didn't scare him. To have neighbors to say good morning to and locals who knew him and his mate by name.

And most of all, to have his demon—his soul's perfect match —always at his side.

It was the kind of life dreams were made of, and Matty was going to enjoy every minute.

AUTHOR'S NOTE

Thank you so much for reading Unleashing Mayhem! I hope you enjoyed your time with Matty and Nightmare.

Ohhh my sweet Matty and his wonderful, terrible Scary. I'll admit I was really nervous starting their story. I knew people had connected with sweetie pie Matty early on, and I was anxious to do his story justice. But once I got started, these two flowed so well, and they've been such a comfort to me. I love a terrifying creature who's soft for his person, and I love a tender human with secret dark pockets. Together they just shined.

What's Next?

First up will be my new contemporary omegaverse series, *Extra Credit*. The first book, *Overeager*, will be releasing in August. It's alpha student x omega teacher, age gap, first times, no mpreg. I'm very excited to share it!

On the paranormal side of things, I have plans for a new series with a few different otherworldly creatures and their human obsessions. Our first book will feature some familiar faces, and the rest is still revealing itself to me.

If you're too impatient to wait, you can read WIP chapters as I write them on Patreon.

If you want to stay in the know, you can sign up for my newsletter for updates and news on upcoming releases. And I can always be reached by email if you just want to say howdy. I love, love, love hearing from my readers!

graebryanauthor@gmail.com

ABOUT THE AUTHOR

Grae Bryan has been reading romance since she was far too young to know any better. Her love for love stories spans all genres, and there's nothing she finds more exciting than all the fictional worlds she has yet to explore.

She lives in Arizona with her family, who graciously share space with all the imaginary men in her head. When not writing or daydreaming or parenting wild children, she can generally be found reading more than is healthy, walking her monster-dog, or cuddling her demon-cat. She loves all things gothic, cozy, lovely, or strange.

Find her online: graebryan.com
    Patreon: patreon.com/GraeBryan
    Facebook: @GraeBryanAuthor
    Instagram: @authorgraebryan
    Sign up for her newsletter: graebryan.com/contact
    Join her Facebook reader group: Grae Bryan's Reader Den

ALSO BY GRAE BRYAN

Vampire's Mate Series

<u>Roman</u> (Book One) – Danny and Roman

<u>Soren</u> (Book Two) – Gabe and Soren

<u>Lucien</u> (Book Three) – Jamie and Lucien

<u>Johann</u> (Book Four) – Alexei and Jay

<u>Wolfgang</u> (Book Five) – Eric and Wolfe

Colin (Book Six) — Colin, Fox, and Dane

<u>Cassian</u> (A Vampire's Mate Novella) – Blake and Cass

Demon Bound Series

Wreaking Havoc (Book One) — Sascha and Kai

Inviting Bedlam (Book Two) — Ivan and Nix

Calling Chaos (Book Three) — Cooper and Chaos

Unleashing Mayhem (Book Four) — Matty and Nightmare

Novellas

An Unwitting Bargain - Benny and Helio